# SURVIVAL OF THE FITTEST

"You know . . ." He interrupted me and leaned back in his chair. "I look at you and I say to myself, 'Just how serious is this woman about being a doctor?' "

"Excuse me?" I demanded.

"I mean," he continued, "I look at you with your long flowing hair and your pink fingernails and your cute little skirts and I say to myself, 'Why, she's just here for the hell of it.' " His blue eyes took in my entire body. "Isn't that right? How badly do you want to be a doctor? Tell me!"

JONI LYNN SCALIA, M.D.

# The Cutting Edge

BERKLEY BOOKS, NEW YORK

This Berkley book contains the complete
text of the original hardcover edition.
It has been completely reset in a typeface
designed for easy reading, and was printed
from new film.

THE CUTTING EDGE

A Berkley Book / published by arrangement with
McGraw-Hill Book Company

PRINTING HISTORY
McGraw-Hill edition published 1978
Berkley edition / April 1983



ISBN: 0-425-05598-1

A BERKLEY BOOK ® TM 757,375
Berkley Books are published by Berkley Publishing Corporation,
200 Madison Avenue, New York, New York 10016.
The name "BERKLEY" and the stylized "B" with design are trademarks
belonging to Berkley Publishing Corporation.
PRINTED IN THE UNITED STATES OF AMERICA

*To my husband, Les*

# Author's Note

About three years ago a good friend asked me, "How come you never write anymore?" At the time the answers were obvious and included: "Because I had forgotten how," "Because it was something I no longer did," and "Because I didn't have the time." And, indeed, my writing, like many other things, had been eliminated and replaced by the encompassing medical life I had been leading for twelve years. This was a life that left little room for anything but the business of being a doctor and being married to a doctor. But today I no longer practice and if I chose to do so, I could perhaps forget those twelve years of my life. It would be easy, certainly. I don't have to deal with medicine on a daily basis any more. I don't have to give it a thought. But then, there are the people who do still deal with medicine daily: the neophytes and the established physicians who feel as I do, but have no voice, because to speak out in medicine is to put one's cherished career in jeopardy. This book tells about being a doctor, about the process of medical education, about the development of professionalism. There are parts of the book which are uniquely my story because I am the woman I am, and because I was educated at a time in which being a woman in the surgical field was an unfashionable position. It was a time when there were quotas, a time when women were, at the very least, unappreciated, and, at the very most, despised by many members of the profession. But the people and the incidents in this book are as important today as they were then; not because they happened to me, but because they happened at all.

# PART ONE

# 1

"Desert Medical," the voice came over softly, "this is two six three four."

"DMC, go ahead."

"We're coming in with a two-month-old male, possible DOA."

"Can you repeat, two six three four?"

"That's a two-month-old male, possible DOA." The voice was completely calm; no background noise, no sirens.

"What's your estimated time of arrival, two six three four?"

"We have an ETA of approximately ten minutes."

"That's ten-four, k.u.b. nine six one."

"Ten-four."

They were hauling dead cargo, and they were taking their time.

The kid was incredibly dead. He was dead as nothing else is ever dead. There cannot be a sight more gross than that of a dead child. Everything seemingly perfect: skin, fine little eyelids, everything perfect but for a slight abnormality of color; a little too pale, a little too violet about the mouth, a little dullness over the eyes. And the skin temperature a little too cool.

The babysitter had gone in to check on him and found that he wasn't breathing. She became hysterical and called for an ambulance. The police were with her at the house, although she was unable to make any kind of statement. Both parents worked. Neither could be reached by phone. The mother, working in the middle of the aircraft plant, thirty miles outside of town; the father, at one of the copper mines—a two-hour drive. They had sent police cars for both of them.

The mother arrived first. She was young. Possibly eighteen. Mexican. She followed the nurses into the room where the body was laid out. The nurses had it displayed with its head on a pillow, eyes closed, sheets covering the small torso. The sheets were folded neatly under his chin as though he were tucked in for the night.

The mother approached the stretcher slowly, quietly, on tiptoes so as not to awaken him. She clutched her purse in front of her and then eased onto the stool alongside and placed her purse below his feet.

"Miguel?" she whispered, leaning over him. "Niño?" She lay her head down on the pillow and began stroking his cheek.

I walked out and stood in the hall, waiting for the scream. It never came. She emerged from the room dry-eyed several minutes later, and we sat down together in an empty room.

"It was one of those crib deaths, wasn't it?" She looked at me directly.

"I can't say for sure. It's possible."

"He was healthy. Nine pounds when he was born. Strong as a horse." She smiled proudly. "A healthy baby. He had a little cold yesterday." She looked around the room briefly. "I read about it in the paper; about this crib death. I always thought, what if that ever happens?" She got up from her chair and walked across the room, stood for a moment and then spun around. The tears were rolling down her cheeks and her nails were digging into her purse. "Why?" she whispered. "Why did he die?"

One of the nurses stuck her head in the door. "The police just called. They have located the baby's father."

The mother looked at me and started fishing in her pockets for a Kleenex. "He's going to take this bad."

She was right. He came rushing in, shoving the nurses aside and looking wildly around him. He spotted the entrance to the room surrounded by police and nursing personnel. He barreled toward them and pushed his way frantically into the room. He ran toward the stretcher and then stopped short suddenly, lurching back in horror. One look was enough. It was true. He whirled around and threw himself against the heavy double doors, elbows bent, arms shielding his eyes, fingers grabbing his own hair. He sobbed and shook. Gradually he stopped, and still facing the doors he dried his eyes on the side of his sleeve, pulled the door handles violently, and ran out into the parking lot. I tried to follow him out but he swung at me and told me to leave him alone.

I poured some coffee and sat down in the nurses' station.

"Dr. Scalia."

"Yes."

"There's some guy on the phone who wants to talk to the little lady doctor. I think that's you." She handed me the phone.

"I guess it is, kiddo. I guess it is."

# 2

The first memory I have of medical school is of cockroaches. The county hospital had eight floors, stretched for four city blocks, and had the largest roaches in the city. It was a breakthrough in public health when one poor nursing student went to change a Phisohex dispenser one morning and found the biggest mother roach ever to be seen by man shoveling in the soap and burping happily over the magnificent repast set before her. The entire medical staff had been happily scrubbing their hands for the last decade with roach shit and then standing by, saying "Don't touch me, I'm sterile."

The medical school itself was approximately two city blocks from the hospital and was the site of the basic science building, where I was to spend the next two years of my life. The building was relatively new and looked very benign on the outside, which is very often true of things that are slowly destructive and ultimately go on to kill you.

The first-year class met in a large lecture hall on the fifth floor. We were handed a mimeographed sheet telling us what we could expect that morning. Like most mimeographed sheets, it told you nothing. Like a headstone; you get the "born" and the "died" and the vital statistics, which aren't vital at all. It's only the stuff that was left out which was of any importance, but you couldn't put it under a heading so it was omitted. The first heading on the sheet was WELCOME. By the time everybody was seated, the total anxiety level in the room was powerful enough to have put the entire Seventh Fleet through the Panama Canal without a lock change. Boy, did I need a welcome.

I was still tired from the day before, having just arrived in the city and immediately gone apartment-hunting. My mother had come in with me to help look for a place and we had spent the morning going through the files in the student affairs office. We finally found what we thought sounded like someplace reasonable. "Utilitarian dwelling, basement of two-family house. Private entrance, walking distance from the hospital." We decided to drive over, which was a good thing. Walking distance from the hospital meant that if you started out Sunday night after dinner and ran all the way you could make it in time for an eight-o'clock lecture the next morning and still squeeze in a sweet roll.

The lady of the house showed us the private entrance, which was located in an alley between two garbage cans and a pile of dog poop. "Watch your step," she said cheerfully. The door swung open to reveal the entire apartment.

"This is it?" I looked at her.

"It's very compact," she explained. What she meant was that if you closed the toilet seat it could double as a kitchen table. There were two gas burners, a bed of sorts, one window with chicken wire running through it, and two Salvation Army rugs on the cement floor. "How much is it?"

"Sixty-five a month," she said with a straight face.

"We'll take it," my mother said with an equally straight face, unable to pass up the obvious bargain.

It took me the rest of the day and the evening just to clean the place up, shop, and move in my belongings. I tried to find a place worthy enough to display my new seven-hundred-dollar microscope, which was obviously the most expensive item in the building, including the roof and the foundation. I finally decided the valuable piece of equipment would be better off left in its case. That way at least I knew the lenses wouldn't mildew. I had room out in the alley for my car, which was another real plus. The car was white when I went to bed; the next morning it was black, covered with a layer of soot from the neighboring apartment incinerators.

I got to lecture on time and waited nervously in the buzzing hall. Finally the double doors at the front of the lecture hall opened and then, ladies and gentlemen, in walked a white-haired man in a snow-white coat—the first in a long succession of white-haired men who are the very core and substance of the medical profession. Without white-haired men, there would be no Medicine.

As part of the welcome the formidable gentleman in the front of the room informed us that we would be having a group Rorschach. This was accomplished by projecting the entire series of ink blots on a giant screen. The Rorschach was followed immediately by a written personality test that included such discriminating questions as "Would you rather be in a pit of lions or summering on the French Riviera?" and "Do you often feel that you are ugly and people are laughing at you?" I answered yes to everything. Apparently this questionnaire was supposed to be designed to ferret out those of us who were blatantly crazy and had somehow gotten past the interview committee, which was equally crazy but somewhat more influential. Alas and alack, as we would see in subsequent weeks, these experts let one get by.

We all noticed her right away, and indeed it was impossible not to. In her brightly colored, mismated outfits, she crawled along the floors of the lecture halls, between the seats, apologizing profusely for her lateness and her inability to find her books. She was the butt of many a joke, and the unfortunate bearer of the nickname "The Sore Thumb," for reasons which were obvious to everyone. For reasons which were not obvious to everyone, nobody made any attempt to help her. No faculty member, no class member.

One morning she didn't come to class. Nobody missed her. Nobody misses one more person at an early morning lecture. The next time we saw her face it was on the front page of the newspaper. She was being carried away, one wrist handcuffed to a policeman, the other arm waving above her head as she babbled frantically at the popping flashbulbs. The photographer caught it all. The terrified, confused face, the large popping eyes—and, in the grain of the news photo, you would swear you could see the droplets of sweat under her nose as well.

"The Sore Thumb" was on the top floor of a building and ready to fly—something she had wanted to do all her life, and, after all, she had the grades for it. But that was yet to come, and we were only up to item three on the mimeo sheet, COFFEE.

This was given a fifteen-minute time slot during which everybody went to the bathroom and had diarrhea. Refreshed and ready to press onward, we came to our last item for the morning: the Tour of the Anatomy Labs. At last, we all thought, we would get to see the cadavers.

The lab tour was conducted by Herman, the faithful. He was the caretaker/watchman who had The Key to the lab. Herman made Igor look like Danny Kaye. He had the whole thing, right down the line: the rumpled gray fatigues, the shuffle, the jingling keyring, and of course the cataract in the left eye. Warner Brothers had missed a real find. Herman, I knew in my heart, did not sleep in a bed at night but in fact occupied a hook somewhere in the bowels of the building along with the rest of the dead who had found their final resting place as pickles in a briny barrel.

I found my appropriate laboratory, which was N-T. Life is merely an alphabet and you have to learn to live with the letters. Learning to live with N-T was not easy. We had, for example, one young man who didn't like women in the class and demonstrated his displeasure by sticking his foot out every time I walked by and whispering obscenities in my ear. He had just recently learned to walk on twos and couldn't handle too many new stimuli at once. He was however nicely balanced out by the fellow across the room who brought his lunch every day and ate and dissected at the same time, occasionally forgetting what exactly he was holding in each hand. I don't want to dwell on this, but on our first day we never did get to see our cadavers; we only got to meet our lab partners, which was equally horrifying. At least you knew you could count on a cadaver not to pick his or her nose. Your lab partner you couldn't count on for anything except maybe a six-inch blade between your left fourth and fifth intercostals, once he or she found out where they were located.

Orientation having been completed, we all made the mad rush to the medical bookstore, where we deposited our collective lives' savings into the rapidly moving hands of Lou the Bookseller. We received in exchange shopping bags full of books, the medical syllabus for the entire year, and a ticket to hernia city.

# 3

We started the year with introductory anatomy. Hey, baby, I'm gonna make you a star, 101A. Hang a big MD right on your dressing-room door. But first we have to go through this little procedure. It's a temporary procedure of course, and it isn't really an introduction, it's more like an interruption. You are being asked this morning and for the next few mornings to interrupt that which you know to be real and to come just a little further with us while we introduce you to yourself. It isn't really your entire self—it's just your body. But it isn't really yours—it's your cadaver's. It was your cadaver's, now it's yours. Actually it was never really anybody's; cadavers were always cadavers, they were never really people. Once you realize that you need have no fears and no guilt. That which is real is what you see before you; there were never any other realities. This is such a pleasant exercise and such a simple one and we'll continue it throughout the full four years, and after a few weeks with us you'll be able to accept just about anything.

The metal containers crashed open one by one in the laboratory, affording us the privilege of seeing all nine bodies in the room simultaneously. "Jeez, it's nothing," a voice behind me said. "It just looks like a mummy." It did. It looked very much like a mummy, but it smelled a lot worse. This incredibly pungent chemical odor pervaded the room. Whoever invented this mixture deserves a lot of credit. Not only will this stuff peel the skin right off your face, it will cling to your body and your clothing forever. You stink, and you know it, and everybody else knows it but it really doesn't matter. There are just too many other things to worry about. Introductory anatomy is a totally leveling experience. You feel like a moron and you know nothing.

Our days started out with morning lectures in which the chairman of the department, who knew everything, stood in front of the lecture hall with fourteen pieces of colored chalk and drew in great detail and at lightning speed what appeared to be the interchange for the Brooklyn–Queens Expressway as seen from a helicopter at 5:00 P.M. on Friday and then announced that this diagram was the network of nerves from the spinal cord to the left arm.

After lecture you went directly to lab, where you and three equally competent lab partners argued for half an hour about whether a given structure under your probe was the lateral femoral cutaneous nerve to the thigh or the medial femoral circumflex nerve to the back. Finally, when you'd all had enough, you called the lab instructor over to find out which maven was correct. "What is this crap?" he would say professionally. "What the hell have you done here?" We all would look surprised. "Do you guys realize that you have destroyed every important structure in the left groin and have chosen to retain and label a piece of fat?" We shrank into the corner, demoralized and guilt-ridden. He looked at us with disgust and walked away.

Our other introductory course was biochemistry, given on alternate days, which we referred to as Biochemistry Given On Alternate Days. Biochemistry was very interesting, but not to us. By *us* I refer to the small group of which I had become a member. In medical school you form attachments fast, and like seeks out like. This group to which I am referring consisted of four or five members. We all had several things in common. We had all had so much college chemistry that we could have taught the course; we were all reasonably bright, having skipped every conceivable grade the New York City school system would permit; we all sat in the back row; and we were all obnoxious.

"Who is it this morning?"

"Dr. Potato Head."

"Not good. That means we have to stay."

Dr. Potato Head was Dr. Glass, an enormous white-haired man with silver-wire glasses. He was the chairman of the department, and his lectures consisted of a series of grunts punctuated by an occasional fart. You didn't walk out on Dr. Glass—he had eyes in the back of his head, hence the term of respect.

Dr. Molecule, on the other hand (who tried for six consecutive lectures to give meaning to the structure of the glucose molecule), was easy. You knew it was only a matter of time before he would twist himself completely awry in a last-ditch effort to demonstrate those hydrogens, and then it was out the back door. We'd head down to the beach and stuff ourselves with Nathan's hot dogs, raw clams, and french fries. After all, we reasoned, we needed our strength.

One morning we arrived in anatomy laboratory, opened our metal coffin, and found absolutely nothing inside. Our cadaver was gone; claimed by a relative. Claimed. Somebody knew him. Somebody was going to bury him. How could that be, we all questioned? We had all been assured that these bodies had been in storage for several years, that these were all forgotten members of society. How could it be unless, we reasoned, Herman the Labkeeper was not as we thought, just another pretty face? Was he perhaps supplementing his income these snappy fall evenings by giving free rides through Central Park in a black hansom cab?

Having one's cadaver claimed in the middle of the semester was a serious affair. Hours of destruction had gone into that body, and it was the only source we had for study for the practical. One did not merely start over. "I ain't got no body" was very badly overworked that week until our group was reassigned to other people's remains.

I was switched into this kid Les Newman's group. There were only two on his cadaver. It was a really lucky break. Les was a nice guy and had the best-looking body in the room. And his cadaver was in excellent condition. He and his partner had been so meticulous with their dissection that when exam time came around everybody came in from the other labs to use their specimen for review. Les was also the only one around who had been able to reproduce the drawing of the Brooklyn–

Queens Expressway with the same rapidity with which it went up on the blackboard. At exam time everybody came in from the other laboratories to copy his notes. You could tell that Les was one of those people who did things right the first time. He joined the group in the back row.

# 4

The days all blurred together and it was winter. Sloppy, slushy, bone-cold New York winter. We pushed our bodies through the filthy snow, urged on by that burning little coal deep beneath our collective breastbones known as fear. Exams were the specter before us. Our forms were visible in the laboratory windows long after it had become dark in the streets below. We were more afraid of failing than of being mugged, and we had good reason to be. It was common knowledge among the other med schools in the city that our exams were impossible.

There was no question in our minds about what material we were responsible for. We were responsible for everything, including the lesser tributaries and the one percent of the time it was found on the left. We memorized the lab manual and tested each other by picking any portion of any sentence from any page and reading only half. If you couldn't supply the other half you were in trouble. You had to know it cold.

We reviewed and rereviewed and by the time we had our last laboratory session we were almost prepared. Our last lab was attended by everyone, as it was to be a special demonstration lab given by Folberg of "What is this crap?" fame. The demonstration was of the uncovering of the bones of the middle ear within the skull of the cadaver, a process so delicate and refined that it was relegated to instructors only. We stood by in awe on that morning in November as Folberg, with the dexterity of a diamondcutter and the aplomb of Toscanini, struck the single crucial blow which sent pieces of temporal bone flying out in all directions. When the dust cleared and he stepped back we all leaned over to witness the exposed, completely intact bones of the middle ear—the malleus, the incus, and the stapes. It was practically biblical.

It was time for finals. The rest of the world had long since ceased to exist and there was nothing on our minds but passing and making it to the next semester.

It was early early morning. Les and I were going in for some last-minute minutiae. As we came off the elevator we could see one of the guys running down the hall, his white coat flapping. In the dim light we had difficulty seeing who it was. As he got closer, we recognized Fred Horowitz, one of the graduate students. Fred was a really hysterical guy with a constant supply of gossip, one-liners, and an arsenal of jokes that were usually at someone else's expense. When they weren't about you, you would laugh your ass off. We hadn't seen Fred in days, but then again we hadn't seen anyone in days. Fred ran up to us and stopped.

"My God," he said, his face contorted and flushed, "did you hear?"

"Hear what, Fred?" We continued walking down the hall.

"President Kennedy's been shot. He's been taken to Parkland and they don't think he'll live."

"Sure, Fred," I said, opening the door to the lab. "Listen, we'll catch the punch line after lunch."

# 5

Exams are a learning experience. That's what professors always say. They are right; we learned a lot from the anatomy final. We learned who took uppers and who didn't, who'd move a tag on the practical exam so that everyone else behind him got the answer wrong, who'd steal your notes, who'd steal your sweater, who'd steal your microscope.

The best experience of all about exams, however, is the after-the-exam bullshit. This occurred of course after the exam, and it occurred in the hall outside. It went something like this:

"I failed, that's it, it's all over." The party speaking would drop his books in a heap on the floor and lean limply against the wall. The doors would open again.

"Oh Jesus Christ, what a goddamn off-the-wall exam. Was that off the wall or was that off the wall?"

Enter the bullshitter in the form of Morey Callahan casually leaving the exam room and lighting up a cigarette right outside the door.

"Morey. Whadja think? Was that impossible or what?"

Morey, who even at that early stage of his career was one of the best rookie bullshitters ever to hit the profession, would take a long drag on his cigarette, shrug his shoulders, and say "Actually I thought it was a gut; a real piece of cake."

"Oh my God, you're kidding! You've got to be kidding. What about question thirty-two? What did you put for question thirty-two?"

"I don't remember. That wasn't one of the three I wasn't sure of."

"Three?" The simultaneous shrieks were audible well down the corridor as the doors opened again and more people emerged. "Three? I left the first seventeen questions blank."

One of the really great things about high-grade bullshit is its timelessness and durability. It matures with the individual, like a talent, and what in your first year of medical school is a "piece of cake," in your first year of medical practice is "Mr. Mahoney, I want to say that although this was one of the most challenging and difficult deliveries of my career, we have for you a fine and healthy son." Once a bullshitter, always a bullshitter.

Les and I passed our exams. Anatomy and biochemistry were over and after a brief recess for Christmas we returned for the second half of the first year. Physiology, histology, and neuroanatomy.

Physiology was a nightmare unless you derived some sort of pleasure from killing large numbers of dogs and cats. I personally barely survived the experience, but I was one step ahead of the animal—who never survived.

We had new lab partners for physiology. Phil Minetta, Gary Maxwell, Les Newman, and me. We were assigned together, and in those first few days if anybody had said we were destined to become friends, we would have all said simultaneously, "Not on a bet."

Phil was the most serious person I had ever met. He sat in the front row and never cracked a smile. We got into a fight in the lab on the first day and didn't speak to each other for a week, making life very difficult for everyone. Les and Gary, on the other hand, managed to amuse themselves by running a steady dialogue.

"Nice jacket, Gary. Not on you, but nice anyway."

"Listen, Les, I've been meaning to tell you. You know that tie you had on yesterday? Wide. Very, very wide. A very wide tie."

Phil tolerated the three of us. One of these days, I thought,

I'm going to tell him what I think of him. I got my opportunity one rainy afternoon, when we had an armload of data and had to prepare a collective notebook for the lab instructor. Gary dropped off his data, leaving Les, Phil, and me. Phil suggested his apartment because it was most convenient. Neither Les nor I had ever been there.

We worked for hours without a break. I couldn't stand it any more, and finally Les said, "Hey, I've really had it, Phil. Let's finish tomorrow."

"Okay," he said. "I'll make you a drink before you go." Phil had enough liquor in his kitchen to stock a bar. He poured me a Chivas over ice and some hundred-proof vodka for Les. After half the glass, I was numb. [Four feet ten and eighty-nine pounds can't absorb too much liquor.] I looked around me. Phil was on his second drink and so was Les. They both looked fine; therefore I reasoned I must be too. "You know, Phil," I said in a voice slightly louder than I had anticipated, "you're a goddamn stiff."

He looked at me squarely. "Who's a stiff?"

"You are, for Christ sake. God, you never laugh or fool around or anything."

"Is that so?" he said. "Have a little more scotch, Joni."

"Thank you." I reached out my glass without getting up. He poured me another huge drink and one more for himself. I took a large gulp. "I mean the way I look at it, you never have any fun. You think he has any fun, Les?" Les nodded an exaggerated no. I looked at Phil. He was smiling.

"He's smiling. Look at that, he's smiling. What are you smiling at?"

"I'm smiling because you can't hold your liquor."

"Is that so?"

"Yes, that is so."

"Well, we'll see about that." I stood up abruptly and fell over. They caught me before my head hit the floor. They were both laughing hysterically. "Let's go to my house for supper," I said to the carpet. "Let's get some steaks and have a big dinner." "Sure," they said, "sure." They walked me back to my apartment.

I now lived within walking distance of the school in a regular building with a doorman. Several weeks before, someone had tried to make me a statistic in my basement flat. They kicked in both outer doors and when they couldn't get past the third one tried the window. The chicken wire probably saved my life, or maybe it was the screaming. Who knows?

We waltzed grandly through the lobby of the apartment and up in the elevator as I planned our meal and sent everybody out for ingredients. They left me in the apartment on the couch, and while they were out shopping I lit the broiler. The oven hadn't been used in a week and a piece of aluminum foil was still sitting on the bottom from the last steak that I had broiled; it was full of old fat and caught fire almost immediately. Phil and Les arrived at the same time the fire department did. Someone else had seen the smoke coming out from under the door. I had fallen asleep on the couch and had to be walked into the hall. Half our class lived in the building and got a chance to see me half shot in the hall, smoked out of my apartment, and in the company of two men with grocery bags. The rumors were quite numerous and exquisitely detailed.

After both the smoke and my head cleared we went back to Phil's, where he cooked us a magnificent dinner and a lot of coffee. We sat around and talked for the rest of the night. We became inseparable. Phil eventually taught me how to drink, but I never really taught him how to laugh.

# 6

It was at the very beginning of my second year that I met the first of the white-haired bastards. Edward Oberon was chairman of the micro department. He ran a tight ship. Yes, sir. He had a tight jaw and lines in the corners of his eyes and tight thin lips. I can only speculate about his rectum.

We were about two days into the course. Two days of watching bacteria swim by under the microscope, two days of staining ourselves with vital dyes, staining our lab partners and our clothes, staining our desks. We eventually stained the bacteria on our slides, but it took quite a bit of doing.

Our laboratory had the misfortune of having Dr. Oberon for a full-time instructor. Everybody else had graduate students for assistants and, since they were really only two lessons ahead of us anyway, they never got excited if we made a mistake. Oberon didn't tolerate mistakes. He didn't tolerate errors of any sort, particularly human.

One morning a graduate student appeared before us instead of Dr. Oberon. He told us that there would be no lab that morning. Why would there be no lab? We were all going to be vaccinated for TB. "Vaccinated for TB?" said I. "What for? I didn't know there was a vaccine for TB." I whispered to my lab partner, "Did you?" He shrugged his shoulders and tapped me to indicate that I'd better pay attention.

"So if you'll all just line up," the grad student was saying, "we'll do this quickly and then you can have the rest of the morning off." Everybody cheered, got up, and started filing toward the front of the room. I picked up my books and started out the door.

"Miss Scalia, where are you going?" It was a small lab and I was the only girl, making me immediately noticeable.

"I'm going to the library."

"Your BCG. You have to have a BCG this morning."

"I'm not taking it," I said.

"You're not taking it?"

"No. I'm not taking it. I don't even know what it is."

"But all the students get it," he yelled after me. I continued out the door. "Dr. Oberon is doing a study and all the students have to have it."

I didn't dare turn around, for I truly couldn't believe what I had just heard. There was a note in my mailbox the next morning: *You will report to the office of Dr. Edward Oberon, room 315, at 9:00* A.M. That's okay, I thought, folding up the note, I'm ready for him.

I had spent the entire afternoon in the library reading about BCG. Bacille Calmette-Guerin. A very interesting preparation. The most interesting thing about it at the time was the amount of conflicting data regarding its benefits as compared with its liabilities. The bottom footnote, "Recommended for use only in high-risk personnel," bothered me a little. The one reported death bothered me a lot. At that point in my life I was naive enough to consider myself as worth somewhat more to the world than another arm to vaccinate. Besides which, I thought Oberon was an incredible bastard for trying to pull off something like this. I arrived at nine o'clock with my armamentarium of references, prepared to discuss the matter.

I was admitted to his office, which was as I expected a tribute to himself. "Come in, Miss Scalia, come in." He did a great Boris Karloff. He indicated a chair in which I took my usual precarious seat on the edge so that my legs would reach the floor.

"I understand, Miss Scalia," he said, leaning forward across the desk, "that you refused to take the vaccine yesterday morning."

"Yes."

"There is of course some reason for it." His mouth gave a brief smile, but his eyes were dead on.

"Yes, to tell you the truth." I began reaching for my papers.

"Some very good reason," he interrupted me.

"I have here an article—"

"You know, Miss Scalia," I couldn't believe it; he interrupted me again and leaned all the way back in his chair, "I look at you and I say to myself, 'Just how serious is this young woman about being a doctor?' "

"Excuse me?"

He was fixed in his chair, his fingers intertwined in front of his mouth with the exception of his thumbnails, which were balanced against his bottom teeth. His red school ring stood out like a flag.

"I mean," he continued, "I look at you with your long flowing hair and your pink fingernails and your cute little skirts and I say to myself, 'Why, she's just here for the hell of it.' " His blue eyes took in my entire body without moving a micron. "Isn't that right, Miss Scalia?"

He didn't wait for an answer. He didn't have to; he was the big leagues and I was only a bat girl. He was the great soaring hawk contemplating his prey, knowing that he had her before she even knew she was being considered for dinner.

"Just how badly do you want to be a doctor, Miss Scalia?" he asked. "Tell me."

"Very, very badly. More than anything." I was squeezing both arms of the chair, but he already had my entrails out on the table and was picking them over at his leisure.

"Then you don't have any funny ideas that are—shall we say —antimedicine or anti the administration of drugs, do you?"

"No. No. I don't. It isn't anything like that."

"Good. That's good." He was out of his chair and walking toward the door. "Then why don't you roll up the sleeve of that pretty blouse and we'll get this BCG out of the way."

"Yes. Yes, of course." I grabbed my purse and left my papers on the chair. He flashed his secretary a big smile and held the outer door open for me like the true gentleman that he was.

My arm festered for weeks, just like everybody else's. When the damn thing finally scarred over into its final shape, I had the insane thought that if I took a magnifying lens and got up really close the scar would read in bas-relief "You have just been fucked by Eddie."

Violated or not, I made it through micro without contracting syphilis, which is always a good thing. Who'd ever believed you got it off a slide? We moved into the second half of the second year. We were ready to start with the heavies.

# 7

Pathology. Introduction to death.

The chairman of the department had been dead for years, which is probably what qualified him so eminently for the position. He had that pasty complexion that only comes from chronic underexposure to light and overexposure to formaldehyde. His good looks, however, were only surpassed by his personality and his lectures. These consisted of a chronological account of who had done what in pathology since the beginning of time. Material carefully researched, of course, consisting largely of personal communications, unpublished data, and academic trivia not to be found anywhere else except on the final exam, where it made up ninety percent of the questions. Let's hear it for the kids in the first row with the tape recorders.

Dr. Furth informed us that our initial responsibility in pathology was to attend fourteen postmortem examinations, "not more than three of which under any circumstances are to be performed by the medical examiner." What's the big deal with the medical examiner, I thought to myself.

The county hospital was the seat of the county medical examiner's office. Every unexplained death and every death by foul play made its way into the back entrance of the hospital past the red arrow and under the sign that said simply MORGUE.

The freshly dead have their own definite odor. It is pervasive and sickening. To the uninitiated it is undefinable and falls simply under the heading of "Oh my God, what is that smell?"

The morgue was in the subbasement of the hospital, down a flight of noisy metal stairs and through a heavy swinging door with a single window of wire-reinforced glass. The door opened into a long corridor with rooms staggered on either side. The far end of the hall to the right was a dead end. To the left, a huge floor-to-ceiling stainless steel door. It said REFRIGERATOR.

We entered the corridor to find it filled with a noisy group of men. Rough-talking, rough-looking, some with guns in business suits, some in uniform, some with cameras. I turned and whispered to Les, "What's going on here?"

"I don't know. I guess we'll just have to feel our way."

We became a part of the group in the hall and could see that they were part of a long line overflowing from one of the side rooms. We were pushed into the line and eventually shoved through the open door. It was clear we were in the wrong room.

The bodies of three naked men lay face up on stainless-steel tables. The room itself was huge, tiled in white, with overhanging lights placed strategically above each table. People were milling among the bodies. Directly in front of us and leaning over the table was the partially naked torso of another man who was, however, very much alive and smoking a cigar. "He took it right behind the ear," he said, pulling back some hair from the corpse's left ear. "And your exit," he went on, moving toward the other side of the table, "is right," he blew on his cigar, "right here. Right above the left eye. Gimme a probe; I'll show you." By now he was on our side of the table and in full view. He was in fact naked only from the waist up, his shirt having been thrown across a chair. He was about fifty, balding, with large coarse features. What kind of a ghoul, I wondered, would wander around the morgue with his shirt off like he was on a golf date?

"Now this guy," he said, moving on to the next table, "never had a chance."

Les and I couldn't get out the door we came in, so we had to file out with the rest of the crowd past the last body and through the door on the far end of the room. On the last table lay a robust-looking man with flaming red hair and a handlebar mustache. He looked the picture of health, and if you didn't notice the six small punched-out black holes in his chest, you would have sworn he was about to sit up and slap you on the back. Two morgue attendants unfolded a sheet and went to cover him. "Okay to move him, Doc?" The question was asked of the cigar-smoking nudist. "His wife is here."

We pushed open the door and got back into the hall, which was now almost empty. "Doc?" Son of a gun. We decided to try our luck with one of the other rooms; we wanted to get in at least one autopsy. Les and I went in separate directions to look.

I was halfway down the hall when I heard the screams. They were muffled, but well audible. Was it human? An animal, maybe? There were a few guys left in the hall talking to each other. They had to have heard the noise as well, but they seemed completely unaffected by it. The sound turned into a wail. It was a desperate sound. A call. It was coming from the stairway where we had entered. The other side of the heavy doors. Les was not in sight.

I walked in the direction of the cries and pushed open the stairway door. There was an abutment at the foot of the stairs; a low concrete wall that came out between the two sets of stairs and formed a little three-sided room. One side was glass, the same reinforced type as on the stairwell doors. A woman stood before the window. She was beating her fists slowly and dully, her face contorted with pain and anger as she viewed the body of her dead husband, whom she had sent off to work only hours before.

He was a butcher. He was expecting an early delivery of meat, and he and his partners went in early to receive it. When they opened the back door of their shop, three other men wearing ski masks rushed in and gunned them down, dragging their bodies into the shop and leaving them on the slatted wooden floor behind the counter.

Her grief finally overtaking her, the woman fell against the window and sobbed. Her palms against the glass, she pressed her fingertips to the pane as if somehow by touching it she could transmit the pressure through to him. I let the door close and stepped back into the corridor. "This is a mob hit," I heard someone say behind me. I ran down the hall and finally saw Les. He was waving to me from one of the doorways.

My relief was exceedingly short-lived as I entered the room. Les was standing by the doorway watching as one of the morgue attendants and what I assumed to be one of the pathology residents lifted the body of an old woman from the white metal gurney on which it lay, and dropped it on one of the tables with the holes around the edges.

"You medical students?"

We nodded. He introduced himself. He was indeed a resident.

I couldn't stop staring at the body on the table. Some little old lady with white hair just lying there naked on the table. Her skin was totally white and wrinkled like a chicken's. "Why is her back so purple?"

"That's dependent lividity. When you die all the blood settles to the most dependent position. It's a very important point. The ME will talk about it for hours."

"What's the ME?"

"The medical examiner, Dr. Varone. You'll meet him."

"I think we've already had the pleasure," Les said.

"Okay, now the first thing you do is take a good look at the body. You kind of do a brief physical." Not brief enough, I thought.

"I'm just going to kind of zip through this one if you guys don't mind, cause I'm in a hurry today."

"Sure." We both nodded.

He picked up a large scalpel, and without further ado made two huge slashing incisions under each of the woman's baggy breasts. They came together in a V. He then started at the apex of the V and slit the entire abdomen open down to the pubis. The fat and muscle jiggled apart. I grabbed what I thought was the wall. It was Les.

The resident slipped his knife under the skin covering the chest, and filleted it back. He did the same to the abdomen, and then reached for what looked like an Exacto knife. With two sudden curved incisions he had cut through the ribs on both sides. He flapped up the breastbone with short jerking movements, slipping his knife along the cut edges. The puffy gray lungs were suddenly visible. He reached again for the scalpel and walked down toward the woman's legs. He stopped and faced the torso. "We take the organs out en masse." He reached his gloved left hand through the large abdominal incision and dug around in the pelvis. "Once you get a good grab on the rectum, it's easy."

I wasn't quite sure yet whether I was going to throw up, pass out, do one and then the other, or just stand there with my nails dug into Les's arm. The resident continued vigorously, unabashed. He grabbed the rectum, bladder, and uterus and cut through them with his knife. The large arteries and veins to the legs were next and then both sides of the diaphragm, the kidneys and adrenals. He stopped. I took what I'm sure was my first breath.

He moved up the body to the chest cavity and then, with his hand resting gently on the lungs, he severed in one swipe the large vessels to the neck, the trachea, and the esophagus. He stopped when he hit bone. As we had watched, within very little time the woman had been completely eviscerated. The resident now carried her organs in a cluster, like a string of onions, and dropped them in the sink. He looked around him briefly, saw what he wanted lying on the morgue stretcher, and reached for it. An old blue chenille bedspread that had obviously come down from the ward with the patient. He balled it up in a wad and stuffed it into the abdomen. "Fills out the body better," he said. He then reached for a large upholstery-type needle, threaded it with some cotton twine, and with a series of whipstitches closed his incisions. "I just have to take out the brain and then we can examine the organs in detail."

He again reached for a scalpel. He turned the head sharply to one side and made an incision starting behind one ear. He continued it around the back of the head to the midline, turned the head in the opposite direction, and cut up behind the other ear. He slipped his knife between the scalp and the skull and separated them. He tugged and separated, the woman's forehead wrinkled, creased, and then totally disappeared as he pulled the entire scalp forward inside out and flapped it over her face. That did it.

"Excuse me, I'll be right back." Les looked at me as I wobbled out the door. I don't really know how long I was out in the hall but I eventually heard the sound of an electric saw and figured he was cutting through the skull.

I got back in time to catch the removal of the brain and the replacement of the upper half of the skull. It was all very neat and cozy, like the top of the cookie jar, fitting the rough edges in till they set right. The resident pulled the scalp back over the woman's head, fitted it snugly and closed the scalp incision.

"Now." he said with a relieved sigh. "We can get to the examination of the organs."

The "post" took three and a half hours from start to finish. I was actually finished about three minutes after the start and didn't recover for two days, during which time I did nothing but drink Coke because I couldn't look at food. I couldn't get that goddamn smell out of my nose. Les, whose father was a doctor, was not similarly affected. As he said, "My father had his office in his house and we learned to eat through anything."

# 8

The actual labs started the next day. Gross lab consisted of a number of rooms lined with specimens of previously removed organs. They were preserved in plastic mounts and labeled for teaching purposes. It was an overwhelming display: livers, lungs, kidneys, hearts. I reached for one of the specimens on the lower shelf. *Cancer of the colon: early* it said. A small segment of bowel had been opened to demonstrate that among the normally velvety folds there was a small area of gray tissue which was different from the rest. Not very impressive, I thought.

I put it back on the shelf and took the one next to it. *Cancer of the colon: late*. I turned it around a couple of times to get my perspective. It was confusing. It was hard to tell what I was looking at. It was just a formless gray mass, very irregular, somewhat like clay that had been left out overnight.

"Excuse me," I said to the lab instructor. "I don't understand this. It says 'Cancer of the colon.' Where is the colon?"

He looked up, scanning the specimen quickly. "Oh, it's been totally destroyed by tumor. That's just tumor mass you're looking at."

"You mean," I began, "that the tumor mass got that big by itself?"

"Not by itself. It got its blood supply from the colon, which it parasitized and invaded and then ultimately replaced."

"I see," I said, putting it back on the shelf. Very impressive.

The instructor looked up. "We're going to have organ recital in about half an hour over in the hospital if you are interested. The specimens are all fresh and you can put on some gloves and get a better idea about things. They look a lot different than the preserved material." Organ recital? Jesus Christ, what was organ recital?

I went to find Les, who was similarly engaged with his one piece of plastic. It contained a large gritty-looking oval slice of something. In the upper corner was a shallow excavation. *TB with cavitation: right lung*, it said. "Thank God for labels," Les said as I came up behind him.

"Hey, want to go to organ recital?"

A group of us walked over to the hospital. The events of the day before had been almost forgotten until I saw the building again. The three dead guys, the old woman, and half-naked ME; it didn't seem like it had actually happened. We walked down the metal stairs to the morgue past the glassed-in viewing room. The fingerprints were still on the window.

Organ recital was a joint conference in pathology and medicine given for the interns, residents, and medical students. It was held in a large circular room. The seats were arranged in the fashion seen so commonly in the old black-and-white pictures and in the early lithographs. "Medical Students Attending a Lecture." Only it wasn't black-and-white, it was living color; in this case the reference to anything living was altogether inappropriate. If there were a bizarre award, this department had to be the no-contest winner.

In the center of the room was a large table covered with powder-blue towels upon which some meticulous pathology resident had neatly displayed the internal organs of a human being.

"This is a forty-two-year-old female," the resident began his presentation.

I leaned over in my seat. *This* is a forty-two-year-old female? This? A pair of lungs, a heart, two kidneys, and a liver? What are you going to do when you're through here, put her hat on and give her carfare home?

"She was first seen in our institution," he continued, giving her complete medical history, her course in the hospital, and finally the events leading up to and including the time of her death. "I think," he said, "if you will all come down here and get a look at this, you can clearly see what killed her."

See what killed her. Yes, I thought, getting out of my seat, I'd like to see what killed her, see what was responsible for her having the final insult of being the star of organ recital. Something tangible did this? Something you can see?

The table was in view now. The fresh organs were glistening under the light. All in perfect configuration, but the cut surfaces instead of being completely smooth were speckled with grayish-white dots. "Miliary TB," one of the residents said immediately.

"TB?" I said, "who the hell dies of TB any more?"

"This lady right here," said the intern who had been taking care of her. "And we missed it."

We attended organ recital every day. It was a most incredible learning experience. It was right there for you, laid out for you. Death and disease: you could touch it, you could smell it, and you could hate it. The interns and residents who had taken care of these patients while they had been alive had to come and present the case histories and view the remains. No ego-tripping in this department. No ego-tripping and no points.

Organ recital had its drawbacks and over and above those one might expect. There was always the element of surprise during one of these conferences. Particularly if you were a woman.

The first time I saw Alexei Skolinsky, he was standing in the hallway of the hospital basement, screaming and stamping his feet. "Idiot! Nincompoop!" he bellowed. He was a short, stocky man with reddish-blond hair, blue eyes, and pink cheeks. A veritable cherub. "You have destroyed the specimen. You have ruined my presentation."

By this time he was directing his remarks to the refrigerator, since the object of his fury had obviously decided it was time for a quick exit. He whirled around on his heel and seeing only me, his eyes narrowed into bright blue slits. He was a totally frustrated being. He zipped around one more time, surveyed the hall, threw up his hands, and with a "Bah!" rushed away. A head appeared from one of the doorways.

"You must be Idiot Nincompoop," I said politely.

"Yeah," he said. I recognized him as one of the pathology residents.

"Who is that?" I asked, with the emphasis on the *is*.

"Are you kidding? The Mad Russian? Alexei Skolinsky? Himself? You don't know him?"

"No, thank God."

"He's a maniac. Unfortunately he's a genius; an authority on the liver. His conferences are worth a million if you can live through them."

"I can believe it."

"No you can't. But don't worry. Alexei likes girls."

Alexei did like girls. He liked to pinch them and embarrass them and throw bloody livers in their laps. And when they ran screaming from the room he would seize the opportunity to run shrieking after them: "Go ahead, run away. You'll never learn about the liver." (Which he pronounced *liwer*.) Needless to say, most of his hospital conferences went unattended by the female members of the class.

But attend or not, we were screwed either way. If we didn't go, there was always the perverse chance that we might be recognized during one of Alexei's formal weekly lectures at the medical school. He would actually interrupt his discussion, ask for the slide projector to be turned off, step down from the lectern and scan the audience. From then on, it was a matter of time. "You. Blondie. You. Yes, yes, you. Up. Stand up." Some poor female would rise slowly from her seat. "Why," he would begin slowly and quietly, "have I never before seen your face?" Any attempts at excuse were futile, to be sure. "Is it because perhaps, you, in fact"—he would pause here for a rest and then come in for his blinding finale—"have never been at one of my conferences?" (Which he pronounced *conferenzes*.) "Is it true? Could that possibly be the caze? Because if that were true, I would know it was only because you considered yourself already an authority on the liwer and therefore were totally prepared to give a conferenze yourself, which is what you will do in fact tomorrow at ten o'clock A.M. over in the hospital. You may now take your seat, expert."

There was only one girl in the class who wasn't afraid of Alexei. That was Elsie Friar. Elsie was my ideal. She was easily six feet tall. She was the one you called when you needed somebody to help you roll your cadaver. She was the one who could stand up in middle of a lecture and say to the lecturer in her best Brooklynese, "Hey, listen, I don't think that's right what you just said," and the lecturer would stop and consider the possibility of error. She was the one who slapped one of the guys clear across the stacks on the second floor of the library for saying "shit" in front of a nun who was looking for a reference book. She was the only one in our class to develop tuberculosis and spend a year of her life in a hospital bed swallowing twenty-six pills a day and being helped up and down because she was too weak to stand by herself. "Shit," I thought to myself when I went up to visit her, "goddamn germs have no respect for quality."

# 9

Although it would appear that we spent a great deal of our time looking at organs, preserved and otherwise, this was really only half of it. The microscopic pathology was the other very important half.

Whereas in histology we had learned to recognize normal cells and tissues, now we were learning to recognize abnormal cells and tissues. *TB* and *Cancer* were no longer adequate diagnoses; they were guesses, like "I bet it's CA." Adenocarcinoma, breast, metastatic, right lung; carcinoma, right lung, primary, small cell variety; astrocytoma, grade IV, cerebellum. Those were diagnoses. Those were specific diagnoses made under the microscope and made only under the microscope. We studied our bezorkies off. There was a patient on the other end of every one of those diagnoses; an incorrect call by a pathologist could mean the loss of a leg or a breast or a patient.

But we were only students, and our knowledge or lack of same carried no immediate consequence. We did what we were told and we went where we were assigned.

One of the things that we were required to attend was the

final lecture in pathology which was traditionally given in our institution by the medical examiner.

He came fully clothed to this event, which was a two-hour slide session of his most interesting cases. This included your run-of-the-mill train accidents, elevator-shaft mishaps, shotgun blasts, only of course at close range, street-sweeper manglings, and a whole host of other memorabilia that this man—who obviously enjoyed his work—went to great lengths to photograph and recreate in their best details.

People floating in the East River for two weeks, victims of a stampeding crowd—it was wonderful. The entire room was in a state of shock for days. But it was really the finale, and he obviously saved the best for last, that is still printed behind my eyeballs.

"Here's your typical Lysol abortion," he said, flashing on a slide. A young Puerto Rican girl lay dead on the floor, the rubber tubing still protruding from her vagina, her nightgown pulled above her hips. "This is what the inside of her uterus looked like," he said, flashing on the next slide. There was nothing but bloody slush on the screen. "They all look like this; all your chemical ABs," he said. "I've got a lot of these." He flashed at least ten more. All young women in various stages of nudity, in positions that would have been impossible to maintain in life. Preserved forever in thirty-five-mm color on a background of dirty basement and apartment-house floors. Several guys got up and walked out.

I'll remember those slides as long as I live, and I'll remember them the next time somebody comes by with his or her big Right to Life poster and tells me what a sin it is to have a legal abortion with a sterile instrument.

The Right-to-Lifers; the Bible-beaters; the guys who worship their own sperm. They have perfect families. Little blue-eyed, freckled-faced kids who all pray together and love God and wear perpetual smiles, because they are wanted children. Preserve the fetus at all costs. Carry the pregnancy to term at all costs. The cost comes high. The cost of denying a woman a legal sterile abortion comes pretty damn high. You can't get much higher than a dead girl on a basement floor. Unless you want to consider the children with the third-degree burns and the skull fractures and the welts and the impetigo scars from being beaten with wire hangers and burned with lighted cigarettes. Or maybe the other little babies who have been fortunate enough to have been carried to term so they can lie in their cribs starving and screaming until they die, only to be thrown out with the potato peelings and tamped down into the trash can as waste; that's part of the cost. Is that high enough? I guess not. I guess that's not good enough when you've been ordained by God, and what you really want to do is not save the baby, but punish the mother. Punish her by making her live with her "sin." Only she won't live with it, she'll die with it. But I guess that's okay too, because the "good" people don't perpetrate errors like accidental pregnancies, and really, those people are the only ones worth saving. "We have a responsibility to the fetus: a responsibility to human life." Wonderful. If that's really true, if you have this burning sense of responsibility, this overwhelming need to do good, well then do us all a big favor: spare us your gospel, your self-proclaimed sanctity, and your perfection. Keep it to yourselves and don't wreak any more harm than you already have on those of us who are only human and do occasionally make mistakes.

# 10

Our next big subject in the second half of the second year was pharmacology. Pharmacology; drugs, pills, and medicines. Medicines. At last some medicine, any kind of medicine; liquid, tablet, or suspension, what did it matter? Finally, finally when your mother called up and said, "Listen, Aunt Gertrude is taking digitalis, what does it mean?" you knew what to say. Unfortunately you usually said too much, because armed with your new repertoire you felt obliged to lay all of your information out at once, complete with side-effect warnings and contraindications. A veritable compendium of terrifying information. This practice very often sent Momma and Aunt Gertrude screaming out of the house prepared to bludgeon their family physician of thirty-five years, which in some instances was not at all a bad thing. We really got into pharmacology. We knew the methods of action of the drugs, the sites of action, the duration, the breakdown, the excretion. We loved it. It was the first real upper.

Physical diagnosis was next. The first glimpse of promise, the first step in the laying on of hands. Nicely said, but let's face it, physical diagnosis in the early days is playing doctor. It is looking in people's blouses, it is looking down their pants, it is grabbing everything everybody always told you not to grab, it is saying "Excuse me," "Pardon me" about a hundred and fifty times in the course of an examination. It is "Did you see that guy over in bed three?" What guilt. You feel like a fraud. You are a fraud; you have no insight at all into disease; all you are doing is learning what is normal. What a normal heart sounds like. What normal breathing sounds like: in a thin chest, in a muscular chest. What are the normal sounds we make? What does a normal abdomen feel like? What organs can we feel from the outside, and how good are our eyes and ears and hands? It is a mechanical, structured process done with no understanding, but it is basic foundation for making the diagnosis. If you don't get this right, you won't get the rest right.

I guess that's why we were such easy prey for the medical-equipment salesmen. The more doctorlike equipment you had and carried, the more you felt like the genuine item. At least you knew you would look like the genuine item. Your stethoscope was the ultimate hallmark. You could tell who the guys with class were by the type of stethoscope they carried. That's what we thought, anyway. The best stethoscope is the biggest stethoscope and the biggest stethoscope is the one with the most heads. We were lucky we could distinguish heart sounds from gas in the first few days, but we all rushed out to the store.

"Hey, what's this for?" someone would ask. "Oh," the salesman, who could see us coming for blocks, would reply casually, "you don't need anything like this at your stage of the game, we usually only sell these to the cardiologists." Like taking candy from a baby.

"Well, I might as well get a good one and keep it for life," the sucker would say. "By the way, what are the other two heads for?"

The salesman would then give his explanation of the wonders of the lugubrious three-headed instrument, which only the strongest of necks could support under the best of circumstances. The explanation eventually clinched the deal. "This, of course, is your regular bell and diaphragm to distinguish the low- and high-frequency murmurs." Everybody nodded knowingly. "Your second head here is for your slightly more sophisticated use."

"Such as?"

"Well, for example, let's say you wanted to examine a sandhog while he was taken ill doing a repair job on the Lincoln Tunnel. In the event of a cave-in you wouldn't get any interference from the sliding rock and the background screams."

"And what about the third head?"

I missed this explanation as I was paying for my el cheapo special at the counter, but I figured that for the price quoted the third head had to enable one to distinguish a grade one over six mitral stenosis from two roaches fucking on the bedside curtain.

Naturally, everybody had to have a black bag in which to put all his new toys. And again, who else but a medical student or Marcus Welby carries a black bag? Nobody else carries them. Because if they did, people would think they were medical students. Interns, for example, do not carry black bags; they traditionally carry everything in their pockets. Their notebooks, their penlights, their tongue blades, their list of normal values, their lunch tickets, their shirt tickets, their paychecks, their tourniquets, their reflex hammers, their lab slips, their tape measures, their car keys. A resounding crash in the middle of house staff rounds seldom if ever is cause for the turn of a head. Everybody knows it's just somebody's pocket giving way. Residents are above all this. They never carry black bags; they don't carry anything. That's what they have interns and medical students for. "Have you got a penlight?"

We spent weeks examining each other and terrifying each other. "I think you've got a big liver." "I think you've got a murmur." "I think we should continue this later in my apartment." The Student Health Service was suddenly besieged with second-year medical students (known worldwide for their neuroses) who had to be seen immediately for their presumably enlarged and noisy organs. But even if we found a large liver or an abnormal heart sound, we didn't know what it meant. We hadn't gotten up to that yet. God, the frustration. We didn't know anything. When we finally hit the wards and got our first patients, we were definitely the largest group of stumblebums ever to have crossed under a caduceus.

Les's patient vomited on him immediately and ruined his new houndstooth pants. Cheryl Foster's patient died right in the middle of her saying "Could you take a deep breath, please?" He obviously couldn't. And my patient looked at me and said, "You're a doctor? You?"

We would all meet after examining our respective patients and methodically go over their physical findings with our learned preceptor, who was probably about a hundred years old. I think he was one of the first doctors ever made and he had to have had one of the first stethoscopes ever made; it was like a Stradivarius. He would question us. "Did you hear a murmur in this man?" You didn't know. Two minutes before you were sure, but now you weren't so sure; maybe he did have one. "No, I didn't hear one." "Good. He doesn't have one." Everybody lied a little, but nobody knew it, except the preceptor. We got better. We didn't get as good as we thought we were, but we were a lot better than we had been.

By the end of the rotation we were all arguing and debating the fine points between a grade three and a grade four murmur, and speculating whether the critical abnormality was best demonstrated in the left lateral decubitus position or lying face down in a hammock swinging from the ceiling. After six weeks of basic training we were ready for the big time. We were ready for the third year.

# 11

We started the third year with medicine, and there were three in our group: Les, myself, and Waldo Macelroy.. Waldo was the oldest guy in our class and a good ten years older than I was. He had previously worked in public relations for the Dooley Foundation. When Dr. Tom Dooley had gone to Laos, Waldo had gone to Laos with him, and when Dr. Dooley died of his cancer, Waldo figured that even the best PR man in the world didn't have a chance against a good solid group of malignant cells, so he enrolled in medical school. The faculty didn't get off his back from the first day he got through the door. They called him Jungle Doctor, and they gave him more than the usual hassles. But Waldo, he just took it all in, with his big Texas smile. When Waldo was a gentleman, he was all gentleman, but like all complex people, he had another side. When we elected him president of the class, he was probably the first in the history of medical school to start off his acceptance speech with "Shit, guys, we're all the fuck in this together." Waldo actually gave new meaning and dimension to the word *shit*. When he said it, it had about three syllables and a drawl.

We met in this unbelievable cafe for breakfast every

morning before we went to the wards. Waldo insisted that you had to have a good Texas breakfast before you went to work. His definition of a good Texas breakfast was three sunny-side-up eggs with bacon, a side order of ham, two orders of toast, a glass of orange juice, a glass of milk, many cups of coffee, and as he said every morning, "Just bring me the check and a mop." He insisted I eat along with him. "Shit, honey, you look like a stick." I didn't look like a stick for long, that was for damn sure, because the only thing that Waldo thought was more important than a good breakfast was a good lunch.

The "restaurant" in which we dined was on the same block as the hospital, and enjoyed the same state of cleanliness. We never died from anything we ate there, which proves the point that dirt is very rarely in itself fatal. Waldo had mastered the art of eating and telling filthy jokes at the same time, and Les spent most of his breakfast spilling his coffee from laughing so hard. So did the rest of the place, because Waldo told it, in his best Texas fashion, for the whole room. After he finished what were probably some of the grossest stories I have yet to hear recreated, he never failed to lean across the table and say, "Ah hope ah haven't said anything to offend you, honey. Eat your home fries."

We were a very interested group.

We'd bought our medicine textbooks weeks before, in anticipation of and preparation for the great days that lay ahead. I had purchased Harrison's *Principles of Internal Medicine*. "You have to read the first four-hundred pages of Harrison before you even hit the ward." That was the word, or "the Gospel according to Murray Feinberg," who was one year ahead of us. Les purchased the other great text, Cecil and Loeb. We argued all the way home from the bookstore. "You can read my Harrison, if you want to," said I.

"What do I need your Harrison for? I have the better text."

"You don't have the better text! Everybody knows that Harrison is the better text."

"Everybody knows that only the first four-hundred pages of Harrison are worth anything; I'll read your first four-hundred pages."

"You don't know anything."

I read the first four-hundred pages like it was the Bible. It *was* the Bible. Chapter I: "Approach to the Patient." The History and Physical Examination. The Art of Medicine. The

Physician's Responsibility. Chapter II. Pain. Fever. Headache. Backache. Pain in the Chest. This was really it. The Word. The Real Stuff.

We began our first day with an introductory talk, given by the head of the department of medicine. Heinrich Lindemann, M.D. Heinrich Lindemann was the very specter of Medicine: the embodiment, the aura. He was shockingly white from head to toe. He was white and sterile and cold. He was sharp like a blade. He was the Future. The Mold. The Ultimate Cookie from which we were all to be cut. In His own Image created He us. He spoke in a monotone. He addressed us as "future physicians." He reminded us of the "awesome responsibility" that Medicine was; that being a physician was. There was dead silence in that auditorium. When we were dismissed we could hardly breathe.

It was probably some measure of good fortune that we could hardly breathe, because the smell in the hospital elevator wasn't anything you needed at full strength. We rode up in the clanking metal car to the fifth floor, where the three of us were assigned to Male Medicine. Male Medicine at the County certainly seemed a far cry from what Heinrich was describing. The ward had all the dignity of the men's room in the Times Square subway station. Some of the patients were handcuffed to the peeling metal beds in which they lay. This was not because they were being tortured but it was because they were in fact dangerous, and instead of a nurse at their bedside, they sported a uniformed officer. The ward consisted of about twenty beds, all in the same state of decay, lined up against the walls, with curtains between them. That isn't actually correct. There were runners for curtains, but many times no curtains were present. There were some touches of gracious living, however; a barber came around every morning to shave the patients. As we emerged into the large ward the barber was in fact already busy at work shaving a patient who had been dead for at least two hours but whose body had not yet been taken downstairs. He seemed quite unflustered when the nurse informed him of his error, and he picked up his mug of soapsuds and moved on to the next bed.

We found our intern in the office marked DOCTORS ONLY. Steve Creighton. Steve must have been sick the day Heinrich gave his lecture. He was delighted to see the three of us. Small wonder. From that day forward, he never again drew another tube of blood or did another blood count, and that accounted for about three-quarters of his working day, because Creighton would draw blood on anybody for anything. "This guy looks bad; let's get another hemoglobin." "I want a sickle-cell prep on this guy, three times." "Why times three?" "You got to get it times three." Creighton had to get everything times three. Oncc wasn't enough for him to know that he had made the diagnosis, or had not made the diagnosis. We called him The Vampire. As if things weren't bad enough, the needles in the hospital were definitely holdovers from World War I. Old metal needles, dull as hell: you could bounce them off the wall. Les and Waldo and I went down to the surgical supply house and bought boxes of disposable needles. What we really wanted to do was dispose of Steve, but the possibility seemed unlikely.

Steve was a great con artist. He had to be, because after a week we all refused to do anything for him. He started making us deals. We all got sucked in at least once. He'd come into the office.

"I've got a really interesting patient that just came in. Really interesting."

"What's he got?"

"Oh listen, I think you want to make the diagnosis yourself; this is a challenging case."

"Oh yeah?"

"Yeah. Listen, if you work up the patient, you know, do the history and physical and the lab work and urine, I'll let you put the work-up in the chart and present him on rounds. It'll be a real feather in your cap."

"Okay, where is he?"

"Bed ten, Mr. Haversham."

Mr. Haversham was ninety-eight years old and had just had a massive stroke to which he was entirely entitled. The only thing interesting about Mr. Haversham was that he had lived to the age of ninety-eight, and I had never really seen anybody that old before. Steve did it at least once to all of us, and after that point he truly could have had the one reported case of rabies in the entire world caused by a bite from a rubber duck and we would have refused to take the patient.

We'd do our morning chores, and then make rounds with Creighton, two other interns, and the medical resident.

We really did have some interesting patients. As a matter of fact, we probably had the single largest collection of rare diseases around. Our institution specialized in the diagnosis of rare disease. If you had something rare, they'd find it. They'd test for it, and retest, and eventually they'd make the diagnosis. Making the diagnosis was what was important. Making a rare diagnosis was even more important, because then you could publish it. You had to push for that almighty rare diagnosis. The patient? The patient wasn't important, it was the diagnosis that was crucial.

Charlie Aldrich was a thirty-five-year-old man who had come in with some headaches and dizziness. He had been in the hospital for over a month. He had a blood pressure that made your hand tired before you could get the cuff up high enough to stop the banging in your ears. They had been collecting his urine, and recollecting his urine, and drawing his blood, and sending him to x-ray, and he hadn't had one milligram of anything to lower that astronomical reading. "Why isn't Mr. Aldrich getting any medication?" we asked our resident. "Oh, you can't give him anything, it will interfere with the laboratory work, and we have to send his urine all the way to a lab in California to do the tests." Les and I went crazy. "He's going to stroke out." The resident was tolerant. "Now take it easy; you medical students always get hysterical over everything."

They found Mr. Aldrich dead on the bathroom floor one morning. The lab work came back a couple of weeks later. "What do you know? He had it; he really had it." The resident was jubilant.

After our rounds with the interns and residents we would all nervously await the coming of our preceptor—The Attending. The Attending was a doctor who had a practice in the community and came in twice a week to donate his knowledge and teaching skills to the medical students and the house staff of interns and residents. We hit it big with our Attending. With Leonard Matheson, we hit it big.

He was a very tall man: maybe six-three. His back was straight and his eyes were front, and when we first saw him coming down the hall we all fell over our own feet to get out of his way. Everybody rustled around, grabbing for the chart racks, grabbing for x-rays, and generally moving in a state of panic. He paused at the door of the ward. "All right, let's get this outfit together," he said and marched into the center of the room. Matheson would stand quietly, look up and down each bed, pivot slowly on his heel, assess the other side of room, slowly, carefully, taking his time. Then he would face our little cluster of bodies and say, "You have a patient with a problem for me?" Everybody breathed simultaneously and the residents began their presentations. What the patient came in with, his history if he could give one, what his physical findings were, what the lab work was, what diagnosis and treatment had been instituted. The whole thing. Matheson didn't interrupt. He always let you give him the whole story. But then we never knew what might happen next. He might say, "If this is the patient in bed eleven that we are talking about, and I assume it is, the reason why your therapy has not been working, Doctor, is because he does not have heart failure but he has a tumor in his lung, and his breathing will not improve no matter how much digitalis or how many diuretics you give him." We would just stand there.

"His chest x-ray is normal," the resident would say.

"Would you like to venture a small wager?"

The resident would gulp. "It's normal."

"Maybe the x-ray you saw was normal, but that man's x-ray is not normal. Look at his color. Look at his color: the man has a tumor." He had a tumor. You could bet your ass on it. It was right on the films.

It wasn't a one-time thing. Matheson's intelligence and clinical know-how was not a one-time thing. Learning was an ongoing, ever-expanding way of life with him. He was never satisfied until he was satisfied. He didn't want any of us to be satisfied with anything but the best and the finest level of thought and care. He never missed a subtlety. He'd listen to the patient. When he took a history, he knew just where to cut it, just when to let the patient talk, just how to get that one piece of information that nobody else had obtained and that you couldn't get in a hundred years of ordering anything times three. We loved him. We damn near worshiped him. We worked our asses off for him so that when we gave a presentation it was as fine and thorough and complete as we possibly could have made it. What he gave to us nobody else had to give, because he was one of a kind.

# 12

My troubles began with an early-morning visit on the wards from Heinrich Lindemann himself. His electrifying whiteness was even more apparent up close. He walked in, waved his hand to motion that he wanted the medical students, and we followed him into the ward.

He picked up a chart and approached the bed. He said a few words to the patient and then turned to our group. He asked me a question. I gave him what I thought was an appropriate answer and he looked at me with utter disdain. He said about three more words, put down the chart, and left. That was it. "Was there something wrong with what I said?" I asked Les and Waldo. "Was that the wrong answer?"

"I don't know, Joni. I don't think it was right." The resident turned around to me and said, "It's too bad you blew that question. He'll grade you on it."

"Grade me on it? On one question?"

"Yup, one question. That and of course being a girl. Heinrich hates women."

I worried about Heinrich, but only briefly.

A couple of days later we were all standing around waiting for Matheson to arrive. We were very excited. We had a great patient to present. Les had discovered a patient with malaria; he had been on the ward for two weeks, undiagnosed by the residents. Les had stayed one night and waited up with the man until he had finally gotten a chill. Les drew a blood sample immediately, made a slide, and looked at it. The parasites were there. It was a coup.

There was a crash from the other end of the hall.

"What was that?" We looked down the corridor. I could barely make out a small group of people. Steve looked up from the chart rack and squinted. "Oh, that's just Dr. Baldwin having a tantrum."

"Who's Dr. Baldwin?"

"Alice Baldwin."

I took a few steps down the hall. There was a gray-haired figure with a broad back standing on the other side of the chart rack for Male Medicine II. (We were Male Medicine I.) I could only see the figure from the waist up. The hair was close-cropped at the back. "I don't see any woman down there."

"That's Alice." There was another crash and the chart rack was pushed into the wall. The figure turned around. She was wearing Red Cross-type shoes, a midlength gray skirt, and a short white coat. She made a rapid turn and entered one of the rooms at the far end of the hall.

"God help somebody," said Steve. Matheson arrived at that moment and we all became lost in the fever and romance of malaria in a twenty-three-year-old merchant seaman. Alice Baldwin was temporarily forgotten.

We spent six weeks with Dr. Matheson on Male Medicine and then the whole group switched to Female Medicine. We were all looking forward to it. It could have been terrific. It might have been great, it might even have been good, had it not been for one thing. We no longer had Matheson for an Attending. We now had Dr. Alex Doropolis.

Dr. Doropolis could have been an ad for the Wet Look. His hair was perfectly fixed in one position due to the quantity of grease he obviously carefully applied each morning along with his after-shave, which incidentally could have felled a trunkless elephant at fifty yards. Dr. Doropolis tried to impress us with his knowledge.

The patient was a twenty-one-year-old black girl who came into the hospital with fever and a hot swollen left knee. Doropolis made a diagnosis of acute rheumatic fever. He then took the floor and for one half-hour lectured on rheumatic fever. He was emphatic. He was assertive, he was grandiose. He was incorrect. We all knew he was incorrect, having been through rheumatic fever only the week before at great length. We had read everything that the library, the current journals, and the publications from the Society of Rheumatic Diseases had to offer.

Doropolis took a drink from the water cooler and perched himself on the corner of the desk. A real sight. "And now, Miss Scalia," he said, ostensibly looking at my name tag but in actuality trying to decide whether it was more profitable to look down my blouse or up my skirt. "What is your opinion of this patient?"

I looked up, startled, having been counting the blobs of dust under the table for the last ten minutes.

"My opinion of the patient?" I said hesitantly.

"Yes," he said, ever pompous. "What do you think of my diagnosis?"

I could see Les sitting behind him. His eyes widened as if to say, "Don't do it."

I did it. I couldn't help it. He was asking for it. He'd done a lousy job; somebody had to tell him. I systematically took apart everything he had said, simultaneously of course supplying him with the appropriate reference source that contained the correct information. I called him on the one pertinent physical finding that he had neglected to discover in his rapid examination, and I arrived at my diagnosis of arthritis secondary to gonorrhea. I took my seat. The tension in the room was more than considerable. Waldo, who had several times tried frantically to stop me with hand signals, was sitting tapping all ten fingers at once on his thighs. Les was looking up at the ceiling, attempting to keep from biting the stem off his pipe.

Doropolis was a column of anger. "You have much medicine to learn, young lady," he said, and peremptorily dismissed us.

# 13

Our ward rounds were interspersed with formal lecture material, given in the good old lecture hall, our home away from home, by various members of the department of medicine. One very notable talk was given to us by Dr. Daniel Loo. Dr. Loo was an authority on diabetes. He was short and squat with white hair that flopped about in all directions, and small wire-framed glasses that sat astride his sharp little nose. He was in constant motion from the moment he entered the room. Forward and backward motion. Side-to-side motion, as he wandered helter-skelter in front of the blackboard and behind the large counters that separated the lecturer from the students. We couldn't hear him. We couldn't hear a thing he said. He said it all to his sleeve. He said it to the floor. He gave at least one fifteen-minute set of remarks to the left leg of his pants. Every once in a while we caught a word. "Diabetes." "Fat." But then he was barreling by again, mumbling and snorting like a little rhinoceros.

"Did you get any of that?" I said to Les.

"Not one goddamn word."

I got Dr. Loo for the final exam. I had a patient with cirrhosis of the liver. Dr. Loo didn't want to discuss cirrhosis.

He wanted to discuss diabetes; the ins and outs of diabetes, what the latest work was that was being done in diabetes. He did not want to know what I knew, he wanted to know what I didn't know—or in this particular case, what I didn't hear. What about my patient? What about the history and physical exam and treatment? He didn't want to know about that. I must have asked fifty people. "Did you have Loo for an examiner?" "No," they said. "No, thank God. He fails everybody."

I was worried. Les said it was silly to worry. The final was only part of it; the ward work was what was really important. That was true, that had to count. My ward work was good. Hell, it was more than good, I knew that.

It was the day after the exam. I got a note in my mailbox to go to Heinrich's office. I was glad. Maybe I was going to be asked to take the final exam again. I sure hoped so.

The minute I walked through the door of his office I knew I didn't have a chance. Not only was I guilty of having answered incorrectly, God knows, but more important, I was guilty of something else. What was it? What had I done that was greater than having screwed up an exam? What was it that could account for the look on his face when I sat down in his office? That was it! I had sat down in his office! In the sanctum sanctorum. I had dared to take a seat in his most professional presence, in my fur coat, with my red woolen dress and my long hair, looking like the person that I was instead of the person that he thought I should be.

It was the same look he'd given me on the ward. It was a look that said "How dare you; how dare you think you can be a doctor?"

"Sit down." He said, "I've called you here today to discuss your grade in medicine."

No, I thought, you're wrong, Joni, you're reading him wrong. You got in here because you have brains; the other stuff can't really matter.

"You have failed the rotation," he said. "You have failed, and you have failed badly. Unless you are able to improve yourself with a summer of concentrated study, you may consider your career as having come to an early close."

There was nothing between us but his words; they occupied the whole room.

"Have you anything to say, Miss Scalia?"

Did I have anything to say! Did I have *anything* to say? Did I have anything to *say*? Did *I* have anything to say; that was it, did *I* have anything to say about what was happening, about what was going to happen? Did I in fact have any say at all? The answer was as obvious when I thought about it as it had been in the office of Edward Oberon. I knew there was a familiar ring to the scene. "No. I have nothing to say."

"I'll send you a copy of what reading materials you are expected to cover and to whom you will report when the remainder of the school year has been completed."

I left the office, wrapping my coat tightly around me. I needed a fur coat; I was really cold.

When I got back to the apartment, Les and Phil were there. They were sitting on the couch. As soon as I saw them, I started crying.

"What's wrong?" Les said, coming toward me.

"I failed. I failed medicine."

"What are you talking about?" Les said. "How could you have possibly failed medicine?"

"I failed. I just came from Heinrich's office. They're going to make me take it over."

Phil had gotten up and had paced over to the window. "Fuckers! Lousy bunch of fuckers."

I was whirling around the room in my fur coat, waving my arms, crying and screaming. "What is it? What is it with me? What do I have to do? Who do I have to be, just tell me, for Christ's sake, I'll do it."

Les grabbed me. I was completely hysterical. He looked at me. "I want you to stop crying. Then I want you to sit down, and then, when you have it all together, I want you to call Matheson on the phone and find out what went wrong; because if he knows he will tell you."

I looked at my watch: 4:30 P.M. "It's late," I blubbered.

"He might still be in his office," Les said. Phil was playing with the Venetian blinds. I went into the kitchen and blew my nose in a paper towel. Goddamn bastards. Wring the life out of you. You could be a goddamn mediocre know-nothing son-of-a-bitch, but if you were a man you could sail right through. Mediocre and lazy and know-nothing, but it was okay because nobody noticed and nobody expected anything from you.

"Why the hell do I have to be superlative, why do I have to be magnificent just to qualify as average?" I was screaming again.

Les came in with the phone book.

"Here's Matheson's number. Call him."

I did. I called him. His nurse put me through and I blurted it all out. I wanted to hear it from him. I had to know if he had been the one: someone I respected so totally. He was quiet after I stopped talking. He finally said something.

"I'm sorry to hear that, Joni, I really am. You can be more than sure that it didn't come from me."

"Thank you. Thank you very much." I hung up. Phil and Les were standing right in front of me.

"So?" Les said. "Was it him?"

"No. It wasn't him; thank God it wasn't him." I walked out of the kitchen, temporarily relieved for no good reason. It was then that I heard Les's voice, quiet as usual, coming from the kitchen. "That little Greek prick." Instantly, of course I knew that he was correct. The little Greek prick. But what about the great white Popsicle, and the little gray rhino?

I was in emotional turmoil for days. My fury was truly only surpassed by my embarrassment. The enormity of failure in medical school is unparalleled. To have failed medicine is not to have failed a subject, a rotation, it is to have failed—period. At this point in time, your medicine has already become your totality. It has become your whole life. But you don't know it; you don't see it. You only see as far as the next page, the next section, the next chapters. And when you finish those, there are always more. More to get through, more to learn. More to understand, to assimilate, so that gradually you become one with the printed words, and the diagrams, and the examples, and you don't even remember having read them because they are now a part of you; they have become you, and you have become them.

Besides which, everybody knows the kind of people who have to repeat courses in medical school: the total yutzes. The shleps, who can't even tie their own shoes, the incredible shmendricks who still carry school bags and, even to the most untrained eye, appear to have never made it as far as puberty. And most of all, the shmegegges. These are the guys that fail. I knew that. And now I was going to be a part of this elite coterie.

My rage overtook me, and for days, months, and—I confess—even years afterward I dreamed at night, and fantasized during the day, as to how I was going to take my revenge on the little Greek prick and the great white Popsicle.

I would call up my Sicilian father and say "Hit him."

"Sure, baby," he'd say and he'd hang up the phone, knowing exactly what I wanted without a word having been spoken.

Doropolis would go down in a blaze of bullets; splattered all over the street, his lunch of moussaka and rice still in his gullet. And when they brought him into the emergency room, with lights flashing and sirens going at full scale, I in fact would be the doctor on duty. The remainder is too disgusting to dwell on; however, one of my other real favorites still flashes by every now and again. In this fantasy, I am doing a tapdance across Heinrich's floury face to an original ballad entitled "Yes, I Have Something to Say." I punctuate all the downbeats by kicking him in the left temporal region, and for the finale I make my stethoscope into a giant slingshot and fire him like a stunning white missile into the orchestra pit. I like that one because it has a lot of class. The little gray rhino I'd bring down with an elephant gun.

The only thing, I rationalized later on in the evening after about thirty-seven glasses of vodka, was that nobody knew that I had failed. Nobody needed to know, really; after all, a lot of kids stuck around the hospital during the summer for special projects. That was it, I would be doing a special project. The next morning, I took myself and my head into school to pick up my mail. In the hall I met Mike Reilly, one of the class clowns.

"Hi ya, Cutie," he said, putting his arm around me. "Listen, I heard you took a dive in medicine. That's a real shame. Really the shits."

# 14

I had very little opportunity to worry about "what I was going to be doing instead of my summer vacation," since the introductory lecture in surgery began the day after the medicine final.

We all met in the lecture hall, Phil and Les and I. Having been temporarily separated during our medicine rotation, we managed to get into the same group for surgery.

There was a young burly guy with black curly hair standing behind the long desk in the front of the lecture hall. He had two basins in front of him and there were towels laid out beside the basins. "Who the hell is that?" said Phil. Nobody seemed to know.

"Good morning, I'm Dr. Silverberg. I'm with the department of surgery. Let's have a volunteer up here, please." Mike Reilly naturally volunteered, and everybody applauded appropriately.

"Fine. Now," Silverberg said, pulling something out from beneath the table, "if you will just stick your hands right in this pot." Reilly hesitated, but only briefly, and then plunged both hands into the pot. They came up totally black.

"What is this crap?" Phil whispered.

"Now, if you will permit me, I'm going to blindfold you and ask you to wash your hands in this basin, using the brush, and I want you to tell me when you think they are clean."

"Oh for Christ's sake," said Phil again, sinking down into his seat. We watched the whole procedure, and Reilly finally finished and dried. His hands were clean. Silverberg looked a little put out but thanked him, and then launched directly into his lecture about sterile technique and the principles of asepsis. Phil was losing his mind and kept shifting around in his seat.

I had actually been reading about this subject the night before. About the history of surgery, about how things were done before anyone knew anything about preventing infection: before the concepts of sterility, before rubber gloves, before people even knew about washing and doctors helped carry infection and death from one person to another with the touch of their hands. I bought both surgery texts.

Silverberg was finishing. "Thank Christ, let's get out of here; this guy's an asshole." Phil reached for his books.

"Before you leave," Silverberg was saying, "I want you to pick up these sheets telling you where to report this afternoon."

Les and I picked up a sheet for Phil, who definitely felt it was beneath him. When we got outside, Les started to laugh.

"Hey, Phil, look at this."

We scanned the sheet until we located our respective names. They were in the left-hand column. On the right was the matching name of the preceptor who would be in charge of us for the surgical rotation. *Marvin A. Silverberg* it read.

"Oh, Christ," said Phil.

We arrived on the surgery ward shortly after one thirty. Dr. Silverberg was standing in the middle of the ward with his hands on his hips, surrounded by an intern and two residents. He glared at us as we came through the door.

"Nice of you to get here. Where the hell have you guys been?"

We all stopped in the doorway. The mimeographed sheet had distinctly said one thirty.

"You might as well get it straight now, you're not here for a vacation, so in the future you damn well get your ass in here on time."

I stood there thinking about the night before. Phil and I had gone out to dinner. Les had to work in the lab. Phil and I had a long talk; actually Phil had done all the talking. I had spent most of the time crying into my veal parmigiana.

"Listen, Joni, you've got to do very well on these next two rotations. Heinrich is out for your ass, and he carries a lot of weight, so don't give anybody an edge."

"What do you mean?"

"I mean, let's have a little less James Dean and a little more Sandra Dee."

"What?"

"You know, big smile, make the guys think you like them, and when you get a guy like Doropolis, don't feel like you've got to call him on his weak points."

"You're crazy. You know how I feel about that kind of thing."

"It doesn't matter how you feel about it, all that matters is that you get through; get around these guys. You know how to do it, I've seen you do it."

"Just what the hell do you mean?"

He smiled very broadly over his wineglass. "You can do it, I've got faith."

I took in a deep breath as Silverberg continued with his version of the riot act and gazed at him adoringly. I didn't dare look at Phil.

We split up after that first day. I would be with Silverberg, an intern, and three residents. Silverberg was in charge of chest surgery, and he had a ward full of post-op patients with problems that I had never heard of. We walked through rounds. He was incredibly thorough. Every statement he made was qualified, defended, explained, and restated. He wanted to make sure you understood everything he was saying, and then unfortunately he wanted to know how much more you knew. If you answered a question correctly, you were in a lot of trouble because he took you one step further and then one more, and if you didn't know the next answer, that didn't stop him either. He wanted to know what you'd do if you didn't know (which you didn't), but you had to do something. "What would you do? What would you do? Think. Come on, think."

Rounds lasted all afternoon. There were x-rays to go over, there were lab results, and then, later, he'd pick everybody's brains. All he cared about was knowing. Knowing was important. You had to know, and if you didn't know you had to find out. The patients were important to him. Time was not important to him. It was 6:30 P.M. and I was still following him around, motivated by sheer awe. "I'm doing a lobectomy tomorrow morning. I want you to scrub so you can get right up close and see what I'm doing. Make sure you know your anatomy." He left the conference room. One of the residents was still there. "Does he ever get tired?" I asked him. "Nope, and he doesn't eat and he doesn't sleep either."

I walked home feeling very very peculiar, very dazed. What was going on? I could have listened for another five hours. Why was it so interesting? Why did I care what kind of procedure Mr. Williams or Mr. Evans or Mr. anybody was going to have, and whether they were going to approach it from the chest or from the abdomen, and what kind of incision they were going to use, and why they chose one approach over the other? Why was that so interesting? I got back to the apartment and Les said, "You want to go for dinner?"

"I've got to read."

I read until I couldn't read anymore. Les brought back a pizza, and I ate and read some more. The book was so thick; how could I read it all in one night? Finally Les said to me, "Hey. What's with you? I think if I put an anchovy on that book, you'd eat it." I looked up at him abstractedly. "I'm going into surgery." It was settled. Somewhere between the section on cancer of the lung and cancer of the upper third of the esophagus, it was settled.

I read everything I could on the lung, on cancer of the lung, on the anatomy, the blood supply, the individual segments, the pathology of the various tumors. But how did you do the operation? I didn't have that in my book, *Introduction to Surgery*. The book was too basic, that was the trouble with it; I had to go get some better books.

The next morning arrived, and I went in for rounds with my intern and residents and then I was excused to go up and watch the surgery. Silverberg was the only one who seemed committed to the principle that you don't *use* the medical students: they're not here to be used, they're here to learn.

# 15

I was so excited. I was actually going to be in on a real case. I ran up the stairs to the operating-room area, eyes aglow like a five-year-old on the subway one stop short of F.A.O. Schwartz.

I passed through the double doors marked NO ADMITTANCE, OPERATING ROOM PERSONNEL ONLY. I got one foot in the door and someone yelled. "Stop. You can't come in here with those clothes on." I was intimidated immediately.

"I'm a medical student, I'm looking for Dr. Silverberg's lobectomy."

"You going to watch?"

"He said I could scrub."

She looked at me dubiously. "God, you're a teeny one." She came out from behind the desk. She was wearing a green shapeless dress, paper booties, and a paper hat that looked like it belonged in the shower. She had a mask tied around her neck by only the bottom two strings, and the mask lay draped across her chest.

"Come on, let's get you dressed."

I followed her to the dressing room. All of the dresses were huge. They hung down to my feet and my bra stuck out the hole for the vee neck. She reached into her locker and handed me a bunch of safety pins. "Here. See if you can get it short enough so you can at least walk. And don't forget the booties. There's a box in the corner. The paper tab goes under your foot, and take off your stockings." She started out the door. I looked after her helplessly.

"The masks and hats are in the hall over the scrub sinks. Don't forget, mask and hat go on before you scrub." She disappeared and I started pinning frantically. She reappeared again in about a minute with a mask and hat. "Here you go, honey, you never would have reached them. Better hurry, Silverberg is already scrubbed. He's in room four."

I was terrified. I didn't want to leave the locker room. I peeked out the door and there was a man standing at one of the sinks. I realized that I didn't have a clue as to what exactly you were supposed to do first. I walked out quietly, trying to look cool, and took the sink next to this older gentleman, an obvious expert. Where was the soap? I didn't see any soap. I glanced furtively at the man next to me. He was scrubbing away at his hands with a nylon bristle brush. His hands were full of suds. Where did he get the soap? Maybe he brought it with him; but not only that, where did he get the brush? I went to turn on the water. God, I felt like a fool. There were no faucets. Where were they hiding the faucets? I stood on my toes to look behind the sink and this large stainless-steel U-shaped handle jabbed me in the thigh. I turned it on with both hands, and the water blasted into the sink and soaked the front of my dress. I wet my hands and concentrated on the guy at the next sink. He inserted his knee into the U-shaped handle, threw his brush into the sink, and washed his sudsy hands off under the spray. He turned off the water, walked behind me, and punched what looked like a Dixie-cup container hanging on the wall. A bristle brush shot out. He returned to his sink and pumped his foot on a rubber pad on the floor. A shot of orange soap came out into the sink. I looked up. Soap dispensers. What a dummy. I was so nervous, they were right in front of me. There were two large ones on the wall. They each had tubing that ran down to the floor so you could control them with your feet and didn't have to touch anything and contaminate your hands. There was a big green dispenser marked *Phisohex* and a big orange one marked *Betadine*. Which one did you use? Maybe you were supposed to use them both, one at a time. My

God, time. I was probably already late. I stepped on the closest pedal, and the orange soap shot out. I got a brush by hitting the dispenser with my shoulder and did my best to imitate the distinguished gentleman on my left. To my horror, as soon as I started scrubbing he turned to me and said pleasantly, "And who might you be, young lady?"

"I'm Joni Scalia; I'm a third-year medical student."

"I'm Dr. Clayborne." I guess he assumed I knew who he was, which I didn't, but he looked important. I resisted my impulse to shake hands and continued scrubbing.

"Do you like surgery?"

"Yes, I love it. I'm going to be a surgeon."

"I see. That's wonderful. Let me ask you—Miss Scales, is it?"

"Scalia."

"Yes. Miss Scalia, as long as you are going to pursue your surgery, I notice you chose the Betadine scrub this morning instead of the Phisohex scrub: Why do you prefer the one to the other?"

I nearly died of fright. I didn't have the slightest idea. I stared down at my hands, which were a mass of little gold bubbles, and scrubbed my thumb very professionally. "Well," I said thoughtfully, "well, it's like this." It's like what? I didn't know what to say. He rinsed off his hands and waited for my reply.

"I think they're probably both good, but I chose the Betadine today"—the answer came to me like a flash—"because I really like the color." I heard his brush drop in the sink. I didn't look up, and God knows I never saw the man again. I finished with my scrubbing, dripped my way into room four with my hands elevated in the air, just like in the movies, and joined the surgery. The gloves didn't fit, they were at least two sizes too large, and I had to stand on two boxes just to get to Silverberg's eye level, but the important thing was that I got to see, I got to see everything. The chest was already opened by the time I arrived, and Silverberg had already isolated the segment of lung that was to be removed: the segment containing the tumor. All preliminary diagnostic measures had been correct. The tumor, isolated and contained within that one lobe of lung tissue, could be removed in toto from the patient. It was great; I loved it. Silverberg explained every step. I was hooked.

I followed the patient postoperatively. Every time the guy burped, I knew about it. I learned from the patient. I learned from Silverberg. I learned that the operation itself weren't nothin'. It was what you did before and what you did after that made the difference. The surgery was the gravy, the postoperative care was the meat and potatoes.

Speaking of meat and potatoes, that resident was right; Silverberg ate once a day, at about 11:00 P.M., when he thought his day was through. I on the other hand ate constantly, and would like to state that no matter what the nutrition books say, Mallomars are definitely the staff of life. Chip Ahoys aren't bad either, and they're easier to eat in the library —where I spent half my life for the next two months.

I didn't see Les much. My afternoons off were spent in the breast clinic, where all the women with breast cancer came for follow-up checks. Weekly, monthly, yearly follow-up exams. I learned how to find the little nodes: where to look, how to palpate. I spent Saturday mornings at surgery conference with the residents and staff, listening to them fight. Not disagree, not beg to differ, but fight, scream, and insult one another. I may have noticed abstractly that in the room of thirty-odd people I was the only girl, but I don't think it really registered. Silverberg introduced me to the chairman of the department. This guy was one big deal, let me tell you, one of the larger minds around. Yes, he had initiated the very earliest work in heart-lung machines; yes, I had read his original paper on incarcerated hernia; yes, I had been cover to cover in the book on intestinal obstruction. Yes, I wanted to go into surgery; yes, I would give a talk on tumors of the soft tissues for a morning conference. Yes, yes, yes. I spent my evenings in the emergency room learning which end of a needle was up and how to sew up a face. Why you used what suture, how you knew what was a no-no, and, most of all, how to tie a knot with one hand and look slick. After a month, I was ready to take on the world. Then I got switched off of Silverberg's service onto general surgery, where I found out that the world needed a lot of taking on.

The chief resident was foreign, he was from hunger, and he really believed that all you needed to be a surgeon was a big ego and a good pair of hands. A good pair of hands he had. He was gorgeous in the operating room. Slick, delicate, technically beautiful, but it all ended there. As soon as he took off his gloves, he was in a totally different category. He was downright dangerous.

I'd been on the service for two weeks. On this service, medical students spent their days doing rectal examinations and drawing blood and running out for sandwiches for the residents. Nobody taught you anything, nobody cared if you came or stayed home, and rounds were an incredible formality where you stood in line and listened, while Dr. Merritt (the chief) gave one instruction after another to the third-year resident, who repeated it to the second-year man, who passed it on to the first-year guy, who told the intern, who told the medical student, who had to do it. Merritt only spoke to the third-year man, and even then he did it over his shoulder.

We were making rounds one morning. We got into the ward and were passing by one of Merritt's post-op gastrectomy patients. The patient was old. He'd had the majority of his stomach removed for what was most certainly a malignant tumor, and they had pushed too much blood and too much fluid during the surgery. The guy was bubbling in bed; his lungs were full from the fluid overload. You could hear him bubbling from across the room.

Merritt stood in front of the bed, checked the man's dressing, checked his lab work, and ordered whole blood. He didn't listen to his chest; he never took his stethoscope out of his pocket, not that you needed one. The third-year resident took down the order and they proceeded to move on to the next bed.

"Wait a minute; you can't give this man any whole blood!" Three rows of guys turned around, and then parted like the Red Sea. Merritt looked across the room at me.

"What is this? You have some objection here?"

"Yes, I have some objection. I always object when you drown a person."

"Well," he stood his ground, "it looks like we have a medical student here who doesn't like surgery."

"No, I like surgery, I like surgery very much, but that man is in pulmonary edema and you're going to finish him off."

He was furious, but he was cool. He said levelly, "Yes, it looks like we have a medical student here who neither understands nor likes surgery." We were in the middle of the ward; everybody was listening. The patients were listening, the nurses were listening, even the roaches were listening. I didn't care.

"You've got a real way with words, Dr. Merritt, like a talent. I think maybe you should have gone into law; perhaps you would have been better at it."

The look on his face was incredible, but it became obscured because the residents closed ranks discreetly between Merritt and me and my little frame became lost in the crowd. We moved on to the next bed. Dr. Curtis, one of the second-year residents, leaned over to me. "You've had it, honey, he'll have your ass for that." The reality of what I had just done was suddenly apparent. My grade! What had I done? I couldn't afford one negative evaluation from anybody; not the chief resident, not the intern, not the elevator operator. I finished rounds in a panic. How the hell was I going to get out of this one? We all dispersed, and Curtis and I went back to the small office so I could get my scut assignment for the morning. Curtis was my only chance. I didn't have a prayer of even getting in the same room with Merritt. We got into the office and closed the door.

"You've got to help me, Dr. Curtis."

"Help you, how the hell can I help you?"

"You've got to talk to Merritt and get him to forgive me."

"You must be kidding."

"No. No, I'm serious. I've never been more serious in my life. I can't fail this course. You don't understand. I *have* to do well."

"I can't help you."

"You have to. Please." I looked at him desperately. It wasn't working.

"Look, I'm only a second-year resident. He eats second-year residents."

I burst into tears and grabbed the table. "What am I going to do? If I fail this course, they'll flunk me out of school. I never meant to say anything like what I said. If I only had a chance to apologize, maybe he'd give me another chance. What's going to happen to me?" I threw myself down on the table and sobbed. I was utterly magnificent. He stood up.

"Look, I'll talk to him. I'm sure he won't listen, but I'll try. Could you stop crying?" He was trying to run out of the office. I continued to weep violently. He stood with his hand on the door.

"Look, I don't know if I can find Merritt right now. Maybe he's scrubbed. I might not get a chance to see him until later; or tomorrow even."

"Tomorrow may be too late," I screamed.

"Right. It might be. I'll talk to him today. If he'll talk to me."

"Thank you. Thank you, Dr. Curtis. You don't know what this means to me." I gave a little shudder, and he backed out the door.

Merritt had a bigger ego than even I had suspected. The idea of reducing a female to tears, ready to lick his blood-stained boots, was, I guess, the highlight of his afternoon. He didn't even ask for an apology, but the royal word was that he was going to let the incident go by. The royal word was usually correct.

The patient, incidentally, expired.

I was up for honors. Silverberg had told me. All I had to do was cinch the oral. There would be no written part to the exam, and we would all have two examiners.

We all studied frantically. Phil and Les were both nervous wrecks. If they hated surgery, which they both undeniably did, they hated studying for the exam even more.

"I don't believe I'm sitting here and memorizing the difference between these hernia repairs. Worthless, that's what it is." Phil had been in a chronic state of pissed-offism since we began, and he was getting worse as exam time got nearer.

"You want me to go over them with you? I really understand them," I said helpfully.

"No."

Les said, "I don't think those are so bad, but do you believe the different loops for the ulcer operations? If I look at it another fifty times I won't know which direction the bowel is going."

"Listen. I really understand that: I really do. Do you want me to explain it to you?"

"No, Joni, I want you to shut up before I wrap this book around your ears."

They hated me. I couldn't understand it. The day of the exam they didn't even talk to me. There were ten of us waiting to take it from the same set of examiners. I was first. When the door opened and I saw Silverberg, I almost jumped up and down. There was another guy who looked like a frog sitting there in the room, who didn't say a word for the whole first half. Silverberg asked me about ulcer disease. I loved it. I told him everything I knew. He didn't ask me anything else.

Then it was the Frog's turn. He presented me with a case history and asked me how I would manage the patient. I was very careful. I didn't trust this guy. It looked like it was going okay, and then he said, "And if he came to surgery, what operation would you choose to perform?"

The patient had ulcer disease. He had deliberately made the history vague and resisted all efforts to be pinned down. I answered confidently, "Well, with that history, I'd do a vagotomy and a pyloroplasty."

There was a gasp from Silverberg. The Frog didn't twitch a hair. "I see," he said.

Silverberg jumped in. "Did you hear the question, Joni? He asked what surgical procedure was the one of choice in this institution, Joni."

"You didn't say this institution."

"We consider this institution to be our frame of reference," Silverberg continued, "and what procedure do we consider to be the one of choice in a bleeding patient without exception?"

"Seventy-five percent gastrectomy," I answered like a little doll.

"Then why didn't you say seventy-five percent gastrectomy?"

"Because we're the only place that does it. A lot of other people don't think you can justify taking out three-quarters of the stomach for a first-time bleed." Silverberg grayed about the mouth.

The Frog took over. He wanted to know which other people from which institutions exactly, in which journal the reference article was, the year, and the page number. I didn't know. He wanted to know how many people bled again from their ulcers after a vagotomy and pyloroplasty as compared with a gastrectomy. I didn't know. Silverberg was sitting with his mouth squashed in his palm, looking at the floor and shaking his head.

"That will be all," You-know-who finally said. Silverberg showed me to the door. He paused. "Joni, why didn't you just give me the answer you knew I wanted?"

I stared at him dumbly.

Les went in next and was in for a long time. He came out

looking sick. He sat down next to me and leaned over to whisper, "He asked about the damn hernia repairs and then some half-assed thing on intestinal obstruction." There were three other guys before Phil, and when he finally came out, he was so pissed off he wouldn't even talk.

The grades came out a few days later. I didn't get honors.

# 16

The next ninety days could have been yesterday. They could have been yesterday, because I remember them with the clarity of yesterday. I remember every smell, every remark, every line in every face, every piece of crap on the floor of the elevator. It's too bad, really, because I'd like to forget the whole damn thing.

I had always liked being a woman. I was always comfortable with it, it was part of my being. To say "I exist" means exactly the same to me as saying "I exist as a woman." I always liked men. I recognized them as being distinctly different, but I liked them.

I never knew that some men hated women. Not some man hating some woman, but some men hating all women. I never knew that some men hated women and were afraid of them and had a need, a real deep-down need to hurt and degrade them. Maybe if I had known that at the outset, it wouldn't have had all the impact that it did when I saw it in full-scale operation.

Our first lecture in obstetrics and gynecology was given by a very eminent professor. White-haired, of course, but thin, well-preserved, very well-dressed, very self-assured. A man who took care of himself.

His locker-room humor was very high-grade. Not the back-slapping kind of humor, but the twinkle-in-the-eye wink, the half smile, the roll-it-off-your-tongue-with-relish type. And he did. He relished every moment of the discussion in his introductory talk, in which he compared vaginal discharges to cottage cheese—which was incidentally one of his favorite foods. He went on to explain how careful you had to be because women became terribly upset when you painted their vaginas and vulvas with that ugly gentian violet medication; it stained their pretty undies and the sheets so badly. It was good top-drawer porno. The guys loved it. He had slides to go with the lecture.

At the time I wondered if I could maybe disappear someplace and take my embarrassment with me. He was talking about me, and you know maybe I'm still furious about it because I'm more angry with myself for sitting there quietly, afraid for my grades, afraid for my future in this great profession, when if I'd had anything going for me at all I would have leaped across all fifty rows of seats and given this man a little example of what perturbed pussy can do. But he was only the beginning.

The department of obstetrics and gynecology ran the school. The chairman of the department was world-famous and had written what was then and still remains "the" textbook in obstetrics and gynecology. The assistant dean of the medical school, the power behind the power, was also an obstetrician-gynecologist. Dr. Lawrence White. A mind like a weasel and a personality to match. With these two giants at the helm, one automatically assumed that a student graduating from our program (which consisted of a ninety-day rotation, longer than any of the other clerkships) knew his or her OB. And that was indeed the case.

Our clinical responsibilities began immediately at 5:00 P.M. We took our bodies up to the eighth floor of the hospital. From this point on, we were divided into two groups. Obstetrics was one group, gynecology the other. The students on OB for the night were in a rotation. A continuous, nonstop rotation.

As each pregnant woman came in ready to deliver, or as in most cases delivering between the sixth and seventh floors on the elevator, a student was assigned to her care. The student monitored her through labor and then performed the delivery without any prior benefit of explanation or demonstration. As

Carter Prentiss, our chief resident, said, "That's what you guys have the book for."

Prentiss was one of the biggest bastards ever to bless our corridors. Carter was black, and for some reason he blamed us all for the fact that he was. Three of the other residents were black, all of the patients were black, and nobody gave a good goddamn one way or the other, except Carter. He had a very large multipurpose chip on his shoulder and he carried it wherever he went.

Not only did we not need Carter Prentiss with his chip, but we most certainly did not need the head nurse in the delivery room, who reported for work every night on a broom. She parked it by the elevator. She hated us more than Carter did, and (bless her heart) she was the one who was supposed to show the medical students the ropes because Carter didn't have time for too many small potatoes in his schedule, particularly any small white potatoes.

Katie addressed all of us as "Doctor," but she made it sound like a swear word. She got us dressed in our special little outfits, stretchy beanies made out of orthopedic stockinette, rumpled baggy scrub clothes, and tennis shoes—designed to assist one in running one's ass off. We looked like refugees from an all-night bakery.

The procedure for the evening was relatively straightforward. If you didn't have a patient, you read "the book." But you always had a patient, because between 5:00 P.M. and eight o'clock the next morning the hospital averaged no fewer than thirty deliveries, and that's a lot of babies distributed among ten unfortunates.

There were ten students altogether. I say altogether because we were all together. We all slept in the same room, occasionally in the same pile, in a filthy little closetlike enclosure that contained three bunk beds.

Five of us in the room took OB call, and five took GYN call. On the following night, we switched. The girls in the group had a choice of spending the night with the men or in the equally tiny call room down the hall which was occupied by Brunhilde Schulz, a second-year resident who was a stampeding Hun, and that was after a night's sleep. We opted for the guys.

The working arrangement for letting a student know of a patient's arrival in the delivery area was very sophisticated.

Katie would open the door of the darkened room where we all lay in various stages of profound fatigue and stupor and scream in her best harplike soprano, "Delivery!" Everyone was instantly awakened and running around in the dark like some kind of munchkin trying to decide whose turn it was. We'd finally push somebody through the door and he or she would run down the corridor trying to find Katie, who had disappeared. Hit and run, that was her technique.

Most often when you got to the end of the hall and saw that every delivery room was already occupied by a patient and a student, you'd stop dead and realize that you'd been had. There would be Katie leaning casually against the wall cracking her gum, hand on her hip, dangling a pair of gloves. "Take your time, Doctor, she's only three centimeters."

The patient got examined a hundred and fifty times. The nurse examined her, then the student examined her. Then the student re-examined her because he wasn't sure of what he'd just felt because he wasn't sure of what he was feeling to begin with because nobody had explained to him how to do an exam properly. But he had to write something up on the chart on the wall for Carter Prentiss to see.

You see, the problem was that when Prentiss came by and examined the patient, if his findings didn't agree with what you had written on the chart down to the last decimal place, you were in for a lot of abuse. So you had to make sure that your centimeters dilated and minus twos and plus ones, or whatever the head position was, represented the correct figure. So you had to make sure that there wasn't any time lapse between the moment you had done your last exam and the moment Prentiss came by to check. So you spent your time running to the door and checking the hall for Prentiss, running back and checking the patient for dilatation and head position, and running up to the bulletin board to change your findings. Prentiss invariably came by when you had walked out of the room for thirty-five seconds to go potty.

If Prentiss walked into a room and found no medical student with a patient he would run one of his whole numbers. He dashed out into the corridor and uttered the two magic syllables that sent chills into the heart of any student who did not want to remain over the summer to repeat the rotation.

"Pre-cip!" he'd scream.

"Precip!" Precip. Precipitous delivery. A rapid uncontrolled delivery without assistance from a doctor, resulting in the baby's delivering by itself in the bedsheets and more often than not resulting in the laceration of the mother's bottom from the rapid popping of the baby's head through her already stretched tissue. "Precip," he'd yell, and doors would open and people would come running with delivery packs and gloves. And when the poor bastard who had been holding up his bladder with rubber bands for the last three hours finally emerged from the bathroom, Prentiss would say, "You. Are you the one that left the lady in room three?"

It was all over. You could shuffle and grovel and wring your hands but it didn't do any good. He had no mercy. He'd make you follow behind him into the room, where he would dramatically approach the bed and throw back the sheet from the moaning patient, exposing her shaking buttocks and her very pregnant abdomen and say, "Fooled you, didn't I?"

One lesson like that was enough. No matter how bad you had to pee you held it till eight o'clock the next morning. At that time there was a very long line for the bathrooms.

But if the nights were bad, the days were in some ways worse. Eight A.M. didn't mean you got to go home, it just meant you got to leave the delivery room. Eight o'clock meant you ran to the nearest shower, changed your clothes, ate everything in sight, and raced back to the hospital to be there in time for OB clinic to start at nine o'clock.

OB clinic, where every pregnant lady in the world who spoke only Spanish came and filled out the questionnaire as a mere formality, since some of them already had eighteen children and knew more than you did about the matter. OB clinic, where you became a master by the end of the day at demonstrating nausea and vomiting, headache and bleeding by charades alone. OB clinic, where if it was your turn to take blood pressures you did nothing but take blood pressures from 9:00 A.M. until the clinic ended at four, or if it was your job to dip the urines for protein and sugar, you sat around like a machine and dipped and dipped and waited for the stick to turn color and then dipped the next one.

By five o'clock your thirty-six hours had come to an end and then, then you got to go home for twelve hours. Until the next day, when you started your thirty-six again when Mickey's hand was on the five. Twelve hours. You could go home and sleep. That is, if you wanted to fail the course; that is, if you could sleep after all the shit that you had taken the night before. Who slept?

The way it worked out, Phil and I were on together in one group and Les was on the alternate night when we were off. We only got to see Les during the day in clinic or in a lecture or conference or whatever godawful event the department had scheduled.

When Phil and I got off at five, we had no intention of going to sleep. We had the evenings carefully planned. First we went to Frank's Bar and Grill, mostly bar, and got loaded. When we had had enough so the checks on the tablecloth represented a solid red line, we went back to my place or his place and cooked dinner and planned how we would eventually kill Carter Prentiss and Katie. After numerous cups of coffee to counteract the numerous glasses of booze, we read until our eyes fell out or one of us fell over. That meant it was time to go home and go to sleep, so we could get up again at eight.

Les did not have to suffer with Carter Prentiss. He had some sort of human being for a chief resident. Some guy named Arthur Meachem who didn't yell or scream or threaten. Apparently this guy Meachem actually explained how you were supposed to do the deliveries. He actually taught. Phil and I sat like two wide-eyed kids around a campfire as Les spun yarns about this great Chief Meachem and the wisdom he handed down to his flock.

The alternate nights on the GYN rotation had their own special flavor. We were still all trundled in together, but when we were up for a patient on gynecology, when that hallway door swung open the magic word you listened for was *incomplete*.

Incomplete. An incomplete abortion. The patient had aborted, "miscarried," whatever, by natural or artificial measures. She now presented herself on the seventh floor of the hospital with cramps and vaginal bleeding.

The routine was exactly the same with every patient. You ran down the stairs to the seventh floor and into the treatment room. You grabbed the chart that had her temperature, pulse, and blood pressure, which you read while you grabbed for a syringe and two tubes. The patient was already up in stirrups. You drew blood from her right arm, bent her elbow, ran around to her left arm and started an intravenous, looked up at her and said, "Did you do this to yourself?" If she said yes, she got antibiotics in the intravenous; if she said no, you checked the chart and if she had a fever you gave her antibiotics anyway because you figured she was probably lying and had used a coathanger to make herself abort. You then ran down to the patient's bottom, put a speculum in her vagina, swabbed out the clots, and looked to see if there was any tissue sticking out of the cervix. If there was any tissue you grabbed a long clamp and yanked it out as you were instructed to do, put a gauze pack in the vagina, and then moved on to the next female.

After the tubes of blood had been run to the lab, which we also had to do, and the patient had been typed and cross-matched for transfusion, she automatically was wheeled over to a large holding area to wait for her D and C. One resident was on every night to do nothing but D and C's until eight the next morning; he averaged between fifteen and twenty a night. Very efficient. His favorite slogan: "You rape 'em, we scrape 'em."

# 17

Phil and I were incredibly sorry for ourselves. We ruminated and philosophized and generally despised every day. But if I felt sorry for myself, I felt sorrier for the patients. I was sorry they were women and I'm sure they were sorry they were women. They were lined up like cattle, with their bottles of urine and their clinic cards, all given the same meaningless eight-thirty appointment so they could sit for hours and hours in one room until somebody could pull up their dresses and listen to their bellies.

I felt sorry for the OB patients because they were helpless. How much more helpless can you be than when you're a pregnant woman in labor? I had a different kind of empathy for the GYN patients, and I guess it is just because of the total lack of dignity with which they were treated.

We had a large cancer service at our hospital. The surgeons were excellent and the residents who took the rotation were excellent. But they lacked something very important; it's called awareness.

Tumor board met once a week in a large room. There were rows of benches for the medical students, a table and four chairs for the gynecologists, and a large pelvic table for the patient, with the stirrups pointing into the room. A patient would arrive from the ward and the resident would present the history of her illness and the diagnostic procedures already undertaken. The purpose of the tumor board was to discuss the patient's malignancy and then to decide on the best course of treatment for her. She stood by and listened until they had finished with the history and then she was asked to step up onto the table.

With twelve medical students looking on, four doctors stuck their hands in her vagina, made their evaluation and discussed their findings, and discussed her cancer like they were talking about odds on the Army-Navy game. All of this in her presence, all of this with her perineum facing the room. I cringed every week.

The last twelve hours of our thirty-six were always agony to get through, and far and away the worst twelve hours of all were Saturday-morning teaching rounds. They lasted for three hours, and that made it bad. You had been up the whole night before, and that made it bad. And they were conducted by Lawrence White, assistant dean, obstetrician-gynecologist, and son of a bitch; and that made it bad. Dr. White threw people out of the ward with the aplomb of a highly paid bouncer.

"Get out, Mister, there's blood on your shoes." "Where's your tie, fella? Don't ever come in here looking like that." He nailed somebody every time, and once he nailed you he never forgot you.

I was standing up, barely, listening to the resident's presentation of a case. I had just made it to rounds, having run down the stairs from the eighth-floor delivery room. My patient had delivered about ten minutes before. I went to pull off my little stretchy hat, and pulled and snapped the rubber band which had been holding my hair. I didn't have time to do anything about it. I zipped down the stairs and sneaked into the back of the group.

Phil was on my right. Rounds started and continued and seemed endless. Phil picked up his left hand to get a peek at his watch. He let his hand drop. It brushed my back. I really can't imagine how it happened, but my hair became entangled in his watchband. Phil didn't know it and jerked his hand suddenly to suppress a yawn. I guess you could have heard me two floors up.

White whirled around and looked. Phil was trying to free his watch. It was obvious where the source of the disturbance was coming from. "You do something about that hair, young lady. That hair is too long. You cut it." I couldn't believe it. I'd heard him yell at others before, but I was never the one on the other end. I didn't say anything. Rounds were finally over and Phil apologized profusely. "Christ, Joni, I hope you don't have any trouble as a result of this."

"Nah, I'll stay out of his way," said I.

Two days later I was walking down the hall of the basic science building with Phil. Somebody came up behind me and pulled my hair. I turned around with my right palm open, ready to take on the wiseass full in the face, whosoever he might be. It was Lawrence White. I think I had that look that Les calls "deadly" when I saw who it was. Traffic stopped on both sides of the hall. "I told you to cut that hair, young lady." He leered at me. "I don't like to think I'm just hearing myself talk." I stared. My mind was saying, What? Are you crazy? Are you some kind of crazy man? My face didn't hide a word; it was obvious what I thought of him. It was obvious to everyone on both sides of the hall what I thought of him. But I guess he couldn't accept it because he had to take it one step further. "What's the matter, sweetie?" he yelled. "Don't you like me?" What the hell was going on? What kind of game was this? I was trying to understand. Why did he care if I liked him? Why did he care if my hair was long? Why the hell did he think he could walk up to me and touch me? I gave him a look that clearly said "Fuck off," and I got a letter in my mailbox the next day stating that I was to report to his office.

"I understand you failed medicine this winter," he said from behind his oversized desk.

"Yes, that's right."

"Well, I'm here to inform you that you are failing OB as well."

"Why? Why should I be failing OB?"

"Your evaluations from the resident staff and attending staff indicate that you are not doing your work, that you spend your time fooling around."

He went on, but I don't really remember what he said. I was aware of what was happening, that I was being set up, that nothing he said was true but that it didn't matter that nothing he said was true. I sat trying to decide what to do and wondering if there was any recourse open to me. And then I knew that yes, there was something I could do about this.

I could see Phil's smiling face looking at me above his wineglass saying, "Get around these guys; you know how to do it, I've seen you do it." I looked across the desk at White, wily egotistical bastard that he was. I took a deep breath. "Oh, Dr. White, I'm so glad you asked me to come in here this morning." I started out with a few controlled tears. "I've just been having so much trouble and I really don't know who to talk to about it." I took in a shaking breath and looked modestly at the floor. "Is it something serious?" he asked, more curious than interested. "Well," I broke into complete hysterics, "I guess I've just been so terribly upset over my failing medicine that I haven't been able to work properly and I just hope it isn't too late for me to correct anything wrong that I may have done. I mean, I just have such a tremendous amount of respect for the department, and for you, and I'm just so ashamed that I've done this badly." I buried my face in my hands. That did it. He was up like a flash, coming around the desk with his hankie, telling me that he was sure that the problems were all correctable and that if I could just do well on the final for OB, he was sure I wouldn't have to repeat the whole year.

"Oh, thank you, Dr. White, thank you," I said, squeezing his hand. "You don't know how grateful I am that you even bothered to take the time to talk to me. And I'll get my hair cut tomorrow." He helped me to my feet. I pressed the hankie into his palm and made my exit from his office as pathetically as I could. I actually had to suppress an urge to retch when I was out on the street.

I stopped by his office the next day to show him my haircut. He liked it. He liked it a lot. He liked me. He called me cutie and honey and sweetie, and hugged me when I passed him in the hall, and I hugged him, and everybody looked at everybody else and wanted to know what the hell was going on. I just smiled and told everybody what a really nice man Dr. White was. Once you got to know him.

# 18

We all underwent culture shock. We rotated through a different hospital.

If I had to guess I would say that the county hospital staff was composed of at least ninety-percent-Jewish staff members. The small hospital we went to was entirely Italian. The obstetricians were Italian, the surgeons were Italian, the anesthesiologists were Italian, the menu in the cafeteria was Italian. Poached eggs parmesan? Only our chief resident was not Italian. He was Southern. We managed to replace Carter Prentiss with Foghorn Leghorn. Eddie Birch, M.D.

Our attending physician was Dr. Louis Leone. "Louie" we called him behind his back. Dr. Leone made Charles Bronson look like Mary Poppins. He was a short, compact man, slightly balding, with large eruptive features. He spoke very softly and never took his hands from the pockets of his white coat. We figured he carried a piece. Louie was very precise; he didn't like mistakes, and he didn't like Birch. Poor Birch, he had his problems. You remember Foghorn Leghorn, that cartoon rooster with the speech problem?

LEONE : Dr. Birch, may we have the first case?

BIRCH : The first case. Ah say the first case is a twenty-five ah say a twenty-six-year-old gravida two, ah say three, para one.

LEONE: Wait a minute, Birch, wait a minute. What are all those numbers? We have medical students here and they may not understand our system of abbreviation. [He rocked back on his heels with his hands planted firmly in his pockets, waiting for Birch to begin again.]

BIRCH: That's a gravida three para one, ah say para one, who came in with a history of two days, ah say one day of cramps and bleeding.

LEONE: Which is it?

BIRCH: Which is what?

LEONE: Two days or one day.

BIRCH: One day.

LEONE: One day of cramps? Or one day of cramps and bleeding?

BIRCH: That's right.

LEONE: Go on, Birch.

BIRCH: She also had some left upper ah say it was right lower quadrant pain.

LEONE: Where was the pain, Birch?

BIRCH: It was ah say it was in her lower that's her left upper.

LEONE: Point, Birch, just point.

Leone was red as a berry. We had twelve more patients to go. Rounds took a long time.

When Louie finally dismissed us he said we would have a conference in half an hour. He hoped, he said, that we were a well-prepared group. Well prepared for what?

Louie got us whipped into shape in about three weeks. He didn't mess around. He didn't care about the book. He didn't care who said what in which journal in 1935. All he cared about was what you were going to do for the patient from the minute she stepped out of the cab with her suitcase. He didn't like bullshit. He'd kill you if you tried to bullshit your way through an answer. He knew his obstetrics, he knew his gynecology, and he knew his medical students. He knew that the most efficient way to get a student to learn was to terrorize the hell out of him or her, whichever the case might be.

Dr. Louis Leone had a thing about tubal pregnancies. The tubal or ectopic pregnancy was his favorite subject, and he beat it to death. He beat it to death so none of us would ever forget to think of it. So none of us would ever let a girl die like so many girls had died in the end bed on a ward, in their own bed at home, or right in front of some dummy's eyes because he didn't make the diagnosis. Because he didn't make the diagnosis before the pregnancy grew and burst open a fallopian tube and she bled to death. We learned to think ectopic. By the end of the rotation if a girl had come in with a fractured toe we would have all most assuredly looked at each other in dead earnest and said, "When was her last period? She could have an ectopic."

We finished our rotation with Louie and it was back to the county hospital for us. Time for the exam, and for all my hours of hard time I basically didn't have an iota of comprehension about the subject of labor and delivery. Not only didn't I understand it, but I didn't give a shit if I ever understood it. I hated it. I hated the rotation, I hated the field, and I hated everybody who was pregnant. If there were no pregnant people we wouldn't have to learn OB. Phil hated it more than I did and the two of us were frankly homicidal. We bitched and moaned and swore.

Les didn't bitch and he didn't moan. He didn't even complain. He sat quietly and read his book. He had been sitting quietly and reading his book for three months. He understood everything in the book and he understood the things that weren't even in the book. He knew about the process of labor. He knew about position and rotation and station and presentation, he knew about complications, he knew how to read pelvic x-rays and take the measurements. He knew about forceps. He knew which forceps you used for what, and when you used them. He knew how to draw them. He knew everything. I hated him. Phil hated him.

Les never really said, "I'm going into OB." It just became blatantly and disgustingly obvious. When Les got honors in OB, he never told anybody but everybody knew. He was the only one in the class who did.

I passed. After the grades came out I went to Dr. White's office and thanked him for his guidance. He was magnanimous and benevolent. He gave me a hug.

I had only psychiatry and pediatrics to get through to complete my year.

# 19

The department of psychiatry at our institution did not have one sane staff member. Everybody who spoke to us was completely out of his mind.

We started our lecture series with Dr. Herman Mann. Dr. Mann was a tall, thin gentleman with a large mouth and a severe crew cut. He leaned over the lectern and spoke to us in a quiet, organized, disciplined, and controlled fashion. He spoke about schizophrenia. A gentle soul who never raised his voice. About three weeks into the lecture series a patient attacked him in his office. He shot the man many times, killing him right on the rug.

Dr. Mann was followed by Dr. Bergenmeister. Dr. Bergenmeister was a child psychoanalyst—meaning an adult who psychoanalyzed children? This man spoke of Tweedledum and Tweedledee with a frightening familiarity. He implied that Rumpelstiltskin had some sort of kinky relationship with the lady with the spinning wheel. He was really into his fairy tales. He lasted for three lectures and was then replaced by a woman who lectured only once and twitched for the entire hour.

We completed our introduction to the course and got our patients. What a treat! My patient was a seventeen-year-old girl who outweighed me and told me that if I got within ten feet of her she was going to cut my tits off. I believed her and asked for a new patient. I was given a seventeen-year-old boy who looked at his feet for four weeks.

Les's patient was a nurse who had been hospitalized for some sort of aberrant behavior. Les never really had a chance to speak with her, however, as she was transferred only a few days after we arrived when one of the orderlies found her in the men's bathroom masturbating a sixteen-year-old boy from the adolescent ward. The adolescent boy, who had been looking good, took a mysterious turn for the worse after she left, which goes to show you that there are some things thorazine can't do for you.

I know Phil had a patient, but he even refused to discuss the fact that he was on the rotation at all. One of the worst cases of denial I have ever seen.

We went directly from psychiatry to pediatrics. Do not pass go, do not even walk on the ward without wearing a mask. Donny Perloff developed one of the worst cases of hemorrhagic measles ever seen in an adult after only one week of seeing patients. Lenny Stern, on the other hand, spent his rotation with both testicles on an ice bag after some large black lady in the emergency room stuck her little kid in Lenny's face and demanded of him, "Hey man, why do his cheeks be so swollen? He look like he got mumps."

It was the thirty-six-hour game again as we spent our nights in the children's receiving ward listening to chest after little chest that was wheezing and crouping, and our days on the wards writing up histories and physicals and making presentations. Unfortunately, our hospital not only led the list for adult rareties, it also had so many rare pediatric diseases that if you didn't know them all, you'd never make a diagnosis. We knew them all and we saw them all. Sickle-cell complications were as common as tonsillitis. We brought the year to a close with our pediatric exam, and for everybody else except the lucky group staying for the summer, the year was over.

I had a note in my mailbox the day after the final. It told me to report to the little conference room on the fourth floor of the hospital. Female Medicine, where I would have my first meeting with my preceptor for the summer. Dr. Alice Baldwin. Why, God? I said to myself as I pictured a pair of giant Red Cross shoes walking over my body, why this woman? I stood staring at the slip of paper. I was to report in two days. Two days. A lot could happen in two days. Dr. Baldwin could get hit by a bus, for example, in which case she would no doubt get up from the pavement, dust herself off, and stomp the driver, but there was always a chance.

Nothing happened, and two days later I got to see Alice Baldwin up close. She was not a soft-looking person. She spoke in short clipped sentences and her eyes darted back and forth over each one of her new little charges, picking out their flaws immediately.

Of course, this was not a difficult task; if there was one group that had flaws, this was the group. There was Herman Klein. Herman-who-always-had-a-question-Klein. Why was the sky blue, why are they serving liver again in the cafeteria, why does every cell have a nucleus, why am I repeating medicine? Herman wanted to be a psychiatrist. Then there was Louis Greenberg. Louis—and I saw this myself—actually brought his transistor radio with him into the operating room when they were doing one of the first open-heart cases in the country because he did not want to miss the bottom half of the eighth inning of the Mets game. Louis will also be remembered for his classic line, "Wow, look at all that blood," which he uttered during the same procedure while leaning over the shoulder of the chairman of the department, wearing his surgical mask covering everything but his nose and mouth. There were two other people in the group, but I don't remember who they were. I've shut it all out.

We reported to the ward daily. The interns and residents were fortunately very sympathetic toward us. They didn't squeeze us for scut work. When I had to present my first patient to Alice, I was nervous. I did it the way Matheson would have wanted it, complete with journal references and a discussion of the diagnosis. She looked at my write-up and then she looked at me. "You do excellent work," she said. That was all she said. I spent the next six weeks plugging away. I spent all my time off with Les. He had stayed in the city for the summer and had a job in the blood bank.

A week before the final exam I got this hot pain in the lower half of my abdomen. The more I ignored it, the hotter it got; the more I moved, the more it hurt. I dragged myself into the emergency room yelling, "Whatever it is, I'm not going to surgery." "Ovarian cyst," said the GYN resident. "Ovarian cyst," said the surgical resident. "I'm not going to surgery," I said as they wheeled me of all places onto the gynecology floor to be "observed."

I didn't like being observed, I didn't like my intravenous, I didn't like being in the hospital. I especially didn't like the idea that Alice Baldwin might think I was a crock, that I might be thought of as malingering because I wanted to get out of taking my exam. I lay in bed feeling enormously sorry for myself. Les came in twice a day and brought me presents and did his impersonation of Froggy Gremlin for me every time he came to visit. I always felt so good when he was there. He was so pleasing to look at. He was tall and thin and had the most beautiful set of features. He was such a classy guy, and he was so nice. I was so out of it I didn't even know I was in love with him.

I lay in my bed reading after Les left when the door swung open again. Alice Baldwin came in. She came over and sat down on the bed. "How do you feel?"

"I feel okay. I'm very worried about the exam."

"Don't worry about the exam. I've spoken with your examiner and we'll move it up a couple of days."

"Who's my examiner?"

"Dr. Doropolis." My ovary must have bled at least another cubic centimeter. "My God, he failed me! I won't have a chance of passing."

She got up and patted me on the leg. "Don't worry, you'll get a fair exam." She walked out. Les came through the door again about a half an hour later saying, "Hi ya, kid, hi ya." I burst into tears.

I got through my exam with Doropolis, and Heinrich gave me the passing grade that I should have had to begin with.

I remember leaving the exam and walking out into the large courtyard at the front entrance to the hospital. Alice Baldwin was standing outside on the stairs talking to Doropolis. I remember thinking that one of the most essential things in life was being able to tell the good guys from the bad guys. When you were a kid, it was easy; you knew the good guys always wore white hats. It got tougher when you got older because sometimes they fooled you. Sometimes they were wearing Red Cross shoes.

# 20

We entered the fourth year in a state of relative calm. There wasn't that much to worry about. If you made it through the first three years at our school, it was "hands off" for the remaining year.

The fourth year was one of specialty rotations and elective periods. We had our regular medicine and surgery rotations and in addition there were smatterings of the medical and surgical subspecialties. The surgical residents in the specialties were a group unto themselves. These were the true wheeler-dealers.

We started out on orthopedics. Rounds began every morning with the chief's arrival on the ward, whereupon all of the junior residents would rally round the chart rack and reach into their coat pockets for some folded slips of green paper. They'd pass them over to the chief, who would count them up and then reach in his own pocket. An exchange of money would take place, as they say, and then rounds would begin.

Female orthopedics consisted of no fewer than twenty-five women over the age of sixty-five with one or more broken hips apiece. Apparently a substantial number of these broken bones had occurred as a result of mishaps on our city's sidewalks.

The pieces of green paper were releases. As in *We release the undersigned from any liability in the event of. . . .* It would seem that these papers were signed by the patient after a little conversation with the resident, who might have told them they were going to the Caribbean if they signed the paper. He might have told them anything actually, since most of them did not know who or where they were and might have thought they were signing the dinner menu. The chief got ten bucks for every slip; the junior resident got five. I don't know from whom—they never tell you anything when you're a medical student—but the patient got a six-week cruise around Ward E, with a view of the ceiling and one leg up in the air providing a nice pelvic breeze. The chief went to the Caribbean.

The plastics residents were not as subtle a group as the residents on ortho. These guys were hungry for cases. I myself saw one of these residents go into the waiting area of the emergency room and stand by the glass door looking up and down the aisles of coughing, miserable people either waiting to be treated or waiting for some family member who was being treated. The resident spotted his man in the third row. A sad-eyed gentleman in his sixties wearing a dark cloth coat and old gray pants. He was leaning over his knees holding his hat.

The resident leaped over three rows of benches, jumped in front of this man, and said, "Hey! Want to get your nose fixed?" The man looked up. Indeed he did have a large and crooked nose. "Come on. I'll get it fixed for you. Won't cost you a dime; we'll do it for nothing." The man continued to stare at him and said something inaudible, apparently related to his reason for being in the emergency waiting area to begin with. "Right. Oh, we'll take care of that too. We'll do 'em both at the same time." The man followed the resident through the glass door to admitting and the young surgeon was out again in less than a minute, cruising the crowd.

"Sir? Excuse me, but have you ever thought about getting your ears fixed?"

We rotated through neurology, radiology, public health, and anesthesiology. I learned only basic material. I learned, for example, that neurologists never panic. "Doctor, there's a lady having a grand mal seizure in the waiting room."

Neurologist, sticking bespectacled head through the door, "You're right, that's a grand mal."

I learned that radiologists can interpret anything that's put before them if you give them proper lighting. "What do you think of this film, George?"

"I think it's a PA of maxillary sinuses with an overlap of the technician's sleeve, who is probably Janet because the sleeve has the mark from Lo Fats laundry on Church Street, which is where she takes her coats. It's normal."

I learned that Public Health people will vaccinate anything that moves and will visit any house in any neighborhood to see a patient regardless of risk to life and limb, and insist that a medical student go with them. "They don't usually hurt doctors."

And finally I learned that anesthesiologists, during those long tiring surgical cases, just really love to grab ass.

We studied patiently, but all we cared about in the last year was getting out. All we wanted to do was graduate and get the internships that we desired.

The internship appointments were all done through a central computer in Illinois. You wrote down your choice of hospitals in descending order of preference and sent your list into the computer. Then you sent the hospitals your credentials and the hospitals sent in their list of preferences for potential interns; again in descending order of desire. On the magic day, you "matched." Or you didn't match—which was another matter entirely. The Reading of the Internships was a public event in our institution, sort of like a hanging. It was presided over of course by our own Lawrence White, who always read the prestigious internship appointments first and saved the notification of those who got into Ozark General for last.

Phil got into one of the better hospitals in the country —which figured, since he graduated number two in the class. We would not see him again for several years. And Les and I both got our first choice.

Les and I had made a number of decisions. We decided that we wanted to stay together for the rest of our lives. There were some other decisions as well, but they had to do with our internship choices, and we chose to take a program that was in an area where there was very little snowfall and in an atmosphere that promised as little abuse as possible. We were happy to have gotten both.

The rest of the year was a steady state of excitement. We had National Boards to take, and we did well; we had small groups of finals to take, and we all did well; and before we knew it it was two weeks before graduation.

"Do you think," said Les one evening over a bowl of won ton soup, "that we should get married?"

"I think," I said, seriously contemplating my won ton, "that we should get married eventually when we both know exactly what we want and what we're doing."

"When do you think that will be?"

"Thursday? You think Thursday's a good day?"

We went for a ring and a license, and we were married by a judge in City Hall on the first day of June. Phil was married several days later, and graduation was on the eighth. We all had a great deal to celebrate.

Graduation was everything we expected it to be. Classless and boring. Nobody wanted to go, but old Lawrence issued a mandate. No showee, no tickee. And he meant it. We all had to attend and receive our diplomas in person. In the basement of a high school.

The proud parents clustered and fluttered about and patted themselves on the back for having given birth to the next chairman of the department of whatever institution their little darling was off to. It took forever to get to my end of the alphabet, but I made my way down the long aisle and up the stairs, trying not to fall over my gown—which, even with the highest of heels and a hem, looked like a shower curtain.

Lawrence White handed me my diploma proudly, shook my hand, and then winked at me. I winked back and walked the rest of the way across the stage. When I realized that I finally had it in my hand I stopped abruptly and did a quick little half turn in White's direction. I could hear Les's voice in the back of my mind saying, as he had so many times and would so many more times in the future, "Don't do it, Joni, don't do it." I turned back and started down the stairs. "Up yours," I said very quietly to my tassel, "up yours."

# PART TWO

# 21

Les and I left New York the day after graduation and headed west. We had one car, two sets of medical textbooks, a case of vodka, and thirty-five cents.

We arrived at our destination and immediately rented an apartment on our good looks and the promise of a double paycheck at the end of the month. We unpacked, which took about ten minutes, and then went to find the hospital.

The internship program we had selected consisted of a group of three hospitals. One county, one Catholic, and one very private. We thought it would be a good idea to see how the nonuniversity community practiced, since we had had enough academia to last us through our next lives. Such naiveté.

We juggled the intern's schedule immediately and had ourselves placed at the same hospital. The County. The hospital was twenty miles from our apartment, which meant that we needed another vehicle. Les went out and bought a motorcycle, which was all we couldn't afford.

My day started at 5:00 A.M. I drove to the County, had breakfast with the residents at five-thirty, rounds at six, surgery at seven, clinic at one, rounds at five, night duty at six, breakfast at five-thirty. I rarely slept but I loved it. I loved the surgery, and I loved being at the county hospital. The private service was a completely different situation.

In the first place, all surgical interns are obnoxious. All interns are obnoxious, but surgical interns are the worst because they are pushy and aggressive; that's why they want to be surgeons. They think they can do anything—they know it, actually—so why doesn't everybody just get out of their way and give them a chance to prove it?

The trouble is that all obnoxious surgical interns mature into obnoxious surgeons, who by definition don't take crap from anybody—particularly not from obnoxious surgical interns. I think you can appreciate the difficulty. The private surgical staff at our institution and I had a wonderful working relationship. They reported me; I reported them. Les had an equally comfortable time with the private internists. He was a "straight medical" intern. Dr. Stacy, head of the program, was wonderful to both of us. "Why do you put up with those two?" The senior medical staff was up in arms at some very temperate cases of insubordination. "Because they're my best interns," Dr. Stacy said, "and you'll be lucky if they're taking care of your patients."

Our internship was in reality no different from anyone else's. It was like one long hard day, with no food and no sleep and nothing to look forward to but a long lousy night. But you do it, because you keep thinking that if you can just get through it, well, all the good stuff is coming up fast. I couldn't wait to be a surgeon.

I had been at the private hospital for about two months. Almost all of the cases were hands-off and all you did was stand around and tie somebody's knots while he said "Too loose, too tight" or cut somebody's sutures while he said "Too long, too short," or every once in a while close an incision while somebody said "Too close, too far apart." Occasionally there was a chief resident's case.

On this particular morning I was third man on a gall-bladder operation. Scrubbing with the chief resident. The anesthesiologist was a real son of a gun who loved to harass the interns. I was tired. It seemed that I was tired all the time.

Being the third person on a gall-bladder is one of the lowest positions in the hierarchy of surgical life. It is your job to stand for however long it may be and retract, with great care, the liver of the patient. This must be done with enough force to keep the liver out of the surgeon's way yet with enough care to prevent putting any traction on the finer and more fragile structures in the vicinity.

The patient weighed close to three hundred pounds and retracting her liver on the two hours of sleep I had had the night before was an Olympian task. My arms were shaking with fatigue and we were only ten minutes into the procedure. I felt a tap on my left buttock. "Doctor," this offensive voice with equally offensive breath stated in my ear, "you're leaning on my patient." It was the anesthesiologist.

"What?" said I, for I was sure that I was not.

"I said you are leaning on my patient."

"No, I'm not." I kept my eyes fixed on the surgical field. About five minutes went by. Another tap. "Doctor," he said in an authoritarian voice, "I told you one time and I'm not going to have to tell you again; you are leaning on my patient!" Two hours of sleep doesn't do a thing for your disposition. I turned around very slowly and looked at him over my mask. "Let me tell you something. Number one, I'm not leaning on the patient; number two, this is my patient, not your patient; and number three, don't you ever touch me again or so much as even speak to me." I turned back to my task at hand, quite furious. "Well, young lady, we'll just see about this."

I turned around again. "Did you hear me? Not another word. I meant that. Don't ever speak to me again."

"Not so much traction, Doctor."

"I'm sorry." I looked up startled at the surgeon, who was across the table from me. He was the chief resident, and I could see that he was laughing behind his mask.

"I'm going to speak to somebody about this young woman, you can be sure of that, yes indeed." The anesthesiologist was addressing his remarks to the oxygen tank, at the top of his lungs. "I don't know who I'm going to tell, but I am going to tell someone."

"Why don't you tell me about it, Fred?" the surgeon said. I laughed behind my mask. Ten minutes later I passed out.

"Go home and get some sleep," they said. I did.

A week later it happened again. This time I noticed my vision starting to blur, and I sat down on the floor before I felt faint. I watched my hands shaking and could hear my teeth clacking together. I was freezing and I couldn't remember my own name. Somebody brought me a Coke and a Mounds bar. I sat on the floor of the operating room and ate the candy and drank the Coke. I felt an almost immediate sickening rush, and in a few minutes my vision had cleared and my hands lay quietly in my lap.

"You've got diabetes, Joni." I sat dumbly in my internist's office two days later. I had Band-aids all over my arms from the glucose tolerance test. I had been stuck countless times for the procedure, since I have the world's lousiest veins. "Your urine is loaded too."

"I don't understand. I don't understand." I must have said it twenty times.

"What about your family? Mother? Father?"

"Hypertension, that's all. Bad hypertension on my father's side. That's it. My parents never go to doctors."

"What about your sisters and brothers?"

"I don't have any. Jesus, I don't understand this."

"It could be the pill," my internist was saying, "sometimes the pill can do it. Let's take you off the pill and then repeat the test. See if it reverts to normal."

I cried all the way home from the office. I cried when I got home. I cried when Les got home. Les was surprised to hear about it, but he was calm.

"It's certainly possible that you have it, Joni. Adult-onset diabetes can present itself this way; you ought to know that."

"I ought to know what? I failed diabetes, remember? I don't know anything about diabetes and I don't want to know anything about diabetes."

"What does he want to do for you in terms of treatment?"

"He said I have to take it easy, and follow a diet, and then he's going to repeat the test in a couple of months after I've been off the pill."

"Oh, God," Les said.

"Right," I said, "one more thing to worry about."

Dr. Stacy took me off general surgery and switched me to a pathology elective. I still took my night call but I had no problems with early-morning cases and I could eat regularly. In three months we repeated the glucose tolerance test. It was worse.

"I'm starting you on medication," my internist said. I was terrified. I didn't want to take insulin; no matter what was wrong with me, I knew I was more afraid of the insulin than of the disease. All I could think of was all the people I had ever seen who had accidentally taken too much and were lucky they had any brain cells left.

"No insulin. I don't want insulin."

"No. Not insulin. You've got insulin, Joni, you just don't put it out fast enough."

"What's it going to be then—something oral?"

"Yes, but you've got to take it on time, and you have got to eat, just like with insulin."

"Well, at least it's not insulin." And then it suddenly hit me. I suddenly realized what we were talking about.

"Eat on time? What about my surgery? I can't eat on time; what's going to happen with my surgery?"

He looked at me. "I don't see how you'll be able to handle it, Joni, if you want me to be frank with you. I think you and I both know that if you had to pick a field that was a bad choice for a diabetic, surgery would be it."

"Don't call me a diabetic. I'm not diabetic. I've just got a carbohydrate intolerance."

He looked at me soberly. He had been telling me the truth. Why don't you ever recognize it when you hear it?

I waited until that evening to tell Les. I didn't want to tell him. I didn't feel like saying it. I already had my surgical residency for the upcoming year. Les and I both had our residencies, and we both had gotten into excellent programs; all of the surgeons who had reported me had suddenly come through with super recommendations for residency.

Les was very understanding, but he tried to get me to be practical. "Well, I guess what you should do, Joni, is give some thought to what else you might like to do." That was it; that was all I needed to hear. I was already upset and I just took off. "What else I might like to do? You don't understand. There *is* nothing else. There is nothing else I care about doing. This is the only thing I want to do. Surgery is not like anything else. It is special, and I am special because I do it well. Don't you understand? I am good at this. I am very good at this!" I was crying. Boy, was I crying.

"I know you're good, Joni, nobody is saying you aren't good, but you're good at a lot of other things too."

"I don't care about a lot of other things; they are all nowhere for me. They count zero. They don't even exist."

"You mean there is absolutely no other field you would even

consider? What about radiology or dermatology? You liked those, you really enjoyed them."

"Sure I enjoyed them. What the hell does that have to do with anything? I'm talking about being a surgeon, and you're talking about being a dermatologist. They're not even in the same universe. Being a dermatologist, you know what that counts for in my book? It counts for nothing. That's no points. Rock bottom. Get it? And you can throw in all the others with it."

"My God, you're a real chauvinist, aren't you? A real surgical personality."

"I'm not a chauvinist, dammit, I just want what I want and I don't want less and I won't take less."

"I don't think we should talk about this any more right now, honey. I think you're too upset, and I think you're just making it harder on yourself."

"Oh, sure. Let's just forget it. Maybe I'll wake up tomorrow and it won't be true. Well, tomorrow isn't going to be any different, and I'm not going to feel any differently." I went over to the sink to wash my face.

"You know, Joni, you're only twenty-three. You've got so much time to think of an alternative."

"Don't bring up my age, goddamn it. Don't ever bring up my goddamn age! You think because I'm young I don't know what I want? I know what I want, I always know what I want. I wanted you, didn't I?" I stood at the sink defiantly.

"Why, you little imp!" Les was staring at me in disbelief.

"See that, think you're so goddamn smart?" I started to laugh. He started to laugh.

"This isn't funny, Les."

"I know. I know it isn't funny."

Within a few days most of the house staff knew that I was having some sort of medical problem. You really can't keep much from anybody in a hospital.

I was eating breakfast with one of the pediatrics residents. He was the original little mother, and at 7:00 A.M. I didn't like anybody's mother. He was one of those people who talked constantly.

"Why don't you go into pediatrics, Joni?"

"I hate pediatrics."

"But it's such a perfect field for you."

"How do you figure that?"

"You're so tiny and feminine, all the kids would love you, you wouldn't scare them, you're so gentle." I felt like stabbing him with my fork. "I hate pediatrics, Norman."

"You'd have a great practice," he continued, unthwarted. "It would be just right for you."

"If I hate it, how can it be just right for me?"

"You only think you hate it, because you don't know anything about it."

"No, I hate it."

"How could you hate pediatrics; that's like saying you hate children."

"I hate children, Norman."

"You can't be serious."

"Look, Norman, I wouldn't make kids better, I would just catch what they had. All viruses think I'm a kid."

"No, that's just in the beginning. Then, after you've caught everything, you get immune to most of the stuff. A little diarrhea every once in a while, you know, but you get used to it."

"*You* get used to it, Norman. I don't see making room in my life for diarrhea."

"You'll change your mind." He patted my hand maternally. "Wait till you have a couple of your own little ones; it's a great field for a woman." He got up from the table. He was wearing a tie with little Dumbos all over it.

"Stay well, Norman." I contemplated my half-dead fried egg and wondered why people didn't just mind their own business. Jesus Christ, a guy with a tie full of Dumbos giving me advice.

I took the medication for a few months. I hated it. I hated having to worry about breakfast and lunch, and whether I ate and whether I didn't eat. I sent a letter to the department of surgery in the residency program to which I had been accepted. I explained my situation and said I wished to be excused from the program. They were very nice. They understood. Everybody understood. Not me, I didn't understand.

In a few months I was doing well. We kept chopping the dose of the medication. I was feeling pretty good. I went for another glucose tolerance test. It was much better.

"You just have to watch your diet now, Joni, and take care of yourself and you'll be okay."

Take care of myself. I'll take care of myself, I thought. I felt fine. I never felt better, as a matter of fact. I had two months left of my internship. Les had finally talked me into writing for applications for programs in dermatology, so that I could look for another residency. That was a good idea —looking for another residency. But not dermatology; I tossed those applications in the basket. Surgery. I'd have to find another program in surgery. Les had a program that wanted him in San Francisco; it was a sought-after residency. I told him to take it, and I'd take my chances on getting in late someplace. I applied to three hospitals. They certainly weren't the best, but they weren't the worst either. The program I finally chose met all my criteria. It accepted me, it was in the same city as Les, only a few blocks away, it had a call schedule of every fourth night, and it would make me a surgeon. Everything else was incidental.

# 22

Starting internship in no way compares with starting residency. It has nowhere the dimension, the magnitude, or the totality. Starting your residency is your personal declaration. It is your yell-from-the-rooftops assertion that you are no longer content to be whoever it is that you are, M.D.: that person is no longer adequate, can no longer fulfill the requirements that you have created for yourself. Your residency says that you now want to be somebody else. You want to be that somebody, whoever it is that is a surgeon, obstetrician, internist, whatever, but *whatever,* whichever, in making your decision you have had to take a stand, you have had to make a choice. And when you made your choice, when you decided beyond a reasonable doubt that this was who you wanted to be, you said something about yourself. You said, "I will give up everything. I will give up anything that is necessary, that might possibly get in the way, that might hinder or impede or in any way reduce my chances of becoming: becoming the surgeon, obstetrician, internist that I so badly want and need to become. Even if that something, someone, somehow is myself. Maybe, perhaps, I will have to give up myself, but it will be worth it because I will have become something better, something that fits the criteria for being "better." It's one hell of a bargain to make.

From day one of our residencies Les and I became two distinctly separate individuals. Separate hours, separate interests, separate thoughts. He went his way and I went mine. He had no time for me, I had no time for him. I had no time for me, he had no time for him; we had no time for anything but "the program."

The hospital that I had taken, in that last-minute grab for a residency, was old and falling apart. The staff for the most part was old and falling apart. They had lost their accreditation for medicine, so there were no medical residents, but they still had a reputation for turning out well-trained surgeons.

When I was first introduced to Tom Flanigan, I was immediately impressed with the fact that this was probably one of the best-looking honchos I had ever seen in my life. He was about six-three, with dark red hair and turquoise-blue eyes. We were introduced in the medical education office by a very proper secretary who said, "Dr. Flanigan, this is one of our new first-year residents, Dr. Scalia."

Flanigan reached out his big hand. "Hi, Wop," he said. "Come on, I'll show you around."

Showing me around consisted of taking me to the ward over which I was to preside. About twenty patients, no intern. All of the patients were men, since it was a union hospital. Flanigan explained, "The first-year resident gets this particular service: It's all hernias and hemorrhoids. By the time you get through here, you'll be able to do a hernia with your eyes closed. We've got very few big cases on this ward, and occasionally you'll get one of the neuro guys' backs to check on, but you won't have neuro for three months. I'll make rounds with you in the afternoon, and I'll be scrubbing with you in the morning. The night call is not bad here. The nurses will not call you for crap; they'll handle just about anything."

"Well, that will certainly be a switch."

He was right. The call was really pretty good, except for the fact that they usually had some pretty sick people in the surgical intensive care unit, and no matter how you looked at it, when somebody wasn't putting out any urine, that added up to no sleep.

Les and I tried at first to get our call schedules arranged so we'd be off the same nights, but it just wasn't that easy, and after a while we didn't bother trying any more. When we saw each other, we saw each other, and when we didn't, we didn't. His schedule was decidedly worse than mine. Where my program was nonuniversity, casual, his was the epitome of structured academic hierarchy.

The guys in his program were as separate from one another as they could be. The whole place was as cold as a morgue, and as usual everybody was understandably impressed with himself. Who wouldn't be? The staff was impressed with themselves; I mean they practiced top-level "university quality medicine." They weren't like the poor jerk out in the street who opened an office and treated patients, my God, those guys were the lepers of the profession; the "local M.D.s" who knew nothing and, as everybody knew, were just in medicine for the money and only did unnecessary surgery. The nonuniversity doctors were inferior; everybody knew that, because if they were superior they would have been connected with the university. They would have been in research, they would have published. Everybody learned this, it was part of the legacy you got handed down to you when you were in a program of this sort. It was part of your ABC's: "University," Yea, "Community," No. It was the good-and-bad list from the first grade, it was the Primer of Acceptable Behavior. It was the biggest crock that has ever been perpetrated, and perpetuated by the few inadequate bastards who can't make it out on the street and who don't know what the hell it means to treat a patient instead of a lab value. But it is mighty, and it is solid, and it's going to be a long time before somebody gets a toe in and kicks the shit in the air.

Les, as usual, managed to steer his way around all obstructions, and maintain his own identity.

I'm not really sure when I started having trouble. Things started off at a rather promising rate. I scrubbed with Flanigan almost every morning. I found out that I was fast; not fast, sloppy, careless—just fast. Flanigan was fast. We started doing our hernias under local, and the patients got up and walked off the table. How fast could I do them? It became a game. Flanigan wasn't a hog. He let me have some cases almost immediately. A gall-bladder, an appendix; Jesus, I loved it.

I loved working with Flanigan. He was so cool. He really didn't know the meaning of an ego problem. The nurses called him by his first name. The chief resident, called by his first name? By a nurse? They loved him. Actually, when you got right down to it, he loved them too; quite a few of them and fairly frequently, and that included half the x-ray department, the operating room, and anybody else who had had the occasion to get close enough to get a full dose of those incredible blue eyes. I was lucky I was so short; I rarely saw them, and spent most of my time addressing my remarks to his left elbow and running behind him down the hall trying to keep up.

Fortunately, Tom Flanigan had a kind of contagious excitement. Maybe you had to be predisposed, but then if that was the case, the whole group of residents was predisposed. It took me about two days to get my feet wet, and that was actually what happened; I got my feet wet. I was on my way home, and walked out of the hospital into a pouring rain. My car was parked about three blocks away, and I came down the hospital stairs already soaked. When I reached the street, I heard a horn beeping behind me and ignored it as I ran down the block.

"Hey, Wop!" I turned around and saw this unbelievable red Corvette. "Get in; I'll give you a lift." Me? Get into that car? That gorgeous, neat car? I paused, still staring at it. He reached across the seat and flung the door open. I got in and pulled the door closed with both hands. "Jesus Christ, you wops don't even have enough sense to come in out of the rain."

"Is this your car, Tom?"

"Of course it's my car."

I turned around in my seat. "God, this is neat."

"Where are you parked?"

"Who cares?"

"Want to go for a ride?"

"Are you kidding?" He wasn't kidding.

We went for a ride. The car took off in a direction which could only be described as largely straight up, and went flying down the street. He hooked into the park, and floored it. The trees went zooming by and I covered my eyes as I got knocked against the door taking a sharp left. "I'm going to throw up." He laughed, delighted, and bombed out again. I felt this terrible grin breaking out all over my face, and I just leaned back in the seat and listened to the engine. We came, needless to say, to a screeching halt back at the entrance of the park. "Enough?"

"Enough. Enough." He drove me back to my car. Man, I thought to myself, that's one crazy driver. I got into my station wagon and drove home.

Les wasn't there. It was his night to work, and I sat there in the apartment watching the lights blink across the Bay Bridge. The rain had stopped. I felt lousy and lonely, and I hated being alone.

We had continuous fog in the mornings. Driving to work was like reading Braille. After a while I got more adept; but looking for a parking place was a real drag. I finally got my very own parking sticker and the next morning pulled into the previously uncharted and unexplored hospital parking lot. There was Flanigan's car, in a space marked HOSPITAL ADMINISTRATOR ONLY, and there, coming around the turn was —wait a minute! I stepped on my brake and backed up. It was! It was an XKE, a dark green XKE. Jesus, now that was a car. A Corvette was sharp, but an E, oh my God!

Somebody honked at me. I pulled into a space. I made rounds and went up to surgery to scrub, after a proper breakfast of all protein and no carbohydrates; I had already gained five pounds from making sure I was well fed all the time.

Flanigan was scrubbing. I grabbed my mask out of the box and started tying it. "Hey, Tom. Who owns the green XKE?"

"Tim Harris."

"Tim Harris?" Tim was a second-year resident, on his second marriage and still supporting a first wife and two kids. "Gee, I would have thought it belonged to one of the staff."

"Those old guys? Strictly Buick Rivieras and Continentals. Check out the parking lot. Except for Paul Grove. He's got a Ferrari, but he's a young guy."

"Yeah, but, well, I guess maybe Harris is a wealthy guy."

"Tim? He hasn't got a pot to pee in."

"Well then, I don't understand; how can he afford it?"

"It's simple; you could afford one too."

"Oh sure, maybe if my whole family died and each left me fifty cents."

"Look, you want a car like that?"

"Sure I want a car like that. Only I think probably in white or silver." Flanigan turned and looked at me, hands poised and dripping.

"You get your husband to go up to the credit union at the

university. He fills out a little form, you borrow the money, and you walk in and buy yourself whatever you want."

"Oh, that's really great, but how do I pay off the money?" He dropped his brush in the sink. "I'll tell you about that later." I finished scrubbing and followed him into the room.

I put on my gown and gloves. It was a hernia under local. Tom and I chatted with the patient and asked him how he was doing. He wasn't doing well. For some reason, although I gave him enough xylocaine to amputate his leg, when I made my skin incision, he promptly left the table.

"I felt that," he said.

"No kidding," we said, as the instrument stand went flying through the air. We just put him to sleep and started over.

I made my skin incision and all was well. As soon as we finished, I found Tom over at the scrub sink. He was scrubbing for "real surgery," which for me meant something where you got to open the abdomen.

"Tell me about it now."

"Tell you about what now, Wop?"

"About the money. About how I pay off the money."

"I'll put you on the schedule."

"What schedule?"

"The medical call schedule. The medical guys will pay you a hundred bucks a night to take call here for them, because they don't have any residents. You almost never get called, and if we juggle the schedule, a lot of times you can get it the same night you're on for regular surgery call, so you really get an extra night in."

"Medical call."

"Don't worry, nothing ever happens around here. Besides, the medical guys are on backup and they're just grateful we're here at all. All you have to do is call them and they'll come in. It's an easy hundred bucks.

"You talked me into it." I walked away from he sink, a small contemplating figure. "I think silver. I saw a silver E once; it was just unreal."

Actually, what was unreal was Les's reaction to my proposal about the car. We were driving to the Chinese laundry that night; we were both off call, and I figured I'd bring up the subject of the car casually, so I could get a feeling for the climate.

"Les?"

"Yes."

"I want an XKE."

We almost had an accident. However Les managed to recover at the first stoplight and repeat, "You want an XKE."

That was what I wanted to hear. Real encouragement. I immediately launched into my explanation about the credit union and the call schedule. "You want to moonlight?" He looked at me in disbelief. "I want an E," I said.

The first night I took medical call a guy came in with complete heart block. What I didn't know about complete heart block—what I didn't know about cardiac arrhythmias in general—could have filled an entire text. That's why they have medical residencies, I kept saying to myself; they have surgical residencies so you know about gall-bladders. Medical residencies they give you so you know about heart block. The best part of the evening was when I had to put in a pacemaker, using the portable x-ray unit in the ICU, which had all the lighting conditions of a slum, receiving my instructions over the phone since the cardiologist was on the other side of town.

"Nothing ever happens around here," I muttered to myself as I tried to decide which goddamn wire went where. "Easy hundred bucks," I thought, as the patient's cardiac pattern came across the oscilloscope. "Praise be to God," I thought as a voice I recognized as that belonging to Arnold Pierce, cardiologist, said over my shoulder, "That looks good."

I bought every book in the world on cardiac arrhythmias after that night, but Flanigan had been basically correct; nothing else ever happened.

I got the car in dark blue with a dark blue interior. I would have had to wait for a silver one. The car was a two plus two, which allowed ample room in the back for my Doberman pinscher puppy, Nero, who was very rapidly becoming very large. From my point of view, the back seat put the car in the category of a utilitarian vehicle, kind of like a station wagon rather than just a frivolity. A seven-thousand-dollar practical vehicle. I would be paying it off for the rest of my life, but when I pulled it into the parking lot and the entire physician and nursing staff came out to give it their blessing, well, I knew it just had to be worth it. Flanigan was standing out there smiling. He had just hooked another resident.

# 23

Although most senior house staff functions smoothly and with a certain amount of style, we all know that interns need to be closely supervised. Our problem child came in the form of Melvyn Fried. Melvyn the Intern. Melvyn was going to be a psychiatrist, which in retrospect was a pretty good choice since already, at the very outset of his internship, he was a master of making his problems everybody else's.

My first exposure to Melvyn was on night call while he was doing his rotation through the emergency room. Any patient admitted to surgery by the intern was to be seen and re-evaluated by the surgical resident. At 11:30 P.M. I received my first phone call.

"Hello. This is Melvyn Fried. I'm the intern in the ER tonight."

"Yes, Melvyn?"

"I've just admitted a patient to your service."

"Okay," I said. "What's he got?"

"He's got a bellyache. I put him to bed."

"What do you mean, 'a bellyache,' Melvyn?"

"You know, he got some pain in his belly tonight after dinner."

"How old is the patient?"

"Fifty-three."

"EKG?"

"What?"

"Electrocardiogram, Melvyn. What does his EKG look like?"

"Oh, I don't know. I didn't do one."

I switched on the light in the room, hoping that would help me hear better, or at least differently, and started reaching for my clothes. "You didn't do one, you say; his vital signs are totally normal, I assume."

"I didn't take his blood pressure but his pulse was. Wait a minute, I'll check."

"You didn't take his blood pressure. Does he have all his pulses?" I couldn't find my skirt.

"His pulse."

"Pulses, Melvyn, *pulses*: that's plural. You know, the arteries, the big red ones that run to your arms and legs, the four things that stick out at right angles from your body?"

"Oh, I'm sure they're okay. I didn't specifically check them. Listen, he looks fine; I don't think that there's any need to bother getting out of bed . . . Oh, hello, you must be Dr. Scalia." I was standing at his right elbow.

"Can I see your work-up, Melvyn?"

"Oh, sure."

"I don't suppose the patient has an IV running."

"No."

"I didn't think so." I picked up the chart. The history began. "This is the first admission of a 53-year-old white male with acute onset of abdominal pain following a meal of a ham-and-cheese sandwich and Campbell's tomato soup.

"At the age of 3 . . ." it went on to say, and continued through the patient's growth and development, including his first erection.

"Melvyn, where is this man?"

"Bed four."

"Thanks."

In bed four was Mr. Logan, looking green as a pea and smiling like a stoic. "Hi, Doc," he said. I did a history and physical. Mr. Logan had appendicitis. Acute appendicitis. Very acute, very appendicitis. Mr. Logan in fact could have written the textbook chapter for acute appendicitis; he was truly one of those patients who come in wearing a sign: "I have appendicitis, please take me to surgery." Mr. Logan's abdomen was so classical that Mrs. Polowsky, who worked in the laundry, with a fifth-grade education to draw on and only *Days of Our Lives* for a medical reference, could have made the diagnosis from under a pile of sheets.

"You need to have surgery tonight, Mr. Logan," I said.

"Yeah," said Mr. Logan. "I figured it's my appendix."

In the following weeks, I was inundated with patients. Just me and Flanigan, and thirty guys to take care of. It took me forever to make rounds and change dressings and write orders. I couldn't really complain, though, because Flanigan was as pressed as I was, but I needed somebody to help out; an extra pair of hands and feet. The phone rang one morning in the doctors' office. I was doing my charts. It was Flanigan.

"Hey, Wop, I've got some good news for you."

"I could use it."

"I got you an intern."

"Fantastic," I said, slamming my chart closed.

"Take a little workload off your small body."

"That's really great."

"It's a kid named Fried; the medical resident says he can spare him." I spilled my coffee in my lap.

Melvyn's clinical awareness only dealt with problems from the neck up. What, I wondered, would he be like in a ward where all the patient's problems were from the waist down? I didn't have long to wait, because bright and early the next morning there he was in the office, fumbling with the charts. Well, I thought, at least he's here.

"Morning, Melvyn."

"Hi, you can call me Mel," he said shyly.

"Fine." I felt bad. Just a sweet kid, needs a little guidance. "Have you made rounds?" I inquired. Traditionally, the intern should have made his rounds, changed the dressings, and been ready to discuss what problems, if any, had arisen during the night.

"Well," he said, "I had a rough night: I only got eight hours." Eight hours. Jesus Christ, I hadn't had eight hours in over four years. "That's why I've only done one dressing change," he explained.

"Okay, Mel," I said bravely. "Let's make rounds."

I grabbed the heavy metal chart rack. Melvyn ran around in

front of it attempting to be of assistance, and ran it over his left foot.

"You okay?"

"Yeah," he said, hopping around the nurses' station. We finally got into the ward and were approaching the first bed.

"How's Mister Winchell this morning?"

Mr. Winchell, like half the other patients on the ward, had had a hemorrhoidectomy.

"Well, he's a little depressed."

"His behind, Melvyn, how's his behind?"

"Oh, it's fine."

"Did you look?"

"No, I asked him."

We tipped Mr. Winchell over on his head, and he was indeed fine, from a surgical standpoint. In the second bed was Mr. Forsythe, two days post-op, left inguinal hernia.

"This is the dressing change I did," Melvyn said proudly.

"Good morning, Mister Forsythe, let's have a look at that wound." I pulled back the covers and was greeted with Melvyn's—pardon me, Mel's—dressing change: a giant gauze pad, firmly affixed by two pieces of heavy adhesive. The top strip connected Mr. Forsythe's left thigh to the skin of his penis, the bottom half his left thigh to his left testicle.

"Jesus," I said.

Mr. Forsythe was looking up helplessly, as I continued to stare at his crotch. "Doc?"

"Yes, yes."

"Mind if I ask you a question?"

"Sure, absolutely." I let the covers fall back discreetly.

"Who's going to take that bandage off tomorrow?"

I thought for a moment. "Not me, Mister Forsythe, not me."

# 24

I was sitting on a stool in the operating-room area, dictating my operative report. A particularly challenging case of internal hemorrhoids on this Monday morning. The elevator doors opened violently, the metal cage having been thrown with force.

Flanigan came hurtling out of the elevator, pulling an old white-metal gurney. Jay Bates, one of the second-year residents, was behind him, directing the foot. They ran by me. "Anesthesia!" Bates yelled as Flanigan burst into one of the empty operating rooms.

The man on the stretcher was an incredible sight. He lay on his back like a big fish, gulping and sucking for air. His lips were blue-black and his belly stood up on the stretcher like a big air bag. His open pajamas had fallen over onto his legs and his flanks were splayed over the edge of the narrow stretcher; they were red-violet and splotchy. An anesthesiologist came out of one of the rooms. "In there," I said. All the personnel from the workroom followed her in, running.

It was ten minutes. I had the definite feeling they needed me in there like a hole in the head, so I just sat perched on my stool, waiting. One of the scrub nurses finally came out. She grabbed a pile of blue towels.

"What's happening?" I said.

"It's all over," she said. "Ruptured aneurysm. He was dead before we got him on the table."

"Ruptured aneurysm." I let out a half whistle. A ruptured aneurysm; I had actually never seen one before, although I had certainly read about the subject enough. Aortic aneurysms. I thought of all the autopsy specimens I had ever seen; that's what they all were, come to think of it: autopsy specimens.

The aorta: blood vessel cum laude; just a big tube really, like a big red snake. Starting out in the heart, turning and twisting its way through the diaphragm, running down through the abdomen, where it branches and ends. Chugging along at the hectic pace it leads, expanding and contracting, delivering fresh blood daily. Never resting, never a day off. In health and youth, like a smooth rubber hose, soft and pliant. In old age and disease, rough and warty like an old leather strap. All the products of metabolism depositing on its walls like rust in a water heater, like barnacles on a boat, till the walls become narrowed and stiff so the blood has to force to get through: has to be pushed harder against those unyielding walls. Soon the walls become weak and the weakest spot balloons out under the strain of the constant chug, chug. The blood pushes to get by and then one day it finds a crack in the wall.

The patient would get some back pain, maybe some leg pain. Maybe he'd go to see somebody about it and when they examined him they would feel the big pulsing mass, like a bomb ready to blow at any time. Maybe the patient would be lucky and have the aneurysm surgically bypassed and the blood flow restored successfully, and his aorta would keep chugging along.

But maybe the patient wouldn't see anybody, and maybe the bomb would go off when he was walking the dog, or reading the paper, or standing at the sink. Then there would be nothing but the exquisite sudden pain, the rapid shock, and death within minutes.

Flanigan came out of the operating room. The door hit the back wall.

"Shit," he said. "Shit, goddamn it to hell." He paced across the floor and threw his scrub hat into the laundry basket. "No good?" I offered.

"Why in the holy hell didn't we do him yesterday; why the hell did we wait?" His blue eyes were bloodshot.

"What happened?" I said.

"What happened? What happened is he blew the fucking thing right in front of us on the middle of rounds: not ten feet away, and everybody was standing around picking their ass." He kicked the heavy laundry basket.

"Careful, Tom," I said. "You hurt that foot and you won't be able to drive that fancy car."

He looked over at me, trying to decide if he wanted to take out at least part of his anger on me. He smiled.

"You should have been down there, Wop, you would have been all over him."

"You think so, huh?"

"Yeah. Come on," he said, grabbing a white coat off the IV pole. "I'll buy you a cup of coffee."

# 25

It was my first day on neurosurgery, and I had the immediate pleasure of meeting Dr. Frank Haver, neurosurgeon. He was a very brisk little man, graying at the temples, with horn-rimmed glasses. He carried all his equipment in a tiny zippered case which he kept tucked up beneath his left arm when he walked, leaving both hands free for comment. In his case, free hands were a necessity, since he had a comment to make about everything. He was one comment after another; one slash, one jab, one shaft after another. There was never any conversation. Conversation implies that another party has another voice. That wasn't so. Haver's delivery was sarcasm, pure and simple; it never varied. He was always on, and he demanded an audience. The hospital floor was merely a setting for his wit; nobody was safe, not even the patients.

"So?" he looked at me. "Are we making rounds this morning, or are you waiting for a meeting of the short people of America?" No smile, just a steely glint in his myopic gray eyes.

"We have a patient in ICU," I said, "a motorcycle accident. Forty years old, comatose; I don't really know that much about him. Jerry's up there with him right now."

"Jerry?" he said with exaggerated surprise.

"Jerry who?" He could have blown out a candle with the *who*.

"Jerry Mackey." Jerry had been Haver's resident for the last three months.

"Oh, yes. Dr. Mackey; one of the great minds in medicine." We walked toward the elevator. That is, I walked; Dr. Haver took advantage of the long corridor to display his nonchalant swagger. Nose slightly elevated, hands cupped in front of his crotch, head turning from side to side, he assessed the world, looking for new material. "I see they've been polishing the floors with last night's leftovers again." He kicked a cigarette butt down the hall. We rode up to the third floor. He assessed my body en route. "Ever thought of teaching kindergarten?" he asked. I smiled sweetly. "Nope, never have." We arrived in intensive care.

Jerry was hassled and tired. He'd been up all night with the patient. His scrub clothes were wrinkled, his hair was a mess, he had drips of dried blood on the front of his pants.

"Hi, Dr. Haver. Boy, this guy is in bad shape."

Haver looked at Jerry. "Dr. Mackey, it's always such a pleasure to see you in the morning, right out of the pages of *Gentleman's Quarterly*."

Jerry was either too tired to care or he was immune, because he went on to describe the patient and his condition.

"He has no family that's been in to see him. He's divorced, he has a seventeen-year-old son." We approached the bed. Haver stopped at the foot.

"So, Mackey, this is what you spent your night taking care of: a forty-year-old motorcycle bum. Hardly time worth spent, would you say? He probably hasn't much more brain function when he's conscious."

The level of anger that was quietly starting to rise as we rode up the elevator had gotten a little higher, and was now sitting somewhere south of my diaphragm. "Uh, excuse me, but he is a human being, you know."

Haver lifted his head, turned to me very slowly, and in his best tone of contempt said, "That really hasn't been established." It was clear that Haver and I were going to have trouble; just how much, and how soon, I wasn't sure. But I could tell we were in fact going to have big trouble.

"Well," Haver continued, "I'm sure that with Dr. Scalia's

expert care and womanly hand you can rest easily, Dr. Mackey. I know that she will do her best to have this man on his feet again—or, pardon me, on his motorcycle again—and riding off into the sunset."

Haver's neurological exam was rapid and was terminated by his viciously scratching the bottom of the patient's feet with his car key. The man's leg drew up rapidly. "Well, he responds to pain, anyway."

We had a few patients more to see, and by the time rounds were over I had one hell of a headache, and I don't get headaches.

I got to lunch early. Flanigan was eating by himself. I sat down opposite him.

"Okay, Tom, what's with this guy Haver?"

"Frank? You having trouble with Frank already?"

"How can you not have trouble with him?"

"I guess Frank can be a little tough at times."

"Tough? He's a monster, for Christ sake: if he saw a dog in the street he'd go out of his way to hit it."

"Now come on, Wop, you're getting excited, and you know how you always screw up when you get excited." He was grinning. I threw my roll at him. He moved his head slightly and it zipped by him, landing on the next table and knocking over one of the salt shakers.

"See that?" He was laughing.

"I'm going to get you one day, Flanigan! I come to you for advice, and you make fun of me. This isn't going to be any joke."

"I *am* trying to give you some advice, Wop. Just don't let him get to you; just let it go by; he doesn't really mean it, he just does it for effect. I actually never had any trouble with him."

"That's 'cause your balls are bigger than his and he recognized no contest."

"Joni Scalia!" He shook his head. "What comes out of your mouth!"

"I'm sorry, Tom," I said, trying to hide in my fruit salad, "but I've only known him for two hours and already I'd like to kill the son of a bitch."

"Well, cool off. The other two guys in his group are very easy going. You'll like them."

Jerry Mackey sat down with his lunch. I looked over at him.

"How you doing, Jerry?"

"I'm doing okay, Joni." He poured himself some milk. "One more day with that guy, though, and I would have folded." He raised his glass. "Here's to being off neurosurgery."

# 26

It was my morning to make rounds with Haver. He came in with his usual splendor, looked at me, and then started out the door. That was part of his game. He didn't tell you where he was going, and he didn't speak to you. You were just supposed to follow him around like the little king. If you happened to have your back to him when he came into the office in the morning and didn't see him arrive, he'd make rounds without you and then come back later and ask you where you were. Rounds were whenever he felt like making them.

I followed him down the hall to one of the back corridors. Rehabilitation medicine. We walked into a small room. There was the usual apparatus hanging on the wall. In the center of the room was a single, large upright frame, made up like a bed, in which lay a thin young man. A woman in her twenties sat beside him. The rest of the room was empty. Haver passed by them and picked up the patient's chart. He flipped through it and scribbled a note. The patient followed him with his eyes, but Haver never looked up. He closed the chart and headed out the door.

"Doctor?" The young man called after him, but Haver had disappeared down the hall.

"Yes," I said. "Can I help you, I'm Dr. Haver's resident." The patient didn't move at all. "Could you come here and talk to me?"

"Yes," I said, approaching the frame. The woman smiled. She was wearing a ring. Obviously his wife.

"Doctor," he said, "I think I felt something this morning. A sensation. I think I felt a sensation in my shoulder: like a burning." I was completely lost.

"Let me look at your chart. I'm sorry, but I'm not altogether familiar with your case." *Not altogether familiar with your case*—there's a little understatement for you. I didn't have a clue in hell what was wrong with him; I hadn't even known he was a patient of ours.

The chart was thick. "Quadriplegia, secondary to diving accident. Repeated urinary tract infections." I felt a real thud. One of those heavy numbers that gets you right in the chest. The chart had a whole series of rehabilitation green sheets, medical white sheets, surgical notes, and every once in a while a sentence or two in the scrawl that I had come to recognize as Haver's. "No change." It was hard to tell from the chart what the patient's status was. In addition, having had only a few weeks of neuro, I didn't know beans about quadriplegia. The man had a spinal-cord injury with loss of function of all the nerve fibers that were located below the level of the injury. He had no movement in either his arms or his legs, and he had a permanent catheter in his bladder, which had become chronically infected. He had been admitted this time around to try and clear up his infected urinary tract, before his kidneys became damaged permanently.

"Mister Hopper," I said, coming over to him, "have you talked about this with Dr. Haver?"

"He's tried, Doctor." The wife spoke with a soft Southern accent. "But we can't seem to catch him; he just kind of rushes in and out: I guess he's terribly busy."

"I see. When was the last time Dr. Haver examined him?"

"About three months ago, wasn't it, honey?" He nodded his head in agreement. "You think you might mention it to him, Doctor?"

"Yes, I will." After I kill him. I left the room. Haver was lying in wait out in the hall, pretending to look out the window, fascinated with the view of the parking lot.

"What was he doing, telling you his life story?" He didn't

turn around, he just stared out the window with his little zippered case pressed against his side.

"No, he just wants to talk to you. He says he thinks he felt some sensation in his left arm."

"What he felt was in his head." He started down the hall.

"How do you know?"

"Because he's got nothing from the neck down, and never will have."

"Well, he doesn't seem to understand that."

"They never do; he'll keep thinking he feels things, getting his hopes renewed. He'll be re-examined, but there will be no improvement."

"Well, they're pretty young. I would think they're going to have a lot of problems facing this. I think somebody should talk to them. I mean, his wife is very concerned."

"She's concerned. Give her six months and she'll walk out on him." I stopped dead in the hall. He turned around to me.

"It happens every time: just as soon as she realizes that he really can't get it up any more when he wants to, she'll leave him." I must have had a look and a half on my face.

"What's the matter, bright eyes?" He was sneering. "Can't you take the truth?"

I was shaking. "The truth I can take, Dr. Haver." I paused, but only briefly. "It's you I don't have the stomach for."

# 27

It had been a long day, and I had been up all the night before. We had two laminectomies in the morning, and I was just finishing my second myelogram. Katie, one of the x-ray techs, was running the fluoroscope up and down, one last time.

"Looks good, Joni, nice and clean."

"Thank Christ." My knees were trembling from fatigue. The phone rang in the little alcove. One of the other techs picked it up.

"Hey, Joni, it's for you."

"Who is it?"

She covered the mouthpiece. "It's God."

"Who is it?"

"Haver."

I took the phone. "Hello?"

"Hello, Joni, this is Dr. Haver. I have a patient who needs an emergency myelogram tonight. He's on two south. His name is Gerard Kurtz."

"You going to take him to surgery tonight?"

"No."

"I thought you said it was an emergency."

"It is."

"But you're not planning on taking him to surgery tonight?"

"No."

"When are you going to take him?"

"Probably Tuesday."

"Tuesday? It's Friday today."

"Look, I told the patient he'd be done today. This isn't just some clown, he's one of the union executives."

"And you told him you would do his myelogram today?"

"I told him *you* would do it."

"You told him *I* would do it?" I was very tired. I was so tired that it took me this long to realize that at long last I had Haver by the balls. But I did finally realize it; Haver never let another resident touch his private patients—especially for a myelogram.

"I see," I said. "Gee, maybe one of the other residents can do it."

"No!" He yelled into the phone. "I don't want one of the other residents; they don't do it the way you do. He's expecting you to do it."

I tapped my fingers on the desk.

"If this guy is so important, why don't you do it?" I asked innocently.

He was at the end of his rope. "I cannot get out there this afternoon. This is extremely important."

"I'm sorry, Dr. Haver, but an emergency myelogram only means one thing to me, and that is that the patient may have to be treated immediately thereafter, and since this doesn't seem to be the case, I'm not going to do it." I hung up.

It didn't take long for it all to hit the fan. When I came back from the weekend, I was informed that there had been a staff meeting, and that if my work didn't improve markedly (I believe it was so stated) within the next six months the hospital wouldn't pick up my contract for the second year of residency. Threats. I hated threats. Shape up or ship out; knuckle under, be a man and follow the rules. Well, I knew Haver was going to make a move; he had to. It was the old fraternity game, and Haver was only the first in a long line of legs you had to crawl under, being paddled on the fanny all the way along. The mentality was the same.

I was in the middle of neurosurgery clinic when my advisor, one of the staff surgeons, came to me with the information about the staff meeting. I sat there and listened. It wasn't this guy's fault, I decided. After he left, I reached for my purse, dug for my car keys, and walked out. I moved out of the parking lot with the damn heavy feeling. I had no place to go with it; this was my number all the way. But what the hell choice was there really? Accept a guy like Haver? Never.

I stopped at the light. There was Solly's on the corner, a neighborhood bar frequented by the residents and other hospital personnel. The light changed, and I pulled into a space in front of the bar. Ten-thirty in the morning—ridiculous.

"Hi, Doc."

"Hi, I'll have some Irish coffee."

I looked out the dirty window. Traffic was heavy. It was two days before Christmas. That's what I needed. A Christmas present, a nice long rest, a nice long rest and some time with Les. We were practically strangers.

"Here's your coffee, Doc. Where are your big buddies this morning?"

"Oh, working hard, I guess." I picked up my glass and then noticed the red Corvette through the open door. Flanigan got out after parking in the bus stop, slammed the car door, and came into the bar. He looked annoyed. He pulled over a chair, slammed his keys down on the dirty table, and ran one hand through his hair.

"How did you know where I was?" I asked, slightly intimidated.

"I saw your car in the street; I was on my way to your house."

"I decided to stop here first."

"All right, Wop, what's going on? You know better than to walk out in the middle of a clinic."

"I know."

"So why did you do it?"

"I quit, I'm leaving. I figure now's as good a time as any."

"What the hell do you mean, you're quitting?"

"I'm quitting. I'm going to be Harriet Housewife. Sleep till ten, coffee and sweet rolls, watch the soap operas, no more 'Yes sir, no sir, may I kiss your ass, sir?' "

"You don't mean that, Joni, that's just bullshit. I know you better than that. But I'll tell you, you'd better get your tail back to clinic. Haver is smoking at the mouth. I told him you didn't feel well, but he's ready to nail you up." He looked at me with distress.

"Well, there's more to this than meets the old eye, Tom."

"I gathered that he's got it in for you, but I was at the staff meeting this morning, and that business about your contract was really overstated. Nobody really wants to cancel your contract. Haver was just blowing off steam."

"Good, I hope he strokes out."

"Joni, sometimes I could just pick you up and shake you." He reached for his car keys. I grabbed for his hand.

"Tom, I appreciate everything you have done for me. Really I do, and I've learned a lot from you. Don't think I'm not grateful. But I'm not going back to clinic." His sharp blue eyes looked very carefully up and down my face. "Don't try to cover for me; I'll handle it."

He shook his head and got up. "You're making a mistake, Wop."

"That's okay, I'll probably make some more." He left and I sat there with my Irish coffee. I took a big sip and burned my tongue.

I took a long time going home. I went through the park. What went wrong? One thing? Many things? Many small things, and then one large thing? Maybe it was true. Maybe I was too young. I was too young: "immature." I tried too hard, worried about too many things that I thought were important but weren't important to anybody else. What happened when you got "mature"? Maybe I should have waited, but how would I know when I got there? I could take the ultimate test: looking Haver in the face and not getting a wave of disgust; thinking he was not so bad. That must be a sign of maturity. I had a long way to go, and then maybe there was a whole other problem: I was a woman: a small woman. "Tiny, petite, cute." I should have taken a lesson and followed the appropriate path. Become a kindergarten teacher, play the flute, wear bangs until I'm fifty years old. Marry a three-hundred-pounder so I could look smaller and cuter longer. But never, never think I was an equal, never think I could look any man in the eye (which I very seldom ever could) and say, "Hey, fella, you've got your head up your ass." That isn't done, dammit, that isn't done. That is rebellion and insubordination, which by definition alone implies that you are starting out subservient, are starting out "less" or "unequal." Maybe I never felt unequal. Maybe I always felt equal. Maybe I even felt that I was better, and that entitled me to demand from everybody else what I thought I could deliver myself. Jesus Christ, maybe I *was* better. Could that be? Could it possibly be that I was in fact better, and that made it worse? Do people who are better fail? Highly doubtful. It wouldn't make any sense. People who are better succeed, or is it people who succeed are better? What difference does it make? What difference does it make anyway; speculation is cheap. I pulled into my driveway.

Les came home about seven o'clock, tired out of his mind. He'd been on the night before. He had the next two days off for Christmas.

I hit him with the news in my usual fashion—as soon as he had one foot in the door. He dropped his package of clean uniforms in the hall and collapsed on the couch.

"How about a drink?"

"Right," I said. I fixed us both something appropriate, and then sat down next to him. He was taking off his tie. I gave him the whole story.

"So you just walked."

"Yeah, I did. Are you mad?"

"Mad?" He shook his head. "No, I'm not mad, I'm just a little surprised."

"Why should you be surprised? I've taken enough shit in the last month to last me the rest of my days."

"Look, don't feel like you have to defend yourself. I'm just saying I'm surprised because I know how much your surgery means to you, that's all."

"Well, so what? What difference does it make?" I started to cry.

"What difference does what make?"

"What difference does it make how much it means to me, if I have to bleed for everything? This is only the beginning. How many more bastards am I going to have to go through?"

"Look, Joni, you knew that before you started. You know what surgeons are like." He got up and went into the kitchen for his pipe and came back with a box of tissues.

"Wipe your nose; surgeons don't cry."

"Ex-surgeons cry."

He sat down again and calmly filled his pipe. The dog came over and put his head on my lap. I petted him automatically. Les took a few puffs and then looked over at me.

"You'd better be sure about this, kid, because if you don't

straighten out with the hospital, you'll have this on your record, and it doesn't look good."

The goddamn fucking record. A running account from day one of medical school. Everything you did. Your future depended on it. Your reputation. Your "good name." Part of being a professional. "A Professional." "Be professional." What a goddamn cross to bear.

"Fuck it."

"Joni."

I stood up on the couch. "Fuck it," I screamed triumphantly. The dog ran under the table.

"Okay, fuck it, but you'd better think about selling your car."

"What?"

"I said you'd better think about selling your car."

"Selling my car?" I dropped to my knees on the couch. "Why on earth would I ever sell my car?"

"Because, sweet baby," he said, stroking my hair, "you can no longer afford to keep it."

I looked at him in utter horror. "Oh, my God, the car payment!" I grabbed him. "I can't sell my car, Les, I love my car."

"You're going to have to. There's no way we can pay for it on my salary."

"No, I can't sell my car. There's got to be some way to make the payment. I'll get a job, that's all."

Les was laughing. "You already have a job."

"No, I mean a real job, that pays real money. A job where they treat you like a person instead of a piece of shit."

"Joni, if you don't go back to the hospital, you won't be able to get a job selling matches on the corner."

"All right, I'll go back. But just to straighten out with them." I went into the kitchen to make dinner. We were quiet for a few minutes.

"Les?"

"What?"

"I hate to say this, but when you get right down to it, I'd probably sell you before I'd sell that car."

"I know."

I went back to the hospital the next morning and asked to see the chief of staff. It was arranged, and I went in and offered my resignation. The guy was a human being. He wasn't satisfied with my resignation for "personal reasons." He wanted the whole story; I gave it to him. I told him how I felt about Haver, told him what the neurosurgery rotation was like for everybody. I didn't think it mattered anyway. He told me that he was glad I had come and that he didn't want me to resign. He'd switch me to orthopedics until he could find out what could be done about the neuro rotation. He actually meant it, but he was making it hard for me, trying to tell me that things would get better, when I knew it was only a matter of time until I'd meet another Haver. I had made up my mind. I wanted out, while I still could get out. I asked him about my contract. He said he wouldn't hold me to it, but asked me again to reconsider. I told him that this was it. We shook hands and he wished me luck.

I didn't feel good when I left the office. I didn't have that great feeling of relief I thought I was going to have. I went downstairs to the radiology department. It was about ten thirty.

"Hi, Joni, what's doing?"

"Not much. Where's Dr. Foster?"

"He's finishing a GI."

"I'll wait."

I sat down in his little office. It was a wreck. Piles of x-rays and papers and books. He came in a few minutes later.

"Hi, Joni, what can I do for you?"

"I came to say goodbye. I'm quitting."

"Finally had enough, huh?"

"Yeah, I guess."

He sat down in his chair and put his feet up on the ledge where the films were. "Why don't you get yourself into a radiology program here in the city? I'll write you a good letter."

"No thanks, Doug; I'm just going to hang loose for a while."

"You'd like radiology. There's no hassle, good hours, you don't have to put up with the surgical mentality."

"And just what's wrong with the surgical mentality?"

He burst out laughing. "I don't know, Joni, you just may be hopeless."

"I just may be." I got up.

"Keep in touch." He put out his hand.

"I will." We shook hands and I left to find Tom. He was definitely the best guy to ask about where to get a job.

# 28

Flanigan came through, as usual; he just happened to know of a job opening in the surgical outpatient department of one of the larger hospitals. The new job was ideal. The money was fantastic, and the hours were even better. Nine to five, five days a week. The job was ideal if you were fifty and you'd just had a stroke. The work was stultifyingly dull. I saw four million cases of hemorrhoids, at least fifty thousand ingrown toenails, I don't know how many cysts behind the left ear, and you can just forget about counting the infected fingers—they don't make numbers that high. I don't think I made a diagnosis that counted in the two years that I worked there. But nobody rode my ass, and nobody shook me at three o'clock in the morning, telling me to haul out of bed. For awhile, that was worth it all: at least I paid off my car. The boredom finally took its toll, and one morning I woke up and said, "Les, I cannot do this any more. I am going crazy."

"Quit," he said.

"What about the money?"

"Screw it, I'll get a job moonlighting."

"What am I going to do?"

"Why don't you try doing nothing for a while? I mean, let's

face it, you've probably been in school since you were three years old."

"Nothing? You mean not work?" The thought was so incredibly alien you might have thought he suggested intercourse with an elephant.

"Sure; take it easy. Do something you'd like for a change."

"But what about the money? I mean, seriously. I make three times as much as you do. We'll be down to near zero."

"We'll be poor, but I do have an opportunity to moonlight, and frankly, you've been miserable for months. I don't ever want to see you unhappy; I wouldn't care what I had to do." He said it so simply over his coffee, just like he said everything else. One sentence, that covered it. He got up from the table. "I've got to go."

"Les."

"What?"

"I love you. I love you." I ran over and squeezed him.

"Look out, look out, you're rumpling my whites."

I gave notice at work, and one month later I was, as they say, among the unemployed.

The idea of freedom was almost as great as the actual freedom itself. Almost, but not quite. Not having to be anywhere at a given time, not having to rush, not having to see anybody if I didn't choose to—my God, that is pure and simple luxury. I took the dog to the park, I hand-painted my furniture, I shopped around San Francisco for the least expensive and most delicious of foods the city had to offer. I learned to sew (skin is one thing, fabric is another), I made friends with everyone on the block, whom I had perhaps never even said hello to in the two years we had lived there; I went swimming every day, half a mile. I had one hell of a time. The old axe, which of course inevitably falls, waited for eight months, and then came in the form of Les's draft notice.

This was really it. Les had gotten a temporary deferment, which allowed him to finish his residency training. And now, the government was reminding him that in very short order he had to pay his dues. The printed form was very interesting; they gave a choice of where he'd like to be stationed. Les had signed with the Air Force, and it had various regions you could put down as your first, second, and third choices. The regions were very specific, like earth, and places like that. We weren't anxious enough, but one of the other residents in the program with Les had just gotten back from his two-year assignment; they had drafted him after his first year of obstetrical residency and he had requested "Northeast United States." They sent him to Minot, North Dakota, where he saw nothing but snow for two years and then made him the base psychiatrist, which resulted, according to him, in "irreversible brain damage" and a morbid fear of anything white.

We were exceedingly nervous about the whole thing. Les put down "Southwestern United States" because he figured at least there was some chance in the world of getting somewhere in California, and the yarns around the campfire in the delivery room about the two years of snow had definitely deterred him from anything that contained the word *north*.

We checked out the possible base locations.

"Look, Joni," Les said one night, "I don't know what's going to happen, but from what I've heard about these military installations, it seems to me that if you don't do some kind of work, you probably won't have a goddamn thing to do. I don't want to scare you, but would you consider something like working in a base hospital if you had to?"

"Sure." I thought about it. What could be so bad for two years? Two years, hell, I could do that standing on one leg.

We got our temporary orders. It wasn't up north, and it certainly was the southwestern United States, right in the middle of the damn desert. We checked out the town. They had a university, a medical school, and a number of hospitals.

"This looks good, Joni. You might even be able to pick up a residency."

I was excited. I was excited because Les wasn't going to Vietnam, because he wasn't going to leave and come back dead like the rest of the guys who kissed their wives goodbye and came back in boxes and envelopes, or didn't come back at all. That was what the excitement was; it was "I don't want it to have to be anybody, but if it has to be somebody, I don't want it to be me."

I thought about taking another residency. The idea didn't really appeal to me. I really enjoyed being home, having my own time, spending my time with Les. I had made quite a few friends; none of them were doctors; some of them didn't even go to a doctor. But, my God, I'd have to do something—I mean, how could I explain it? "I used to be a doctor, but I'm retired now?" Twenty-eight years old? Retired? "I'm a dropout?" That wasn't any good either, because I was too old to be a dropout. Maybe Doug Foster was right; maybe I should give radiology a try. Good hours, no hassle. Radiology was kind of fun, anyway. I'd liked it in medical school. I wrote for applications. What the hell.

I was accepted into the university radiology program and Les received his final military orders almost simultaneously. In one weekend I flew down to the site of our new home, purchased a half-finished adobe house, spent twenty-seven hours looking at floor tiles, and accepted my appointment at the university. We were all set.

# 29

X-ray: radiology. The power of it: the implication, the wonder of it. Being outside and seeing inside. Having all revealed to you without parting a layer of skin. The depth and dimension of it. The ultimate in magic. Now you see it, now you don't, only in reverse. The indisputable evidence: the concreteness, the definition, the suggestion. The presence, the absence, the diagnosis. The ultimate tool in medicine. I loved it. I can't ever imagine medicine without it. It was truly to have been practicing blind. I loved it. I loved radiology but I hated being a radiologist. It was one of the worst years of my life.

Where was everybody? That's what I want to know. Where was the Ancient Mariner? Why the hell didn't he stop me on the way to the mailbox when I dropped my application and say, "Ah, you maketh not a wise move," or whatever people like that say. The Cheshire Cat: where was he with his smiling face? Why didn't he pop out from behind a cactus and say, "You? A radiologist? Don't make me laugh." What went wrong this time? Where goes the blame here? I've been over it so many times, but it's like walking through the ruins of Nuremberg and asking yourself "Let's see, I wonder where I put the coffeepot."

It isn't that I wasn't interested. God knows I went about things with my usual myopic enthusiasm, but it just was not destined to go well. It was a disaster from the onset.

I arrived at the university hospital at 9:00 A.M., July 3. It was already 110 degrees in the parking lot. As I got out of my car and locked it, some guy in cowboy boots said, "Better crack those windows an inch, they'll blow right out come twelve o'clock." I rolled down the windows and walked up the stairs not really believing that people wore cowboy boots.

All the incoming residents were to assemble together: medical, surgical, and so on. It was a medium-sized group. I felt fairly comfortable. We sat waiting for our welcome.

"Welcome." How many welcomes had we all been through by now: how many beginnings, and introductions, and bottom-of-the-heaps? How many more welcomes would there be before we got the one big one that said "Welcome, baby, you have arrived."

An enormous man entered the room. He was easily 250 pounds. He had a large nose and a pair of low-set ears. The thought struck me immediately: this man is an anomaly. I could have cried when he opened his mouth. He was from New York.

Solomon Bernstein. Sol. He was the vice-chairman of the radiology department. He was also in charge of all the incoming residents and he wanted to make sure we all started out on the right foot. Actually, the entire resident staff could have started off on his right foot, which was bigger than his left, and was probably what had given the poor man his attraction for radiology. He talked to us about how important we all were and about other pertinent things, like where we couldn't park or we'd get a ticket, which was precisely where I was parked, and I did, and then he switched over his discussion to radiology and the radiology residents.

Dr. Bernstein said that we were to consider ourselves a consulting service and that we shouldn't get any ideas that radiology was just sitting around and eating doughnuts and drinking coffee and reading films. "I don't want film-readers here," he said. "I want a complete radiologist." What was a "complete radiologist"?

"One more thing," he went on. "I think we have something in our program of which we can be extremely proud. We are probably the only program in the country that offers twenty-four-hour consulting service to the other residents in the hospital."

Twenty-four-hour consulting service; what was he talking about?

"This of course means that one of our radiology residents remains in the hospital at all times on a regular night-call rotation. You are not to be afraid to call him; he is here to help you make your diagnosis. You are to call him before you want any request for a radiograph. We will have only quality work done here at night; we have no technicians after 11:00 P.M.; the residents will be taking all the films themselves."

All the residents in the room applauded. All except three. Me, and the other two suckers who thought they were starting a job as a maitre d' and found out instead that they would be slinging hash in an all-night diner.

I was truly enraged. I was indignant. I had been sucked in. Conned by a New Yorker. I wanted my money back. I wanted another chance. I wanted to turn in my stubs, but most of all I wanted to talk to Les. But Les was at Fort Noplace, in some pinhead-sized town in Texas under wraps like a giant U-2. Totally unreachable.

I knew one thing. I had to get out now. This had been a real mistake; anyone could make one, but why, why was it always me?

Everyone was getting up to leave.

"The radiology residents will please remain. I wish to meet with you in my office."

Bernstein met with us privately. Individually. My meeting with him was about as congenial as the Ox-Bow incident.

"Dr. Scalia, I'll make this brief." Not as brief as I'm going to make it, I thought.

"I don't like women; I don't think they belong in medicine, and I particularly don't think they belong in radiology." That was brief, all right.

"One more thing. I don't like taking physicians in the program who have been out in practice. They are usually hard to deal with and they just don't accept training well like a fresh mind out of an internship."

I really just couldn't believe it. One turkey in the whole field and they have flown him directly out, or maybe he had flown himself, so that he could be in charge of the one program out of hundreds that I had chosen. What, I wondered, were the odds of this happening outside either a Grade B movie or a recurrent nightmare?

"I don't really think I understand," I said. "Why on earth did you accept me in this program?"

He looked at me in dismay. "Your qualifications are so impressive and your letters of recommendation are so excellent"—he threw up his hands in defeat—"I really didn't have a chance with the admissions committee in turning down your application. But bear this in mind," he said, raising his voice to an ominous pitch. "This is no field for lightweights. You have to have stamina to be a radiologist: you have to be strong to stay in this program." He banged the desk for emphasis, and then reached for his pipe.

I was speechless.

He stuffed his pipe with tobacco and leaned forward at me, glaring over that ridiculous nose. "It is my experience that a woman like yourself just won't make it in this program."

That was it. The fat was in the old fire. High noon in the Old West: a direct challenge.

"Is that so!" I said, grabbing my purse.

"Yes," he said between puffs, "that is so."

"Well," I said, standing up in all my minuscule entirety, "we will just see about that." I walked out of the office. He yelled after me, "Don't be late tomorrow. Seven A.M. first conference." I turned around in surprise.

"We start early in this program. We like to beat the surgeons out of bed." He was smiling like the caterpillar in *Alice in Wonderland*; high on his mushroom with his hookah, smoking away. The Cheshire Cat was probably right behind him.

I stormed out to the parking lot. There was a ticket on the windshield. "Shit," I said, grabbing the door handle, which was probably three hundred degrees. I screamed and looked at my left hand, which was blistering before my eyes. Tears rolling down my miserable little cheeks, I turned the lock with my key and used my skirt to push in the button and open the door.

The inside was like a blast furnace. I had no air conditioning. I ran back into the building and got some wet paper towels and dragged them through the lobby, throwing them on the front seat and patting water on the wooden steering wheel. I finally got it cool enough so that I could sit down without turning my entire behind into a marshmallow, and I began the drive home. Home. Home is where you hang your hat. In this case, your cowboy hat.

It was a fifteen-minute drive and the sweat was rolling down my back and legs. At least the house was air-conditioned. I pulled off the main street onto the long road of farmhouses and pastures that led out to our house. The grass abruptly ended at the river bank, which was now a huge dry ditch under a bridge. When the rain came, the river would roll and swell and barrel under the bridge, drowning whoever happened to be sitting and picnicking without a radio and hadn't heard the warnings of flash floods.

The road took off into the hills. Hills of sand and rock and low-lying cactus and shrub. It was the barest of vegetation, lifeless and still in the afternoon heat. I bombed up the driveway and skidded into the garage. The dog was flaked out in the laundry room. I opened the door and faced what surely had to be the emptiest house in the world.

# 30

Les called that evening. I told him what had happened. I really wanted to cry, but he sounded so lousy himself. The drive to Wichita Falls had been a real scenic delight: sand, interrupted by sand, some road, a little sand, one or two state troopers, a few dead possums, and some locusts.

His first day of Air Force briefing had been all instructional. The Air Force had special books for the doctors. "This is an officer, this is a mailman: one you salute, one you don't." Everybody was bored out of their minds. Les was staying in a motel with a dentist from Denver. They were going to hit the big time in about an hour: *Speedball Charlie*. A motorcycle movie at the drive-in.

"You're not afraid to stay there alone, are you?" Les asked.

"Who, me? Afraid? Why should I be afraid?" Why should I be afraid in the middle of nowhere, in a house with seven entrances, all glass, no curtains, no garage doors, and a Doberman pinscher with heat stroke?

"You'll take Nero into the bedroom to sleep with you tonight," Les said, "and you know where the guns are."

"Right," I said.

The guns. I was really glad I had them. My big problem

would be deciding which one to use. The .38 was terrific, but you had to use both hands to fire. And it had only five shots. What if there was more than one assailant? The 9-mm automatic was better: you could get off thirteen shots really fast, if you remembered to put in the clip. The .22 had a nice long barrel; very accurate, but a .22? The hole was so small it wasn't even worth considering. I'd better take all three to bed with me and pray I didn't wind up shooting Nero on his way to the kitchen for a biscuit.

I hung up. Just hearing Les's voice made me feel better. It always did. Besides, it was still daylight and I really wasn't afraid yet. I looked out the back door of the house. There was another house in the distance, but no sign of people moving. I could always scream for help, but who would hear?

When it gets dark in the desert, it's like a stranger rode in with the four-o'clock stage. What was quiet during the day gradually becomes deathlike; and it scares the shit out of you if you're alone.

I went to work the next morning determined that everything would be all right. It wasn't. Sol was in a foul mood. He was having a tantrum in the hall, stomping his huge foot and screaming. He screamed at the technicians. He screamed at the machines. He screamed at me. I screamed at him. He told me to do what I was told, I told him to go to hell. He told me to get out. I told him "With pleasure." I went home and cried for an hour. The phone rang. It was the chairman of the department. He had the office across the hall from Sol's and had heard the racket. Actually, the guy behind the counter at the Walgreen's three blocks down from the university hospital had probably heard it too, but he didn't have my phone number. Dr. Benjamin, the department chairman, was now asking for some sort of explanation.

I told him I thought Sol was a horse's ass. He told me that wasn't nice. I told him Sol wasn't nice. He told me that I had to learn to live with Sol (like a chronic illness). I told him that it wasn't worth it. He told me not to take it all so personally, and to come back in and we'd straighten the whole thing out. I told him I wanted an apology from Bernstein. He told me I'd never get one, but he wished me luck. He set up an appointment between Sol and me for later on in the afternoon.

The minute I walked in the door, Sol started screaming. I screamed back. Dr. Benjamin intervened. We declared a truce,

Sol refused to apologize, and I refused to be screamed at. Some truce. When I finally left the office, I stopped Dr. Benjamin in the hall. "Why did you bother with this mess?" I said. "This is obviously a hopeless situation."

"My wife's a doctor," he said, and flashed me a huge grin. What kind of explanation was that?

My schedule had me at the university hospital for the first two weeks, learning technique. Learning how to operate x-ray equipment for someone like myself did not even enter the realm of reality. I, who could mess up a Polaroid, who could break a curling iron by merely plugging it in, who was afraid of the garbage disposal and who was never able to drive a shift car because of inability to remember the basic H, I who didn't know a watt from an ohm, set loose in a department with thousands on thousands of dollars worth of precision equipment. Equipment with dials and gauges and lights and levers and panels and timers and manuals and automatics.

The first day there I fouled up the fluoroscope. The techs said they wouldn't tell Sol. The second day I fed the film incorrectly into the processor and ruined one of Sol's barium enemas. The techs covered for me. On the third morning when I came in I found that the technicians had made a tight circle around the machines. They made me promise I wouldn't touch anything. I agreed, and just observed for the next two weeks. I explained to the technicians that I had this basic mistrust of equipment; they explained that they had this basic mistrust of me.

At the end of the two weeks Sol gave an exam. I had to present him with one set of films that I had taken completely on my own. I tried for an hour to do a set of skulls; fortunately, I practiced on an empty model skull, since I had my milliamps-seconds up a little higher than I should have. One of the techs came in and saved my life by doing the whole thing in five minutes. When I brought the films out to Sol, he looked at me suspiciously. "You did these?"

"Certainly."

"Well, it took you long enough."

"Good work always does," I said, smiling.

I started on the night-call rotation that evening. The call room was up on the second floor. It was one of those totally darkened tombs with no windows and one light switch which is located—deliberately, I'm sure—at the other end of the room from the telephone. So that when the phone rings, not only do you have no way of getting to it, because you can't see it, but you have no way of getting to the light either.

There was a regular technician on till eleven, but after she went home, I would be on my own.

I read the films from the emergency room, which was a huge joke, because after two weeks in a residency your qualifications are considerably few. The interesting thing about it though is that every doctor thinks he's a radiologist. Every surgeon, internist, every first-year resident, every third-year medical student, everyone who has ever had a chest x-ray considers himself qualified to make a radiologic diagnosis. (Sol, damn his eyes, had a great expression, but I can't remember what it was: it had to do with looking and seeing. He would swear up and down that it took about a year before you actually "saw"; it was all very philosophical and metaphysical, and correct: The first time I realized that I could "see," I was about eight months into the program. The difference was so dramatic that I went in and told Sol. "You're only a girl," he said. I guess that meant I didn't see, and wouldn't until he said I did.)

I got my first call at midnight. The emergency room wanted a hand or a leg or some damn thing. Having already made up my mind what my approach to night call would be, I reached into my jacket pocket for the piece of paper containing the night technician's phone number. "Mike," it said, and the number.

"How'd you like to do a leg?" I said when he answered.

"Sure. Be right in."

Easy enough, I thought. I called him twice more that night and each time he said, "Sure; be right in." By the third call, I was sufficiently sleep-robbed to make it down to the basement. Mike was down there hanging up the latest film. It was a big toe. The emergency-room requisition said "Pain, big toe." Mike was whistling to himself and filling out the envelope.

"Jesus Christ," I said, "don't you mind coming in here for this?" I never did well with sleep loss. He looked over at me and lit a cigarette.

"You don't know what's going on here, do you, Doctor?"

"What do you mean?"

"Sit down. I'll tell you a little story."

I did, and he proceeded to relate the facts of life. It seemed that due to lack of funds in the department some cutbacks had to be made. Sol had decided that the best way to make them was by not having to pay the technicians' time and a half for after eleven o'clock, something he would have had to do if the techs stayed in the hospital all night and took all the films. It was then that Sol formulated this ingenious plan of utilizing the cheapest possible labor available, the residents. The residents, whose collective asses could be run both day and night for the same lousy six hundred dollars a month, without meals or parking. The "night-call consultants." I was homicidal by the time Mike finished talking.

"So, you see, I get paid only if I come in to take a film. You call me once, I get paid once. You call me four times, I get paid four times as much."

I put out my hand. "Michael, you and I are going to make it to the big time." We shook on it. The intern came in from the emergency room. "Is that toe normal?"

"Read it yourself, baby," I said, and snapped on the light for him.

My anger was consuming. It kept me up the rest of the night, of which there was but little left. By the time I got to breakfast, I was in a small rage. I told off my scrambled eggs. That did nothing for me. I got rid of my tray and tried to deposit my hatred with it on the conveyor belt. It didn't work. I took the elevator down to the basement; maybe the change in altitude would do it. We had our usual seven-o'clock conference. I smacked right into Sol in the viewing room. He was checking last night's films.

"Oh, Joni, I'd like a word with you."

I'd like more than a word with you, you penny-pinching bastard, I muttered to whoever might be listening in my head.

"The emergency room says they didn't get a reading on one film last night. It was a toe. Do you know anything about it?"

"No," I said sweetly, "the slip must have gotten lost." I'd like to blacken your eyes, you cheap son of a bitch.

"One more thing."

"What's that?"

"You missed a skull fracture last night."

I stopped hallucinating. "What?"

"Take a look." The films were hanging on the view box.

The fracture was visible in three views. It wasn't even subtle. I was horrified. "I didn't even see it!"

"No, you didn't even look." He was puffing on his pipe, staring at me in that inscrutable big-bird fashion. He was right, of course; I hadn't even tried to wake up when I looked at that set of films. I had glanced over them, decided they looked normal, scribbled down "normal skull" on the ER sheet and rushed my little body back up to bed, aggravated beyond belief that I had to get up to read the films on some drunk with a three-day-old head injury. All the man's teeth could have been missing on the film and I wouldn't have noticed.

"All you guys, get in here," Sol yelled. The rest of the residents grouped around him. "Listen good. Ninety percent of this field is concentration. If you're not looking for something, you'll never see it, and I know you guys, I know you." He was at full volume. There was one of those "Oh, my God" looks on my face: he saw me and he lowered his voice. "I know you, you don't pay attention at night." We all stood around him like a flock of angels. "Now, let's get to work."

# 31

After Les's first day at the air base he came home and said, "This won't be bad." After his second day he said, "You know, it's just me and a guy who was drafted after one year of residency, which makes me the only qualified obstetrician, which puts me on call every night until this other OB gets here from Chicago." He got called in for a delivery and was up all night. After his third day at the base he said, "I'll tell you something, this colonel is such an asshole that I may just have to tell him so."

After Les's fourth day at the base we went out for a Baskin-Robbins and I dropped my hot fudge sundae all over his military cap, which he kept next to him in the front seat of his reasonably newly acquired pick-up truck. ("Good desert vehicle," he said.) He became very upset. "They like you to wear your hat," he told me. What if the chocolate didn't come out? I was laughing so hard at him that he almost threw me out on the highway. The following weekend I dumped a Coke into his Corfam shoes while trying to climb into the front seat with my McDonald's. He threatened to report me to the CIA. I gave him my fries and he forgot about it, but I could see that he was already becoming rule-ridden.

They had rules for absolutely everything on this installation. It was a Strategic Air Command Base, and they would actually shoot you if you attempted to drive through the front gate in an unauthorized vehicle. Les took my car one morning because the truck was in the shop. He failed to stop at the gate because he forgot my car didn't have a sticker. The airman at the gate yelled "Halt," and he kept going. Thirty seconds later he was looking down the barrel of a rifle. "It's the click that really puts your foot on the brake," he told me later.

On day five of his military career Les came home with a severe headache. "God," he said, lying down on the couch and popping two Edrisal, "when the hell is that guy going to get here from Chicago?"

Dr. Sterling finally arrived in the clinic on the designated Monday morning. The clinic volunteer knocked on the door of Les's office. "Major Sterling is here, Major Newman. I'm sure you'd like to get acquainted."

Les put out his hand. "Les Newman."

"Neil Sterling," he said, giving Les's hand a squeeze. "Man, this place really sucks, doesn't it?"

Neil was a rare combination of Phil Silvers, Mel Brooks, and Neil, and he was the only good thing that happened to us in the next two years. He and Les fell in love with each other. They were so seemingly different, but it didn't matter to either one. They had a com-line installed between their offices and they called each other up about twenty times a day.

"This is the general speaking."

"Fuck you, sir."

"Keep up the good work."

They called each other up at night.

"This is an obscene phone call," Neil would say; then he'd hold his nose and make a series of disgusting noises into the receiver. We'd call him up at two in the morning. "This is Mrs. Howsyourass, Colonel Howsyourass' wife," I'd say, "and I just ran out of birth-control pills."

"Take an aspirin instead: they work just as well."

Neil was recently divorced, but his ex-wife called him up every night from Chicago and reversed the charges, just to drive him crazy. He kept getting his number changed, but she kept getting the new one. Neil was the only reason that getting up and going to the base was at all bearable for Les. For me, getting up and going in to the university hospital was scarcely bearable at all. This was chiefly due to the warm and wonderful atmosphere created by the attending staff.

Although Sol was very definitely Our Leader, there were several other members of the department who were in direct charge of our daily lives. The entire staff made a collection of Dale Carnegie dropouts look like winners in a Mr. Congeniality contest.

Dr. Alvin Stein was a little compulsive. I'm sure he counted all his fingers and toes before he came to work in the morning to make sure there were exactly enough digits and that they were all in their proper places.

Dr. Stein did not think that women belonged in medicine. He obviously learned that from Sol. After two weeks of the residency he called me into his office and he told me that he could see that I wasn't catching on like the rest of the residents. He could see I needed help. He would be glad to tutor me. Getting help from Alvin was like taking the cure. He could spend half an hour on one film. He could pick apart every line, every suggestion of a shadow of a hair of an irregularity, and speculate on its importance. He specialized in the minuscule and the microscopic. He kept patients on the table while he reshot and redid and repeated and then made an extra film so he could keep it in his collection of slides to be used for teaching purposes. And he wanted to help me because he knew two weeks into the program that I wasn't catching on. He knew I was starting out with some deficit, carrying that extra X chromosome around. I should be home raising a family, he told me, pulling out his wallet to show me his little angels.

But I couldn't blame Alvin too much. He did not see the world to be full of people, only full of bones.

I can recall, to the day, placing Dr. Stein in his proper perspective.

It was three days before Christmas, and one of the pediatric interns had come rushing excitedly into the department, carrying a small chest x-ray.

"Dr. Stein, could you look at this, please?"

"Certainly."

"It's the latest chest x-ray on one of my little leukemics. She's doing very well, and if this film is okay, I want to be able to send her home for Christmas."

Alvin put the film up and contemplated it for about an

eternity. I looked over at the intern. She was shifting from leg to leg. "It looks pretty good, doesn't it?"

"Yes, I would say it is probably normal." He turned around to face her and said very earnestly, "Listen, would you do me a favor?"

"Sure."

"When this kid dies, would you let me know so I can get a piece of her bone from the autopsy specimen? I'd like to make some slides." He stared at us, not having a clue that he had said anything inordinate. The intern looked like somebody had stabbed her in the heart, and she backed out the door. Alvin looked at me pleasantly. "Nice girl."

# 32

The IVP. What's an IVP? If I just said that I hated them with a fury, would that be good enough? If I said that if I never had to do one again in my whole life, that would be reason enough to get up in the morning? Would that be good enough? If I said it was one of those procedures where you could walk into the hospital as a patient, humming and strumming a tune, and walk out dead, would that be good enough? The intravenous pyelogram. One of the real show-stoppers in diagnostic radiology.

You take an x-ray of the abdomen. It comes out a study in grays and blacks, with outlines softly suggested. Then, by a simple intravenous injection, an oily material containing iodine flows via the patient's circulation to his kidneys. The iodine —being a fairly heavy element—blocks the passage of x-rays so that when you take the next film of the abdomen, you see before you in startling and blinding white the loveliest of outlines: the flowerlike interior of the kidneys and the curved grace of the tubular ureters as they descend from the kidneys and empty into the bladder. Fantastic! Dramatic as hell, visually.

It's a great test; you can get a huge amount of information

from it that can greatly benefit the patient. And you can get trouble like you'd never believe. Very rarely, and I emphasize very rarely, the patient is allergic to the oily contrast. And has a reaction. Why bring all this up? Why? Because I did IVP's every morning for six months. The first week along, I started the intravenous on my patient and injected about a cubic centimeter of material. She looked up at me and said "Aargh," or whatever they used to say in the old Tarzan comics when the guy fell out of the tree clutching his throat and stopped breathing. She responded very nicely to all the appropriate medications that one is supposed to give under these circumstances, which I considered lucky for both of us. The remainder of my patients ran the spectrum from breaking out in hives to throwing up in my face. I looked on each new day as a challenge. The statistics on anything severe happening to any of these patients were probably as rare as finding Arafat at a Chanukah service. But several months later, when this nice little old man with a prostate problem looked up at me as I was about to push the plunger on the syringe and said, "Listen, I don't know if I mentioned to you or not, but the last time I had one of these, at the VA hospital, the doctor said my heart stopped," I decided this was one Sol would do.

We had a theory among the residents. We figured that if the patient had a really bad contrast reaction, we could depend on the staff to react on cue. Sol would remain calm and cool and get the complete study, we theorized, and then he would rapidly send the patient over to the ER so he didn't die in the department. Alvin would wait till the patient was already dead and then take postmortem films. This was only speculation, but what the hell else is there to do when you're standing around waiting for someone to throw up on you? I was just crazy about being the University Resident, comma, First Year.

I came in every morning and checked the blackboard with marked hesitation. Maybe, if I sneaked up on it slowly, there would be only three IVPs. Maybe if it was raining out, one of them wouldn't show. But it never rained in the desert.

IVP was the first column on the blackboard, and it was not a good column, but the second column, labeled VCU, was decidedly worse. I got to the point where I could ruin my day instantly, simply by reading from left to right; so after a while I didn't read the board. I just came into the techs' lounge in the morning and asked for a reading. "Looks good this morning,"

"Only three," "Bad day, Joni. Alvin's on fluoro; that means he'll tie up all the rooms." God, when Alvin was on fluoro or, in other words, when Alvin was doing the GI series and barium enemas, I could forget about getting any rooms to put my patients in for IVPs. Alvin needed another film, or he wanted another look, or he requested a special view. His pick-up rate on duodenal ulcers was probably very low, because if you came into the department with an ulcer it had a good chance of having healed by the time Alvin finished your GI series. Usually by noon I got to start my VCUs.

VCUs are the radiologist's answer to a blue movie. Voiding Cystourethrogram. Voiding, meaning obviously what it means: void: to pee. Cystourethrogram, meaning picture of your bladder and urethra. So we are taking an x-ray, recording on film your bladder and urethra (that channel connecting your bladder with the outside world) while you are voiding. A moving study of a person in the act of going potty. Are you getting the general feel for the procedure? Some poor person is asked to stand up in a drafty, strange room, on a little platform, and urinate, while the doctor (who stands discreetly outside the room at his or occasionally her fluoroscope) monitors the progress of the urinary stream. It's like a screen test. Nobody can ever pee. Could you? The radiologist can watch the patients' poor indecisive little bladders under the fluoroscope, contracting, making a try with everything they've got in the way of muscular structure, but the little socially aware muscular valve on the outside keeps saying, "Wait a minute, you guys, somebody's watching." Patients stayed in the department for hours. We gave them water to drink, we put warm towels on their feet, we turned down the lights in the room and drew the curtains. Getting a successful VCU was really the ultimate in skill. If your exposures were no good, you didn't get another chance. Needless to say, I always had one of the technicians set my technique and push the button for me when I said "Now," just so my hand would in no way touch the machine at the critical moment.

Alvin continued to be on my back. When I got up at a conference, I thought I was to make a diagnosis; Alvin thought I should be giving the Gettysburg Address. I was under the mistaken impression that if you didn't see the abnormality on the film, you said, "I don't see it," and you sat down. Wrong.

Alvin insisted, "You have to talk when you get up there. You have to go through the processes systematically and out loud."

"Why out loud?"

Because that's good conferencemanship.

"Conferencemanship? Is that with one *s* or two?"

"Probably two."

"But look," I attempted to reason with him. "What is the point of discussing everything normal on the film if you miss the diagnosis? If you miss the diagnosis, the discussion is purely peripheral."

Alvin cringed. He shuddered. He shrank from my disrespect for academia. After several severe admonitions I decided that if they wanted me to talk, then I would just have to talk.

It was Thursday-afternoon conference. This was our most difficult conference. It was not just for the residents, but for the staff as well. A visiting radiologist would bring his most difficult cases for the sole purpose of stumping the other radiologists and the residents.

The visiting radiologist had put up a number of films, we had all been called on, and now he was putting up one of his obviously difficult cases. He called on one of the senior residents; he missed the diagnosis. He called on Alvin; he missed the diagnosis. He called on three other staff members and they missed the diagnosis. I was sitting next to Sol. I knew he knew the diagnosis; he rarely missed. I leaned over to him. "I know what that is," I said to him, having been through every radiology book in the library.

"Does anybody here know what disease this is?" the guest radiologist called out to the room, obviously pleased with himself. "It's osteogenesis imperfecta tarda." The entire room turned around. Sol looked at me. "You're absolutely correct, Joni," he whispered. "That's what it is."

"Who said that?" The room was buzzing away.

"I did."

"Would you repeat the diagnosis?"

"Osteogenesis imperfecta tarda."

"That's correct, and that's very good. What year are you?"

"First year."

"How did you know what this was?"

"It's classical," I said sweetly.

I did it two more weeks in a row. A malignant melanoma of the stomach, read from a GI series, which I had not yet learned how to do, and a case of cretinism in a forty-year-old woman. The crowd went wild. I realized that I had in some ways committed an error; whereas before they expected nothing from me, they now expected more. "Ask Joni to look at that film; see if she gets it," Alvin would say. I had to keep following my own act just to stay on top.

# 33

We were conferenced to death. We had morning conferences and afternoon conferences. We had dinner and after-dinner conferences. We had guest lecturers. We had "the case of the week" and "the case of the day."

I learned to recognize people by their bones. By their soft-tissue variations, by the width of their retroperitoneal fat stripes on an abdomen film, by the shape of their stomachs and the outpouchings of their colons. I learned to appreciate what was a "good case," and what was not. I got to know people by their tumors. I had the pleasure of recreating a demise by simply hanging up a series of fourteen-by-seventeen-inch reproductions which followed the growth of a tumor from the size of a barely perceptible pea to the huge goober that it was six months later, visible from three blocks away. You had the whole story right in the manila envelope. You knew the patient like nobody else; you were part and parcel of his medical course. You knew in many instances before the treating physician did when this patient would not be back for future films. You might never have seen the patient, but you could have given his eulogy. You would have said, "I knew him, I read his films."

It was after conference one evening. Everybody had gone home. I was on call and was on my way up to the cafeteria. I passed by the main block of rooms. There was a stretcher out in the hall. Damn, I thought, the ER is starting in early. I didn't see the tech, so I walked into the center alcove between the two main rooms. One room was empty and dark. The second room was dimly lit, and there was a figure in the middle of the x-ray table. It was a small figure. A child of perhaps ten or twelve. It looked like a girl, but it was hard to say because the head had been shaved, and now only a fine stubble of hair covered the scalp. The figure sat crouched, knees bent, shoulders hunched forward. Tiny sticklike arms protruded from the hospital gown and hung limply between her knees. It was a girl. I could see the face, though I could barely believe it. Two hollowed-out eyes that stared straight down at her knees, cheeks that were concavities where healthy, normal flesh used to be. My God, I thought, what is the poor creature doing here? The tech came in. I grabbed him.

"Mike. Who is this patient?"

"That's Dr. Lane's myelogram."

"Myelogram, for what?"

"I don't know; she has some kind of cancer. I tell you, Doctor, I don't know how they are going to do it; she can't lay down; she's in too much pain."

Oh no, I thought, not again. How many times before had I seen these children down here screaming in distress because some incredible idiot had ordered some study on them that did nothing to prolong their lives and everything to increase their pain. Jesus. Not Don Lane, though, I thought; he just wasn't that kind of guy. He was a neuroradiologist and definitely stood out as the one member of the department who didn't know how to play games. He was quiet and straight out, a good teacher and a good radiologist. There had to be an explanation; but I wanted to hear it. I really did. I walked down the dark corridor. I could see the light in his office.

"Don?"

"Yes. Oh, hi, Joni."

"Can I come in?"

"Yes, sure."

"Don, could you tell me about that little girl over in room three for the myelogram?"

"Oh, my gosh, is she here?"

"Yes."

"Gee, I hadn't even said I'd do it, yet."

"What's her history?"

"She's got a neuroblastoma with metastases. She's got it in the majority of her bones, and this morning she lost control of her bowels and her bladder. She has a cord compression, and radiotherapy wants to know what level it's at."

"Why?"

"Why do they want to know at what level?"

"Why do they want to know, period? It's obviously at more than one level; what the hell are they going to do—radiate her whole body?"

"I can't say I really understand their thinking, Joni."

"They aren't thinking. They aren't thinking at all. They couldn't be. Don, if that were me sitting in that chair, I sure as hell wouldn't put this child through any more."

He looked troubled. "How can I say no to them?"

"How can you say yes, Don? How can you possibly say yes?"

"I have to think about this, Joni." He took off his glasses.

"There's nothing to think about. Take a look in that room: That's living death sitting there on the table; that's agony beyond comprehension. Don, I have never seen an expression like that in my life. That child is sitting in there waiting to die. Please. Let her."

He stared at the chart and flipped the corners of the pages slowly. Alan Parker appeared in the doorway. He was the chief of the radiotherapy department. "Are you ready for that myelogram, Don?" He looked up from the chart and met my eyes. I knew what he was going to say, so I didn't wait to hear it.

The complete myelogram was hanging up in the viewing room the next morning, and the patient, Maria Chavez, age twelve, was lying in the morgue.

I pushed through the days ahead, wondering seriously whether my future indeed lay in the world of black and white, and whether I would be completely blind and demented at the end of the year from lack of exposure to normal light and normal people.

Sol came in one evening with an announcement.

It had been decided, he said, by unanimous vote (we didn't

even know there was an election) by the interns and residents at the Veterans Administration Hospital (with which we were affiliated, and through which we rotated as radiologists) that the radiology residents should share the night-call schedule in a regular rotation and see all the patients that came into the emergency room at the VA. That meant that, in addition to our regular night call for radiology, which we now took at the university, we would take medical call at the VA. Sol looked vaguely uncomfortable reading the announcement. He said the radiologists were outnumbered on staff as well, and had been voted down.

Everybody refused to do it, and everybody did it. Except me; I didn't do it. I walked into Sol's office and said, "Dr. Bernstein, I am here to inform you, officially, that I will not take call at the VA."

"You have to. Everybody has to."

"I don't have to. There is nothing in my contract that says I have to do anything other than radiology. And this ain't radiology."

"This is a political problem, Joni; we have no voice in this."

"I'm not doing it, I will not be anybody's intern. I did my internship four years ago, and I have no intention of repeating it."

Sol and I had now gotten to the point where we could disagree without anything flying through the air. I suppose that was some degree of progress.

"If that emergency room isn't covered, you will have to accept the consequences." Sol was ominous.

"Oh, it will be covered."

"I thought you just said you wouldn't do it."

"I won't, but somebody else will if I pay them enough." I got up and paused at the door. "I'm not even going to tell you what I think about this situation."

It was interesting. All the medical and surgical residents who were bitching and groaning about being overworked and overloaded took that money so fast and worked those extra nights so willingly. I was pissed as hell.

Les said he didn't care about the money, but he said he thought the whole thing was outrageous. "I think you guys ought to strike; you're supposed to have house-staff committees and stuff like that; well, that's what they are for."

"The house-staff committees are composed chiefly of medical and surgical house staff, and they voted against us; there are only six of us." I tried Sol's reasoning: it was lame.

"Yes, but if you struck, nobody could replace you. They can't do any of the procedures you guys do; they can't do a GI or a barium enema, and they can't read films."

"I agree with you, but we have no staff backing. Sol I don't trust any more."

"Any more?"

"Well, Sol I don't trust, and Benjamin, he's a very slick number. He smiles and shakes your hand and calms your feathers, but I think maybe he's a double agent."

"Look. He's chief of staff; isn't that what you said?"

"Yes, he is chief of staff."

"How do you think he got there? You've got to be a real pro to get up that high."

So I raged against the night call, but I got no support from the other residents. They were afraid. They were afraid of Sol; he had threatened them. He made it clear that he didn't think much of troublemakers and then told them all what they had to lose by "risking" the loss of their residency; the two guys in my year were draft-eligible. The minute they put their heads out the door of that hospital, somebody was going to slap helmets on them. I, on the other hand (as Sol pointed out to the rest of the all-male resident staff in a closed meeting which I was not asked to attend), had nothing to lose. I had a "rich husband to support me," and it wouldn't matter if I lost my residency. How's that for reasoning? How did I find out about the meeting? One of the techs told me; he had heard the whole thing.

# 34

The question naturally arises at this point: Did Sol and I really need any additional source of irritation in our relationship? Does a dog need fleas?

There was another girl in the program. Adrienne was in her last year of residency and we eventually became friends. Then, in the middle of the year she became pregnant. She became good and pregnant: large pregnant and sick pregnant. She threw up every morning, she missed lectures and conferences, she stayed home, she couldn't do her fluoroscopy because she couldn't be near the x-ray equipment, and she had to have all the guys in the department cover her work and theirs. Sol took it all like a real gentleman. He had something like a nervous breakdown, only it was noisier.

Sol had to blame someone. He couldn't blame Adrienne; how would it look? Screaming at a poor, helpless, pregnant, vomiting female? But he had to blame someone. He saw himself as a victim: trapped by some obscure uterine power invading and taking over his orderly male world, where everybody had a flat abdomen and urinated standing up. What happened was totally predictable: Sol blamed me. Me, the potentially pregnant. Next, banish every female from the kingdom, nip it in the bud; a bitch in time. Oh, God, he took it badly. For the remainder of my residency Sol addressed all his remarks to my abdomen. He scrutinized me every morning. Was I getting a little fat? Did I have that rosy blush to my cheeks? Was I three days late? Every time I went to the bathroom, he knew I was in there throwing up. Every time I ordered a pickle with my sandwich at lunch, it confirmed his worst fears. He knew it was only a matter of time before I would disgrace the department.

Unfortunately, at this point I had already been physically stretched beyond my limit. I passed out doing an arteriogram, I got cold and sweaty if I missed breakfast, and I gained fifteen pounds. And I wasn't even a surgeon. For the coup de grâce, Sol came in to announce one morning that in addition to the regular night-call rotation at the university and the night-call rotation over at the veterans hospital, the residents based at the VA hospital would now have to go spend half of every Saturday at the VA doing IVPs and barium enemas and upper GIs. The VA house staff had complained that they wanted full radiology services available six days a week, and Sol, of course, willingly sold them my body. I now had no weekends off.

# 35

I took my first weekend VA morning call. I then drove back to the university, where I was to spend the rest of my weekend. It was a zoo. Everybody was croaking on all floors of the hospital. The patients in ICU were arresting, the little infants in the premie nursery, who weighed one pound and were so frail we referred to them as potato chips, were blowing out their lungs on the respirators. The kids with one lung already blown out blew out the other lung. And then there was the emergency room.

When I first started taking call, I spent most of my time hiding in my room, in the library, or down in the x-ray department. A film would be done, the tech would call, I'd read it and send the slip back to wherever it needed to go: ICU, ER, pediatrics, whatever. But when we took call for the whole weekend, there were very few places to hide. We couldn't leave the premises. Unbelievable as it may seem, Sol wouldn't let us out the door.

I had a bad auto accident shipped over to the department one Saturday night. Two girls out for a ride, had collided with each other. The girls were both wearing seat belts, and the force, the acceleration with which they went forward trapped in those tight belts, had resulted in incredible pressure on their pelvic bones. The girls were wheeled into the department, screaming in pain. An ER intern had ordered x-rays. "Pelvis," it said on both requisitions. A nurse and an orderly from the ER accompanied the patients. I walked in while the tech and the nurse were both doing their best to transport one girl from the stretcher onto the hard x-ray table. The girl was wrapped in a sheet, and, at the count of three, she was lifted. The screams were incredible. "Oh, my God, they're crunching! My God, I can feel them crunching around. Stop! Please! You're moving my bones."

"What happened here?" I asked the nurse. She related the details.

"Where are the IVs? Why don't these girls have any IVs running?"

"I don't know," the nurse said.

I stood there shaking my head. "This is no good, honey, this is not a good thing." I was getting nervous.

"Do you want to talk to the intern?"

"No, I want two set-ups in here; I'll start them myself." I was still shaking my head. "This is not a good thing." I went over both girls after the IVs were running. Their injuries were remarkably similar. The x-rays of their pelves looked like broken glass. The possibility of one of those sharp fragments of bone tearing into an artery or vein, or the accelerating force of the collision having ripped one or both of their bladders clear off, was huge. In addition, the intern hadn't ordered a chest x-ray. A must: an A-number-one must. One of the chests showed a pneumothorax; the girl's lung was partially collapsed. Either one of the girls could easily have bled to death in the department while the technician was out developing films. The nurse had gone back to the ER. I was upset.

A couple of weeks went by. I had been on call Saturday night, and I still had all Sunday to work. I'd just brought a reading back to the ER. Normal left elbow. It was about 7:00 A.M. I grabbed some coffee and sat down at the desk in the ER.

"We've got a 'flat and upright abdomen' for you, Dr. Scalia."

"Okay, just tell the tech; he'll come and get the patient." I reached for the phone to call Les. He'd been up all night and was still at the base at 5:00 A.M., when I had last spoken with him. I figured I'd call the base and see if he was still there. There was a chart lying on the desk in front of me.

The base put me on hold, and I read the history. It was a familiar history: twenty-seven-year-old female, onset of pain in right upper abdomen and right shoulder, passed out at home, blood pressure was normal when the ambulance arrived, last menstrual period two months ago. Les came on the phone: "Hi."

"Hi. How was it?"

"She's delivered."

"Great. Now you can go home and go to bed."

"Yup, I think I will."

"Listen to this, Les, listen to this and tell me what Louie Leone would say."

I read him the history. "I don't know what Louie would say, but I'd say she's got an ectopic."

"That's what I'd say too." I glanced up casually and swiveled the stool around, replacing the chart on the desk. I was now facing directly through the corridor and looking into the x-ray department waiting room.

There was a woman sitting up in a wheelchair. Her back was to me. I looked at her fleetingly, and as I did, her figure suddenly became limp and slumped forward in the chair.

"So long, call you back." I ran into the hall and grabbed the wheelchair, putting one arm across the woman's chest. "Kenny! Where the hell are you?" He came out of the office. "Oh, my gosh, what happened?" I ran with the wheelchair back into the ER. "Okay, everybody, who is this patient, what's the story?" I wheeled her into a room, and Kenny and I lifted her onto the bed. She was breathing, but she was white as hell. The nurse came in with the chart. "Let's see. Dr. Widener thinks she has a gall-bladder; she's the one for the abdomen films." I recognized the writing on the chart. "Jesus, this is the ectopic. This girl has an ectopic." The nurses were taking her blood pressure. "Ninety over sixty, Doctor."

"All right, let's get an IV up here. Fourteen-gauge needle. Ringer's lactate. And get some blood for type and cross-match." They started scurrying. With a little oxygen and an ammonia ampule crushed beneath her nose, the woman woke up.

"What is going on in here?" a male voice demanded.

I looked up. It was one of the surgical residents: a real arrogant bastard. "Your patient passed out in x-ray."

"What's her blood pressure?"

"One-ten over sixty," the nurse said.

"Hardly shock." He looked at me condescendingly.

"Pulse seventy-six."

"Sit her up and she'll drop her BP," I said. "I think this girl has an ectopic."

"I don't have any reason to suspect that."

"How about her pelvic exam?"

"I haven't done one yet," he said. "She's an obvious gall-bladder: right upper-quadrant pain, had a fatty meal last night, fever; perfect history."

"Well, I'll tell you; I think she gives a very good history for an ectopic, and she faints good, just like an ectopic, so maybe you should have a GYN-type person see her."

"I will when I'm ready. Are you going to take those abdomen films for me?" It wasn't really a question.

"Yeah, I'll take them."

"Oh, thanks for starting the IV on her. You radiologists get pretty good at that, don't you?"

I didn't feel that it was polite to say that I could start an IV in anything, regardless of size, race, creed, national origin, or medical specialty. Including a smart-assed surgeon, if you stretched him out for me, so I just said, "Sure."

The films were of little value other than to rule out the fact that she hadn't perforated an ulcer or anything else that would leave a big dark bubble of air sitting free in the abdomen where it didn't belong. I brought her back to the ER. There were several other cases waiting for films, and the rest of the day was a mess. I didn't see the resident until about six that evening. I didn't bother with hello. "How's that girl?"

"Fine; she's up on surgery."

"Has a gynecologist seen her?"

"No, she's got a gall-bladder; there's very little question."

I was shot down. I was shot down, but it was more than that. How the hell could I be wrong about something like this? I could be wrong because I hadn't examined her, for one thing, but let's face it, this girl was wearing a sign. If I couldn't read signs any more—and, especially, signs saying "I've got an ectopic; get me a gynecologist"—what the hell good was I?

I just needed a good night's sleep. I didn't get it. Somebody needed an emergency upper GI at one in the morning; he had had multiple surgical procedures, and he had perforated something, somewhere, and they wanted to know what.

I did my study with Gastrograffin, a water-soluble material that is harmless if it leaks out of the bowel. The patient was sick as hell and too weak to move from a recumbent position. I tipped the table, I turned the patient, I turned myself. I found the perforation, and I got it in four views. It was gorgeous. I had barely finished when the tech brought in four kids from the emergency room. Another auto accident. This time at least, a surgical resident came with them, and they had IVs. They needed a lot of films, and they needed them in a hurry. I called another tech, and we zipped the patients through.

Suddenly it was Monday morning and it was time to go back out to the VA.

Sol called me up about eight. He was furious.

"Joni, these films from the weekend are such a mess that I may never get them straightened out."

"What's the matter?"

"The studies are incomplete; you've got views missing on three out of four sets of skull series, cervical spine films, lumbar spine films, there are no obliques, there are no Towne's views on the skulls. How can I possibly read these out?"

"Dr. Bernstein, those patients were so badly injured that we were lucky we could get any views at all. Those studies are incomplete because those patients would have lost time if I had done any more."

"Well, I can't make a diagnosis. I've got four sets of radiographs here on four separate people, and I can't make a diagnosis on any of them. This is sloppy radiology; there's no coning and you've wasted space on your films."

"Look, Dr. Bernstein, sir, let me just tell you right now that I could not care less if those studies are incomplete. I don't care if they're neat, I don't care if they're four on one, or two on one, or if the film isn't centered. I don't give a damn about those films. I only care about the patient. Those films are good for only one thing, and that's to help the patient. Am I supposed to knock the patient off so I can give you a complete set of films?"

"Joni, I am not asking you to knock the patient off. I just want a study where you can make a diagnosis. You aren't any help if you don't make the diagnosis." One point for Sol.

"Well, I'll tell you, Dr. Bernstein; it was the judgment of the doctor taking care of those patients that they needed to go directly to surgery, and those were his patients. You don't know what that means; you never took care of patients." One low blow.

There was a temporary silence on the phone. "*Ms*. Scalia, I think this discussion has gone far enough. Let me just tell you that I think you had better pay a little better attention to practicing good radiology."

"Goodbye, Dr. Bernstein." I hung up.

"Dr. Scalia?" It was Phyllis, one of the techs.

"Yes, Phyllis?"

"Walter's got your first barium enema in room four."

"Okay, thanks."

The patient in room four was about eighty-five years old. He was lying on his side staring at the walls and picking at his sheet. A catheter hung alongside the gurney, and the sheets were soiled with feces. The technician was standing there, patiently awaiting his instructions. "Walter," I said casually.

"Yes?"

"When's the last time you had a cardiac arrest in this department?"

"Oh, last year, I think."

"Are you ready to handle another one this morning?" He looked alarmed. "No, ma'am; I'm sure not."

"In that case, Walter, I suggest you get this patient out of here and return him to wherever he belongs."

"Yes, ma'am."

"What's the doctor's name on that requisition?" He pondered it. "Levine."

"Thank you." I went back to the viewing room and picked up the phone.

"Can you page a Dr. Levine for x-ray, please?"

"Dr. Milton Levine?"

"I don't know."

Five minutes later, Levine returned my call. He was one of the interns.

"Dr. Levine."

"Yes."

"This is Dr. Scalia, one of the radiology residents."

"Oh, yes. How did Mister Caruthers' barium enema turn out?"

"Dr. Levine, do you know what a barium enema is?"

"Of course I know what a barium enema is," he said indignantly.

"Have you ever done one?"

"No."

"Would you like to do one?"

"Well, I don't know."

"I ask you that, Dr. Levine, because if you can do a barium enema on Mister Caruthers before he either has a cardiac arrest from the procedure or dies of natural causes, I will personally recommend you to Dr. Bernstein for the radiology program."

"I don't understand what the problem is." He was using his best intern's bravado.

"I know you don't understand what the problem is, Dr. Levine; that is why we are having this conversation. A barium enema is not like a wash, set, and comb-out. You don't just make an appointment and have it done. There are risks with the procedure and, not only that, there is the practical consideration that this patient couldn't hold an enema for three seconds; and I can't do one in three seconds." Levine was quiet for a moment. "Well, I don't know how we're going to make a diagnosis on this patient without a complete set of studies."

"I will give you his diagnosis, Dr. Levine."

"What is it?"

"Old. He is very old. And I think you should plan your work-up accordingly."

"You're crazy. Are you one of the nurses?"

"No, Dr. Levine, but it was nice talking to you."

I finished my work about five thirty and went home to bed.

I woke up the next morning feeling like I had never gone to sleep. My body had had it. I dragged myself into the bathroom and tried to take refuge in the tub. It always worked. Not today; today, I was too tired to reach for the soap. I was so tired that I started to cry. Les was shaving, and, finally, noticed me in the mirror.

"Are you crying?"

"No."

He turned around. "What's the matter?"

"I can't take it any more. I'm tired and I'm getting sick again, and I've got three more years of this to look forward to. I just don't know what to do."

"Why don't you try talking to Bernstein."

"Oh, God, Les, he's such a damn mule. I don't believe he took a program that could have been so neat and loused it up."

"Look, Joni, tell him to kiss off. I'll find something for you to do where you don't have to work so hard. I'm really surprised the whole group of residents didn't walk out a long time ago."

"Yeah," I said, reaching for the soap. "You know, it's a real goddamn shame, Les; I mean the stuff is really interesting. I mean I was just kind of getting into it. I mean, I think I have the potential to be really good at it." Les rinsed off his face.

"You're already good at it. Now, get out of the tub before I climb in on top of you."

I didn't budge.

# 36

It was about two days later, early July and time for residents' conferences, when Sol called me into his office.

"Well, Joni, I think you know that you've done a good job, and I consider you a fine resident. Not that I really had any doubts about you."

I stared at him. What a two-faced bastard.

"You'll be officially at the VA this next year, and I don't want you to take any nonsense from any of the techs out there, or anybody else. If you have any problems, you come to me about it. Oaky? Do you have any questions?"

"I think I have only one thing to say, and that is that I find the program and the way you run it unacceptable to my way of life. I'm tired, and I'm tired of being tired unnecessarily."

"I told you, Joni; I told you, you have to have stamina. I told you that the first day."

"Don't you understand that what you are doing doesn't prove anything? A gorilla has stamina; that doesn't qualify him for anything except being a gorilla. It doesn't make me less of a radiologist because I'm not willing to drive myself into the ground, does it?"

"That's the way I run my program, Joni. If you don't like it, you are free to leave at any time."

"Thank you, I'd like to do that."

"Just send me a letter of resignation."

"Fine." I got up.

"Joni. Did you seriously think that anything you might say, or that any of the other residents might say, would make a difference in the way I ran my program?"

I looked at him briefly. "No."

Dr. Benjamin wanted to see me in his office the next day, for an explanation.

"I heard that you resigned, Joni, and I'd like to know why, and what you plan to do."

"You can ask Dr. Bernstein why."

"I'd like to hear it from you. You seem quite unhappy in the program and a little insecure."

I looked at him. "Well, I think the hours are ridiculous, and I think Bernstein's ridiculous."

"Your health is failing, isn't it?" Your health is failing, isn't it? Was that a line out of a 1935 movie?

"Let me recommend someone here at the university. He's an expert on diabetes and fat metabolism."

"I don't need an expert. I have a doctor, and I have been doing fine with him, thank you, and I would have been just fine here if I didn't have to deal with a bunch of hard-headed individuals."

"I'll give you his name," he continued, unthwarted. He was uninterested in and unconcerned with what I had to say about the program. He obviously thought that an elevated blood sugar meant "syrup on the brain."

I walked past Dr. Bernstein's secretary's office and stuck my head in. "I'll talk to you, kid." Cheryl and I had become good friends. She motioned me to close the door.

"What's up?" I asked.

"Danny's quitting."

"What?" Danny Hayward was one of the other first-year residents. "Why?"

"I think he's got some financial problems. He's going to be working the ER at St. Anne's."

"No kidding? Well, that's interesting. What's Sol going to do to replace two residents?"

"He's going to put the third-year guys on call."

"That bastard; he promised them."

"Yup, they're pretty upset, all right."

"Well, I've just heard this story one time too many, Cheryl, so I'm going to just say adios to these problems and pick up a new set someplace else." I walked out the door.

Les, Neil, and I went out to dinner the evening that I left the program. Neil started telling medical-school stories. Nobody told medical-school stories like Neil. We were screaming. I laughed until I thought for sure my dinner was going to come up.

"Stop it, Neil, stop! I can't stand it any more."

Neil would say, "I'm sorry, no more" and he'd repeat the one phrase from his story that was guaranteed to set us off again.

"Listen," Les said. "Listen, Neil and I are thinking that we'll probably go into practice together."

"God, that's terrific, but I feel sorry for the patients."

"What do you mean? What do you mean?" Neil said very professionally. "Just a minute there, young lady, Dr. Scmurdlap does only quality medicine. I just can't get used to wearing those damn gloves when I do an examination."

"Oh, Neil!"

"Look, I've got it all planned; we open an office right next door to Chicken Delight, kind of a storefront thing with a big flashing sign that says WE DELIVER."

We started laughing again. Only then did it occur to me. "Where *do* you want to practice? Have you given that any thought?"

Les answered right away. "Oh we'll stay here. We still have one more year at the base. And already we know quite a few people in town. I've talked to several surgeons who started out at the base and are now practicing here; they say it's just smooth as silk." Les poured some more wine. I stared at him. "Here? You want to stay *here*?"

"Sure," Neil said. "It'll be fantastic. Everything will just drop in our laps."

"Literally," Les said. They both started laughing again. I stared at my wine glass. Here? He wants to stay here? Les ruffled my hair. "What's the matter, cutie? Why are you so quiet?"

"Oh, I'm probably just tired. You know, I had kind of a bad day today."

"How do you feel about leaving that residency, Joni?" It was Neil.

"Oh, Neil, you know—it was, uh, kind of bad from the first day."

"That guy Goldstein, or whatever his name is, sounds like a real prick. You're better off. Listen, you know, you can put a year of radiology to good use, no matter what you do."

"Right." We finished dinner and went home. Why, I wondered abstractly, would anybody want to stay here?

A few weeks later Les and I were in The Pancake House eating breakfast on a Sunday. The place was crowded. "There's Hal," Les said. Hal was chief resident in gynecology at the university and a friend of ours from San Francisco. We went over to talk to him. "You want to have breakfast with us?"

"Thanks," he said. "I'm waiting for somebody. But listen, you remember, about a month ago you saw a patient in the emergency room? You started an IV on her?"

"Very well. Why? Do you know her?"

"I thought maybe you'd like to know; she went into shock up on the surgery ward before they finally called me. She had about two thousand cubic centimeters of blood in her belly."

"She did!"

"Biggest goddamn ectopic I've seen in a long time. It's a good thing you had blood ordered on her."

"Is that so!" I had all I could do to keep from jumping up on one of the tables. "Listen, Hal, I don't understand, though; how do you know I saw her? I mean, how do you know that I started the IV on her?"

"I don't know how I heard, but everybody seems to know about it."

"Is that so!" I kept saying that.

They had our table for two, and we sat down. "Did you hear that? Did you hear that? She had one. I knew it, I knew it all along. Goddamn; that is really something."

"I think that's cool. I do, Joni."

I was so excited I could hardly decide between bacon and eggs, which I should have had, or Danish pancakes with syrup, which I shouldn't have had. The Danish pancakes were great.

I kept thinking about the ectopic. I kept thinking about how I could never keep out of the action for very long and wondered why that was. It was obvious to me that if I could just get enough rest, enough time to recover, I'd probably be okay. But I needed something good going on. Something where I had a chance to use what I knew. All my surgery had gone to waste. And the radiology? God, what a shame. I needed something good; it had to move, it had to be different and interesting. The emergency room. Now, that just might do it.

I applied for an opening at the medical center. That was not the university hospital; it was a large private facility which had been in operation long before the university hospital was conceived. I would be one of a group of four doctors. The shifts would be twelve hours long, and then it was adios. The work was four days on and four days off. I would make my entire month's salary as a radiology resident after working only three days. I signed my contract and walked out thinking, Well, if all else fails there is consolation in hearing the jingle of change in your jeans.

# PART THREE

# 37

It was my first night to work at the medical center, and suddenly what had seemed like a great idea didn't seem like a great idea any more; I hadn't worked emergency room since I was an intern. I read everything I could for review, but, Jesus, I felt like I had forgotten everything I had ever learned. I drove to the hospital terrified.

The hospital looked ominous. It was a different place at night; it stretched out like a huge concrete snake. The lights from the helicopter pad were turned off, and the only light came from the big red sign that said EMERGENCY. I started up the ramp just as an ambulance unit was pulling in. The drivers got out at a moderate rate, opened the double doors in the back, and assisted an obviously pregnant woman into the wheelchair. My entire colon went into spasm—OB: God, I didn't remember any OB.

"She isn't for ER; take her to labor and delivery," one of the nurses said.

What do you know, I thought, there is a God. I took a few more steps. But what, it occurred to me, what if He goes off work at eight? I walked into the closed door that said DO NOT USE THIS ENTRANCE.

The main emergency area was relatively quiet. Not too many people around. I walked past the admitting desk into the nurses's station. It was an open space running half the length of the room.

"Hi," I said to one of the nurses. She looked at me like I was crazy. "I'm Dr. Scalia; I'm a member of the ER group. Can you tell me where Dr. Layton is?"

She hesitated a moment, not really sure if she should believe me. "Uh, yeah, sure," she said. "Crofts, where's Layton?"

"He's in x-ray."

"He's in x-ray," she repeated unnecessarily, with that look still on her face. "That's way down the hall."

"I know where it is," I interrupted. I really wanted to say, "Could you walk me?" but I thought it might be too much for her.

The walk from the emergency room in this hospital to x-ray was one *mother* hike. Whoever designed the facility was, no doubt, not a radiologist, and in actuality was probably not a member of the medical profession at all. The system of corridors would have stymied the entire company of "Willard." When you considered that during our twelve-hour shift I might have to make the trip twenty or thirty times, it mounted up.

Dr. Layton was over in one of the viewing rooms, intently studying a pediatric chest film. I knew him by sight only.

"Hi," he said.

"Hi."

"Looks like there might be something at the left base here," he said, sweeping his hand over an area that included most of the film and part of the shelf below.

"It's normal."

"What?"

"It's normal," I repeated. He looked startled.

I looked up at him. "Do you want to show me what to do? Where to start?"

"Sure," he said. He glanced back at the film again. "You think that's normal, huh?"

"I know it is."

He followed me out through the maze and back to the ER.

"Did Hancock tell you anything at all about the way we work here?"

"Very little," I said. "I'd like to hear it again, anyway." Anything to stall, I thought; I'd even listen to water running.

"Well," he began, "when a patient comes in they check in at the desk over there; the nurse then sees them and finds out who their doctor is. If they don't have a doctor, they are automatically referred to the doctor on call." We had reached the nurses' desk. "There's a list up here; it changes every day, and sometimes during the day. We've got someone on call for everything here. Medicine and pediatrics, of course; and we've got every surgical subspecialty." I looked at the list; Plastics, Ortho, Neuro, ENT, Chest, Cardiovascular, Ophthalmology. "There's also a psychiatrist, and there's a backup second-call man."

He lowered his voice and steered me into a corner. "What's your name again?"

"Joni."

"Look, Joni, I don't know where you've ever worked before."

"Well, I used to bag groceries at the Safeway."

He didn't laugh.

"What I mean is, I don't know what type of ER you are used to: county, private, or what, but let me just warn you about this place. This is strictly private, right down the line. You don't so much as say boo to any of these patients unless you've gotten a verbal referral from their doctor or from the guy on call."

"What?"

"I'm not kidding. These guys will have your ass for seeing one of their patients if they haven't been called first."

"That could be bad."

"Very often." He nodded his head for emphasis.

"I can't believe that, though," I said. "What if you've got no time, and it's a code or something?" Just saying this did a real number on my head.

"That depends."

"That depends? How can that depend?"

"Look," he said, "use your judgment. I've got to run. Just take it slow; you'll find out who the good guys are soon enough." He was getting his coat. "One more thing," he said. "Don't depend on the nurses here to field anything for you. A couple of them are okay, but the rest will give it to you right in the back just for the hell of it."

I felt terrible. I was ready to pack it in and head home.

"Hey you guys, quit horsing around; we're piling up here." One of the nurses came over, a thin Irish-looking little girl with sharp features.

"This is Linette, one of our lovely ladies in white," Layton said, bowing grandly and backing out the door.

My fear started to dissipate as I began seeing patients. Funny how just going through familiar motions can transport you back in time. I needed to start thinking the way I used to, but everything seemed to be moving so slowly. My head was loaded with values and intervals and dosages; I wondered if they'd really be there when I needed them. I wrote up a physical in the three-inch space they had provided in the chart.

"The patient in room three is back from x-ray, Dr. Scalia."

A huge heavy envelope crashed onto the desk in front of me.

"Here are her films," the x-ray tech said. "Good luck." He smiled wickedly. "You know, there's no radiologist in the house at night." I attempted to ignore him. "Dr. Layton ordered a thoracic and lumbar spine on this patient before he went off duty; she's an auto accident."

The nurse speaking was Alice Spiegel; she seemed reasonable. She looked at me. "You might want to see this other patient before you look at these x-rays."

"Why, is he acute?"

"No, it's just that it might take you a while. It usually takes the guys quite a while to get through a set of films like that."

I laughed to myself. Back films—I could read them in my sleep. I very often did read them in my sleep, come to think of it.

"Mrs. Spiegel," I said with a flourish, "I will be back in five minutes, maybe less, depending on whether or not I take a wrong turn."

The rest of the evening was steady. There was never time to sit, but there was nothing big happening, either. "When," I thought, "is the old axe going to fall?"

At eleven the shift changed. Two nurses and two orderlies came on. They all looked like they were ready to sack in, rather than come to work. I said a brief hello and went to lie down in the end room that we used for gynecology. I fell asleep on the table, curled up under a pile of blankets.

Somebody was shaking me. "No," I said, which is my usual waking response to alarm clocks, clock radios, doorbells, and phones.

"Better get up; we've got a code coming in."

I fumbled around. I am always a complete disaster when I wake up suddenly.

"I'm going to set up," the nurse said. "The ambulance is five minutes out."

"Damn," I said, trying to get off the table without breaking my leg. We had a rule among the ER groups. You don't page a cardiac arrest; you handle it yourself. Once you page it, you have every intern, resident, and what have you down on your neck and it's chaos. I knew that made sense, but it had been years since I'd done a code. I hurried down the hall.

I stumbled into room one, which, although totally empty only minutes before, was now alive with people and activity. One of the orderlies threw a backboard on the stretcher and ran to get some suction tubing. Grace, the head nurse, was running the IV into the sink to clear the line of air. The pharmacy cart arrived directly behind me and immediately began setting up shop. Seals were broken, vials were brought out, ready to be opened at a moment's notice. The defibrillator was plugged in and charged. I pulled open one of the drawers in the fire-engine-red cart that contained all our equipment.

"What's coming in? Adult or child?"

"It's a man. Seventy-eight years old."

"Damn," I said, and grabbed for a large endotracheal tube and a large curved laryngoscope.

"They're here," somebody yelled.

The ambulance drivers raced in the door, their stretcher supporting the lifeless man. We grabbed him under both arms and slid him over onto the table. There was no doubt about his diagnosis: his pupils were large and fixed. Dead man's eyes. "This guy's gone," I said, checking him. The nurses were hooking up the leads to the cardiac monitor. The screen would carry any pattern of cardiac activity if it was present. But I was sure there was none. Grace was putting in the IV and one of the other nurses stuck her head in the door. "Dr. Gertz just called and said he wants a full resuscitation." What else, I thought? Pickles and lettuce to go?

"Get his clothes off and get his head up here."

"I can't get the IV started, Doctor."

"Yeah, well," I said, "do your best." I took the laryngoscope in my left hand and pulled the plastic airway out of the man's mouth. They had taken out his dentures in the ambulance. I slid the stainless steel blade past his gums and behind the back of his tongue and pulled it up out of the way. I strained to see. There was vomit rolling up at me. "Suction, please. Let's get this crap out of the way." We slipped the suction tubing in and rapidly tried to clear out his throat. I was looking for the epiglottis; the gateway to the larynx, the little structure at the base of the tongue that stands up at you and says, "Here I am, right this way." It popped into view, and I slid the rubber tube along behind it.

"You'll have to do a cut-down, Doctor. I can't get an IV in him." I ignored her temporarily and continued to slip the tube in. I made a blind passage, never having identified the vocal cords and, therefore, not knowing whether I had entered the larynx or was several millimeters behind and had entered the patient's esophagus. If I had entered the esophagus, any oxygen we administered would go directly into the man's stomach instead of his lungs.

"All right, blow some air in there," I said, with my stethoscope over his abdomen. A huge belching noise came back at me. I was in the stomach. "Damn! Bag him," I said. I looked up at the monitor. There was no pattern showing and there was no light on the screen. "What's with the monitor, you guys?"

"It isn't working; we're going to get another one from CCU."

"Jesus . . . well, you might as well hit him; use four-hundred." Grace took the paddles from the defibrillator and threw two alcohol sponges over the man's chest. She placed the paddles perpendicularly, taking care not to let her own body come in contact with the man or the stretcher. "Charge?" she said. "It's charged." The body jumped up off the table as four-hundred watt-seconds worth of electricity coursed through it. She checked for pulses; there were none. She paused with the paddles in midair. "Again?"

"No," I said. "Let me start this cut-down."

"What size gloves do you want, Doctor?"

"Screw the gloves," I said, grabbing a blade off the tray and making a slash above the left ankle. I dug in with a hemostat and lifted the vein off the bone. A piece of silk, two fast ties, and a poke with the blade; I was in the vein. I slipped in a short polyethylene tube. Two more knots and it was secure. "Run it."

"My God, you're fast." It was Grace.

"Yeah," I said, "too bad this guy's dead already." I looked up briefly. "All right, let's have it: bicarb, adrenalin, let's have it all." The new monitor arrived from the coronary care unit. They hooked it up. There was no electrical activity. The drugs had done nothing, and we had pushed them all.

"How long was this guy out before you got there?"

"Probably ten minutes. He looked gone when we got to the scene, but the daughter was hysterical so we started closed chest massage right away."

"Okay, let's end this fiasco" I said, still irritated at myself for not getting the endotracheal tube in the right place.

"Are you officially terminating the code, Doctor?" It was the nursing supervisor, who was standing there taking notes, wearing a hat that looked like a dead doily.

"Yes."

"Well, we'll call the time of death two thirty-eight."

"Call it what you like," I said, furious at myself for having gone through the resuscitation on an obviously dead person because Dr. Gertz, whoever the hell he was, had requested it.

Grace said, "Do you want to talk to Dr. Gertz?"

"No, Grace, I don't want to talk to anybody."

# 38

The head nurse in the ER on days was Lottie Deaner. A real bitch. I think she was laid with the first cornerstone of the hospital. She was ready to retire, but she just wouldn't let go. She survived by making life a pile of shit for the doctors she hated and by moving mountains for those she liked. We didn't make it, L.D. and I, not from the outset.

"This kid needs a cast, Doctor."

"Fine. Call one of the orthopedic guys."

"Dr. Hancock usually puts his own casts on."

"Good for Dr. Hancock. Dr. Scalia does not put on casts."

"Most of the doctors do, if the fracture isn't displaced."

"A lot of people do a lot of things that I don't do; and I can't afford orthopedic malpractice insurance, so let's just forget it."

"Anybody can put on a cast."

"Good. Call anybody."

She was angry. She was used to pushing the docs around; she'd been doing it for years.

"You'd better get going. You're falling behind," she snarled at me.

"Falling behind what?"

She went into the bathroom and slammed the door. At the

time, it was not apparent to me what an incredible system of politics and personalities moved and modified the workings of a hospital. So I basically thought of Lottie Deaner as just one more pain in the ass, and continued to treat her as such. About two hours later, she walked up to me.

"Sign this chart."

"What is it?"

"Just sign it. I'm going to send this kid home."

"What kid?"

"Just some teenager of Dr. Benson's; she tried to take an overdose of aspirin this morning. We lavaged her; Benson ordered a salicylate level over the phone. It's normal."

"Okay, put the chart down, and after I see her—"

She interrupted me.

"He doesn't want you to see her."

I stopped writing. "He's coming in?"

"No, he's going to send her home, but I need this chart cleared with a doctor's signature."

I turned and looked at her. "Wait a minute. Let me get this straight. You want me to sign out a chart on a patient I have never seen, and whose doctor is not coming in to see her? A doctor I don't even know? And a patient who tried to kill herself this morning, no less? Just send her home, right?

"She just took a few aspirin. She had a fight with her boyfriend."

"Oh fine, just a few aspirin. So maybe we'll send her home with the same problem she came in with, and tomorrow she'll take Drano because she ran out of ASA."

"Jesus Christ!" She slammed the chart down, her teeth clenched. "You can make more goddamn nothing into something than anybody I've ever seen."

I turned my back on her and faced Mary Wilson, one of the other nurses. She was a very quiet woman who could start an IV in anything and make me look clumsy. "She's really got it for you, Doctor," she whispered.

"You're kidding!" I faked surprise.

"Uh huh, and she can make it miserable around here."

Lottie turned around and saw us talking together. She rode Mary's ass the rest of the day, and then topped it off by assigning her to work the one Sunday that she had requested off. A real sweetheart.

The ER during the week and ER on the weekend are two

different places. It was not until my second shift that I was introduced to weekend ER, and the Three-Way Pass.

A thirty-year-old male came in. He had been climbing around the desert, communing with Mother Nature, and had put his hand on a ledge above his head. The ledge was already occupied by a six-foot rattler. The snake nailed him right between his thumb and index finger. Our young man responded in the only fashion he knew; he screamed for fifteen minutes until somebody found him, his belt cinched to his upper arm, sucking his hand and trying to hold up his pants. He was brought into our little oasis in the desert by Good Samaritans, and upon his arrival it was discovered that he did not have a doctor.

The interesting thing about rattlesnake bites is that the literature is replete with information regarding their treatment. The information, however, is all conflicting and reads something like this:

1. Tourniquet immediately.
1a. Do not tourniquet. It increases the swelling.
2. Release the tourniquet intermittently.
2a. Do not release the tourniquet suddenly; a sudden rush of venom may cause the patient to arrest.
3. Immediately make ¼-inch by ¼-inch incisions perpendicular to each other at the site of the bite, and apply suction.
3a. Do not make incisions—it opens vessels and may destroy underlying structures.
4. Immediately give antivenin.
4a. Do not give antivenin unless you can establish that the patient has been envenomated, which may be graded on a 1-to-4 basis depending on severity, and then not before giving a skin test for horse serum.
5. Pack the hand in ice.
5a. Do not pack the hand in ice; it causes more tissue damage.

This kind of cookbook medicine is definitely not my style, but what could I do? The last snake I had seen was in the Bronx Zoo, and he was behind glass. Lucky for me, I thought naively, we have a surgeon on call. Here comes the Three-Way Pass.

"Dr. Roundtree, this is Dr. Scalia in the ER at the medical center. I've got a guy here with a rattlesnake bite on the left hand, and I'm really not that familiar with viper bites."

"Oh, I don't treat anything on the hand any more; call one of the orthopedic guys." That was pass number one.

"Who's on ortho call?" I asked one of the nurses.

"Dr. Parrish."

"Okay, let's get him."

We finally reached him at St. Catherine's.

"Hello, Dr. Parrish, this is Dr. Scalia in the ER. I've got a guy here with a rattlesnake bite on the left hand."

"Love to help you out, but I'm just about up to my ears at St. Catherine's. I don't handle that kind of thing anyway. I think one of the plastics guys might be interested. Why don't you call Dr. Doran, he's new in town." Pass two, complete.

"Dr. Doran, this is Dr. Scalia in the ER," I began my spiel. "And I'll tell you, if you refer me to anybody else, I'm going to go out into the parking lot and slit my throat."

"Well," he said, "you'll have to call an ear, nose, and throat man for something like that. I only take care of hands." He hung up. I couldn't believe it. *I* was stuck for a doctor.

I went to an anesthesiologist whose only qualifications were that he had once seen a rattler in his driveway and knew they were poisonous, a local neurosurgeon, who had in fact been bitten severely several years ago and almost died because, as he put it, "nobody knows how the hell you treat these," and finally to a local snake farm, where I was told to call L.A. County, "where they know everything." They did: they had the largest collection of cases around.

Needless to say, as I was calling around, the patient's hand was swelling and the patient was screaming his head off. He was entitled to do this, but it was a direct violation of point 6, which states: Avoid any excitement.

"I'm not taking any horse serum," I could hear him yelling from his room. "My cousin almost died from it in 1938."

At this point, I noticed one of the surgeons walking past the nurses' desk. He was on his way out. I recognized him from the university.

"Dr. Daniels," I said, rushing up to him, "I really need your help."

"You do?" he said.

"Yes," I said, grabbing him around his waist. "If you could just see this patient for me, I'd be so grateful."

"You would?" he said.

"Yes," I said, squeezing his ribs. "I'd just feel so much better if you would look at this man's hand."

"You would?" he said.

"Yes," I said. "You know, there aren't too many people I have any faith in."

"I see," he said. Only he didn't. "Well," he looked at his watch, "I'm rather rushed."

"Please," I said in desperation, "This man's hand is in terrible condition."

He hesitated, then said, "All right, I'll see him."

"Bless you," I actually said.

I got my next rattlesnake victim in less than twenty-four hours, but by then I had become the resident expert—along with Dr. Daniels, who was to become my favorite plastic surgeon.

It was 2:00 A.M. Two guys pulled up in a pick-up truck and carried a third man through the doors. Mike and Carl, our physicians' assistants, grabbed him and put him on a gurney. He was breathing, but barely conscious. His tongue was swollen to gross proportions and was protruding from his teeth. It was blocking his airway, and he breathed in short, stuttering gasps. He had on an old Levi workshirt which was the same blue as his face.

"He was bit by a rattler," one man said, and they both ran out the door. Grace was on the shift with me.

"Grace, I want Benadryl, adrenalin, and an IV." I was trying to get an airway in, but his tongue was so big I couldn't get past his teeth. I attempted to pass a tube through his nose, but the back of his tongue was swollen as well. We ripped off the man's shirt. No needle tracks. His pupils were wide, but came down immediately when exposed to a light. His right hand was swollen and white.

"I want to draw some blood," I said.

"What do you want?" Grace asked.

"I don't know. I guess a glucose before the IV goes in; CBC, toxicology maybe." The man gasped alarmingly. "Hike up his chin a little," I said. We wheeled him into a room.

"Do you want a tracheostomy set?" Mike asked.

"Jesus, no; I sure don't, but bring it in anyway."

"How much adrenalin?" Grace asked. I gave her the dose. She drew it up and handed me the syringe. "Aqueous adrenalin one to one-thousand, zero point four cc," she said. "Just give it sub-cu," I said.

"BP one-forty over seventy," Mike said. I checked the patient's lungs. They were clear.

I reached for a tourniquet and put it on his arm. He pulled away. Mike held him and I put the needle in. When I had finished drawing the blood and removed the tourniquet, I noticed a ring of tiny hemorrhages on the skin beneath where the tourniquet had been.

"What the hell?" I thought. I pulled out the needle. The blood from the puncture site soaked the cotton pledget, and even with pressure trickled out from beneath. Grace had a good IV going in the other arm.

"What's with his tongue?" Mike said. "I thought the kid that brought him in said this was a snakebite."

"Who knows? It's got to be allergic; maybe something he took; maybe he sucked the wound and got some local reaction; maybe he bit the snake. Who knows?" The IV was running well, but there was blood running out both puncture sites.

"His color's a little better," Grace said. I looked. It was, but not much. "What are you going to do?" she asked.

"I'm going to hope this adrenalin works. I don't really know what the hell is going on here. His clotting mechanism is screwed, which means it could be a viper bite, which means I shouldn't have given him the adrenalin."

"You think you might still have to do a trach?"

I didn't answer her.

"You want an ENT man?" I stood looking at the slightly blue man with the bleeding needle holes and wanted to be someplace else; anyplace else.

"It's 2:00 A.M., Grace; what I want is for his tongue to come down by itself."

"You want me to call Dr. Reiner? He only lives a half mile from here."

I turned and looked at her. "Okay, Grace, call Reiner. Then, when you're through calling Reiner, call the pharmacy; I want all the polyvalent rattler, moccasin, cobra, and whatever other antivenin they have; I want the blood bank, because he needs to be typed and crossed, although that's probably impossible. I want tetanus toxoid, I want hypertet, I want a gram of hydrocortisone in the IV, I want some more adrenalin, I want a hematologist, I want my favorite plastic surgeon, and I want my mother."

I sat there and watched this guy's tongue for the next half hour; it came down beautifully with the adrenalin, which was then and is still my all-time favorite good-guy drug.

The patient was in the intensive care unit for three days before he started clotting normally. Two hematologists kept track of all his ups and downs. When he awakened, he told us what had happened: he'd been out in the desert blowing grass; it got dark, he got stoned and wandered off by himself. The last thing he remembered hearing when he lay down in the sand was the rattle, but he just couldn't do a thing about it.

# 39

It was a quiet morning in the middle of the week. There were a lot of patients around, but none of them were mine. I was looking through a magazine at the nurses' station, thinking that I still had nine hours to work. Dr. Levine, one of the surgeons, stopped by the station and referred all of his patients to me, saying he would be in his office all day. He was on call for us for the day. I saw a screaming kid go by with a scalp laceration. His mother was insisting that she be allowed in the room with him, to supervise his care.

"You know who's going to wind up with that kid, don't you?"

"Go to hell, Carol," I said.

I almost didn't see them go by, but the ambulance drivers slowed down in front of the desk. "Short of breath," one of them said, "probably respiratory." I looked up at the patient on the stretcher. He sat forward, chin outstretched, gulping at the air, taking in huge mouthfuls while sniffing desperately. I grabbed my stethoscope. Not respiratory. No, sir. Not this. I followed the stretcher into the room.

The nurses were getting him undressed and setting up an IV of dextrose and water.

"No good, Carol," I said.

She looked at me, tearing the cellophane off the tubing. "What?"

"No good. Start a Ringer's lactate and use blood tubing." She stared at me. "Start two IV's, Carol, two big ones."

He was groaning in pain, closing his eyes, trying to block it out and roll with it at the same time. I knew this man; I had seen him come out of the elevator when I was a resident. He was wearing the same sign; it said, "I have an aneurysm, move your ass."

"Where is the pain, sir?" I was yelling at him. His lungs were clear. He had a murmur; at his age, he was entitled to it. His pulses were all there; they were good, down to his feet, but his belly was like dough, and he was tender right where I placed his aorta. I palpated and listened to his abdomen. He was groaning too loud to hear anything.

"Does your back hurt?" I yelled. "Do you have an ulcer?" He couldn't answer. "I want x-ray and lab, now!" I said. The EKG tech had already been grabbed by one of the nurses and was putting her leads on the patient, but he was so sweaty they kept slipping. One IV was in and running. "I'm having a little trouble with this one," Carol said.

"Let me try," I said.

I heard "No blood pressure." The second IV was about in, and the patient pulled off his oxygen mask and vomited.

"Open these IVs," I yelled. The EKG began to produce a tracing. The girl from the blood bank tapped me on the shoulder. "How many units?" she asked. I was watching the tracing. "Till you get tired, Frances." X-ray was coming down the hall; I could hear the big heavy portable machine. The EKG tracing was totally normal. "Is Levine still around?" I asked.

"He may still be in the coffee room," someone said.

"Hang up a plasminate," I said, and ran around the bed into the hall. "Stat chest?" the x-ray tech asked. "Very," I said, zipping around the corner of the hall and into the coffee room. Levine was dumping a packet of sugar into his coffee.

"I need you."

"What is it?" he said, taking a sip.

"I've got an aneurysm in room three."

He stopped drinking.

"Can you feel it?"

"No."

"He's got a history?"

"No." I started out the door. "No blood pressure, tender lower mid-abdomen, seventy-three years old."

"Pulses?"

"He's got all his pulses." We were outside the room. "Sixty over forty," Carol yelled out like it was a ball score for the winning team. Levine had stopped in the doorway. He was staring at me.

"What makes you think he's got one?" A legitimate question; I knew he was going to ask it. He walked in and went over the patient as thoroughly as he could. The x-ray tech was pulling the plate out from behind him. "I want that yesterday," I said.

"Yeah," he said, used to my demands by now, and disappeared out the door.

Levine took the stethoscope out of his ears and looked up at the IVs. "Well," he said, "why don't we draw a hematocrit and see how that comes back. He really could have anything going on in his belly. And let's get some more x-rays."

I walked out of the room with him. He paused in the hall. "Look, I'll stick around; I just have to go over to surgery and take care of something. By the time I get back, you'll have your blood work and we can go from there." He smiled, patted me on the shoulder, and started walking down the hall.

"Dr. Levine?"

"Yes?" He turned.

"Don't move out of here." He looked totally shocked.

"I mean it; I know he's got one."

"You're really serious, aren't you?"

"I know how this sounds," I said, and I did.

"Dr. Scalia." It was Julie, one of the other nurses. "I've got a bad chest pain in room five. He's IV'd and I'm getting an EKG." The x-ray tech came around the corner: "The radiologist says that chest is okay, and there's no air under the diaphragm."

I looked at Levine. "Eighty over forty," Carol said, "and this IV's out."

"Dr. Scalia? This guy in room five?" It was Julie again.

"I'm coming," I said.

"Go ahead," Levine said, "I'll stay with him. Is the crit drawn?"

"Everything's cooking," I said and followed Julie down the hall.

The chest pain in room five was a nice man. He did everything he was supposed to: he had his heart attack after dinner and came right in, kept his blood pressure up, and he stopped hurting almost immediately after his morphine sulphate was given. He waved to everybody as he was being wheeled over to the coronary care unit.

When I got back to the nurses' desk, there was no one around. I found Carol in one of the rooms.

"Where's my guy?" I said.

"Levine's got him up in surgery. His hematocrit was seventeen."

The rest of the day was a real mess. Levine came by about 6:00 P.M. I was bogged down with patients.

He came into the nurses' station and sat down on a desk with a cup of coffee. "Want to know what I found this morning?" he asked.

"You know I do."

"He had a leaking aneurysm." He looked at me, waiting for me to say something. "Right at the bifurcation of the iliacs."

"Thanks for taking care of him," I said.

"Sure." He paused. "He died on the table; you knew that."

"No, I didn't." I paused, and then I said what we were both thinking: "I'm not surprised, though, he never really had a chance."

It was the Sunday morning following the ill-fated aneurysm. I was finishing my second cup of coffee. A voice came over the ER radio. "Seventy-six-year-old male with back pain." Holding my empty cup, I leaned out of the coffee room. The voice continued, "ETA is six minutes." There were background sirens. Maybe it's a kidney stone and they panicked, I thought optimistically. Carol came around the corner. I crashed into her. "Oh, no," she said, "don't tell me you're on today." We looked at each other and then said, simultaneously, "You know, you're bad luck!"

The unit came wailing into the driveway. They unloaded the patient and wheeled him by. The ward clerk looked up: "EKG, lab, x-ray?"

"Right," I said.

The ambulance personnel had not panicked; the man had no blood pressure. Carol was proceeding with the IV.

"Sir, where is your pain?"

"Oh, God, my back." He reached desperately for the plastic oxygen mask. I pulled back the sheets. His flanks were purple. "No, I thought; this cannot be." I felt for his femoral artery pulses. Nothing. I palpated his abdomen. "Oh, God, don't do that." Carol had the IV going. She came over behind me. "Same game?" she whispered. I shrugged in disbelief.

"Same game." We started the second IV. EKG was coming down the hall. Sunday morning; who in the hell would be around? I went out to the nurses' desk. "I want any surgeon in the house; but I especially want Kendall if he's available."

Norman Kendall was a vascular surgeon. He was incredible. He'd put a clamp on your aorta in the middle of McDonald's, if your aorta happened to blow there. I went back into the room. The EKG tracing was coming across the machine. I couldn't believe it, it was one of those patterns: the kind that you see when the patient says to you, "Doctor, do you think I'm having a heart attack?" and you say to yourself, "You bet you are, buddy," but you say to him, "You certainly could be, sir." The cardiac complexes on the paper got taller and more bizarre, and then right under my nose, the guy started to block. His normal pathways of conduction were damaged and his heart muscle was just beating time. He needed a pacemaker. Immediately.

The ward clerk appeared in the doorway. "His internist is on the phone."

"Who is it?"

"Cellini." I nodded and started toward the phone.

"All right, Carol, let's get some drugs; atropine, an isuprel drip, and get the code cart in here." I reached for the phone, which was on the wall outside the room, and pulled it in as far as the cord permitted. By now I had perfected the art of talking on the phone under a variety of unbelievable circumstances and in many impossible positions. I dragged the EKG machine closer to me.

"Joni Scalia here," I said into the receiver. "I think your patient's got an aneurysm."

"It sounded like it on the phone," Cellini said. "I told his wife to send him in by ambulance. I'll be right over; I'm at St. Catherine's. See if you can get hold of Norm Kendall."

"Look, that's not all; he's in heart block."

"Call Larry Heinz; he's on his way over there. He just left

here." Heinz was a cardiologist. I hung up and started pushing drugs.

There was a racket coming down the hall. A call on the hospital PA for "Any surgeon, stat" had its definite drawbacks; every surgical resident in the house was descending, at knifepoint.

"What have you got?" they asked eagerly, clogging up the doorway with their bodies. I was watching the EKG. The atropine had done nothing. The isuprel was being hung; sometimes it helped pick up the heart rate just enough so you could stall for time, but if you gave a little too much, it could really get away from you. I watched the tracing coming out of the machine. The paper was piling up on the floor. "I need Kendall and Heinz," I said to the surgical residents.

"Blood pressure ninety over sixty," Carol said.

"Kendall's not around, but Fletcher is over on Wing 100 seeing a patient." Fletcher was Kendall's partner. A super guy. Calm, smart with A-1 judgment. One of the few guys I would consider calling if anything happened to my belly. Fletcher would not open your belly in the middle of McDonald's, but he'd put you in the front seat of his car and drive you to the hospital instead of waiting for the ambulance.

"I wonder if he heard the page?"

Everyone arrived at once: Fletcher, Heinz, and Cellini. Heinz was all over the patient. He was sweating and fumbling, and he tried to stick an arterial line directly in without any local anesthetic, which is okay, if you don't miss three times. If that doesn't bring up his heart rate, I thought, nothing will.

Fletcher stood at the foot of the bed, talking to Cellini and me and rapidly taking stock of the situation. After his third lousy try, Heinz finally stepped back. "I'll have to do this in x-ray; I need the fluoroscope." He turned to Fletcher. "You want to examine him?"

Fletcher was cool, easy, gentle. He put a hand calmly on the patient's shoulder and then examined his protuberant abdomen. He felt, he listened, he felt again. Then he stepped back into the hall.

"I don't feel one," he said. The patient's sign was now very definitely reading "I'm going to arrest." Somebody had to make a move, but Fletcher said he didn't feel an aneurysm, and Fletcher knew aneurysms—he'd been feeling them for fifteen years. The patient was fat, but I was sure Fletcher could feel a pulsing aortic aneurysm in a pregnant elephant.

"How can he not have one? No pulses, back pain, profound shock, how can it be?" I looked at him.

"He could; he could have one. I just don't feel it." He went back into the room and re-examined the patient. He exited, and then moved out of the way as they wheeled the patient with his portable oxygen and monitor over to x-ray.

"I just don't think he has one," Fletcher said. The patient had a cardiac arrest in x-ray less than five minutes later; he didn't respond to anything. His family consented to an autopsy. His heart was massively damaged, and that was the whole story. There was no aneurysm. Fletcher had been correct.

I don't even know what comes close to the feeling you get when you've made a wrong diagnosis. It's not just being wrong; it's the consequences of being wrong. "Everybody blows it now and then" just doesn't cut it in the emergency room. Fletcher's experience, my God, who can put a value on it? Experience and judgment. They aren't just there, they don't just exist, they evolve; they mature; they develop. They are the very last thing to come in medicine, and there's a price attached. A heavy one: all the nights, all the patients, all the hours and days spent observing and examining and rechecking. For all the bellies Fletcher ever palpated, those were all the times he wasn't at home, or he wasn't at the movies. The "one more case" was one more lunch and dinner he didn't have and didn't even know that he had missed. Just like all the other things that went by all of us, and we didn't even know that we were missing them, and lacking them, and needing them. But that's how you get your judgment and your experience in medicine. You pay for it with your life.

# 40

Football season opened, and suddenly all of the physicians who never referred anything to the emergency room physician now referred everything. When there was a game on you could just about guarantee that you couldn't get hold of a specialist even if somebody's life depended on it, which it very often did.

The orthopedic guys were always the worst. The jocks of the profession were at every season game and had no intention of leaving. The jocks outside the profession, however, very frequently left their games early—on stretchers—supplying us with an enormous increase in the number of orthopedic injuries. Everybody big enough to get into a football jersey was out on the lawn smashing his collarbone, dislocating his shoulder, and dislodging the cartilaginous attachments of his knees. "Ace wrap, ice pack, crutches." That was the standard script, and it was given over the phone. They didn't care how bad the fracture was or how displaced it was, they wanted it wrapped and elevated. They wouldn't leave the game for anything. The same injury on a Monday morning called for an immediate visit to the office and an immediate cast. They'd cast anything on a Monday.

It was Sunday. There was a big game. Every surgeon in town was signed out to me. Every kid in town had split open his eyebrow or his chin. Every adult in town was taking advantage of the gorgeous day by turning over his four-wheel-drive in the desert and breaking his or her skull. I was so backed up with patients I wasn't even trying to hurry. The pile of charts on the desk was approaching the critical mass, and there was only one technician in x-ray.

I had just admitted one patient to the CCU, one patient to the ICU, and one patient to pediatrics. I was writing the last set of orders when this incredible subhuman scream ripped through the corridor. It sounded like a large wounded animal. The chart I was holding jumped out of my hand and clattered to the floor. I turned around. Several of the nurses were running down the hall. I followed them into room two. It was one of our larger rooms and it could house six patients with curtains between them. Instead of rushing into the room, to my surprise, the nurses grabbed the accordofold doors from each end and quickly pulled them shut in the middle.

"Who's in there?" I said.

"It's more like what," one of them said.

"Okay then, what's in there?"

"It's one of those kids from the training center. He ran away and ran right out in front of a car."

"What's that? A reform school?"

"No, it's for retarded kids and adults." Another scream shot through our innards. "Jesus, that is unreal. Who is the doctor?"

"You're gonna love me when I tell you this, Dr. Scalia, but they're all automatic referrals to the ER physician."

"Oh, give me a break," I said, throwing myself against the wall. "How old is he?"

"About sixteen." Something crashed across the room. I opened the doors a crack. He saw me immediately and rushed over to one of the stretchers. He climbed on like a monkey, curled himself up at the head of the gurney and, cradling his left arm, he rocked back and forth.

I walked in very carefully and stood at the foot of the stretcher. The reason for the boy's retardation was obvious from looking at him. He was microcephalic. He had a very tiny head and his base level intelligence was apparent from his expression. So were his pain and his terror. He understood nothing. He had a lump on his forehead, and his left arm was clearly broken. As I tried to approach him, he let go with another unbelievable scream and successfully blasted me out of the room. I stumbled down the hall, laughing to myself. Christ Almighty, I thought, this is so pathetic, will somebody please tell me why I'm laughing?

I walked into the nurses' station. "All right, you guys, we are giving away an award in ten minutes." They all looked at me. "It's the award for patient of the day. I usually like to wait for the full twenty-four hours to be up before making the presentation, but it appears that we have a hands-down winner." I leaned against the wall and started laughing again, but then I realized why. I had just seen the clock. I was going home in five minutes.

I had to work the next morning, and mornings were generally reasonably quiet during the week. It would be the one time that I would have time to sit and discuss patients with the ambulance personnel. I had just finished talking with two of the drivers about a woman who had come in the day before. She was sixty-five years old and had overdosed on unknown medications. She was without respiration or heartbeat when she came in. The resuscitation had been long and complicated; however, she was alive, although not yet breathing on her own. She would walk out of the hospital a week later, but we didn't know that yet.

One of the internists had come into the coffee room and was sitting reading the paper. I couldn't stand this guy. He was arrogant and supercilious and he conveyed this manner to everyone, including his patients, whom he treated like the lesser beings he believed them to be.

The ambulance drivers got a call and got up to leave. The internist looked over at me as they walked out the door.

"You spend a lot of time talking to the ambulance personnel." It was a challenge.

"Yes I do. I think it's very important."

"Really? How do you figure that?"

I looked at him in disbelief. "How do I figure that? Well, they are the first people to see the patient and the more they know, the better they will handle the situation."

"What difference does it make? They're totally unskilled and highly unqualified."

"They're unskilled here, but they don't have to be. If they

are trained properly they are going to make the difference between whether the patient makes it to the hospital or not."

"That's absurd," he said disdainfully. "There's absolutely no evidence that those trainees are anything other than dangerous. They are given a crash course, their heads are filled with drugs and doses, and then they're let loose on the street."

"And how does that make them any different from us?"

"What are you talking about?" he snarled at me.

He didn't know. He didn't have a clue. He would step over a guy lying half dead in the street before he would get blood on his shoes, you could bet on that. And this man who did nothing but office medicine was trying to tell me that it didn't make any difference what happened out in the street. That it didn't matter when a man was sitting in the front seat of his car with his head through the windshield, glass sticking out of his cheeks, whether there was an untrained person or a trained person to assist him. Where an improper movement an inch in either direction could slit his throat, could cause him to leave his entire blood volume on the front seat of the car in the time it would take to extricate him. That he could die in the time it would take to transport him because no one was allowed to start an IV or clear his airway properly so he wouldn't aspirate and suffocate in what was left of his own blood. That by not allowing treatment to be instituted immediately you were standing there holding the door open for death, saying, "Go ahead, he's yours, you got here first."

But it was a worthless conversation. These things always were. He reached for a prescription pad. What would it be? Robitussin? Valium? Aspirin with codeine? He was a soak-it-three-times-a-day doctor. He was a call-me-in-the-morning doctor. He allotted one full hour in his office for each new patient's apointment to give himself adequate time for a good history and physical and treatment plan. I had less than five minutes to do all of those things. If he blew it, he had recourse. A phone call, a change of drug, a re-evaluation in a week, a referral. If I blew it, the patient bought the farm.

I walked out of the room and ran into one of the ward clerks who worked evenings. She was standing with a bloody towel wrapped around her finger.

"Joni, would you look at my hand?"

"Sure." I started unwrapping the towel. "How did you do it?" I asked.

"Broken glass in the dishwasher."

I looked at the laceration. It was deep. I pulled it apart gently. She winced. "Did it spurt, Barbara?"

"I don't think so; it just started pouring out and I couldn't stop it."

"I don't know, Barbara, but just briefly, I'd say you'd better get one of the surgeons to do it."

"Oh no, Joni, don't be ridiculous. I want you to do it."

"Well, look, let's look at it properly." I tested her for function, sensation, range of motion, and then I put in some local anesthetic. She was sitting up watching me, chatting. The laceration was very deep. Deep enough, certainly, to have cut a tendon. I put a rubber band around the finger for a tourniquet. I retracted the sides of the wound. "Wiggle it." She did. The silvery tendons slid by. They looked okay. I looked at the wound.

"I don't know, Barbara, the tendons look intact; everything looks good in there; the digital artery wasn't cut."

"Then sew it up." I had a feeling that said "Don't do this one."

"You're sure you don't want one of the surgeons?"

"Joni, just do it."

I sutured her, dressed her, gave her some antibiotics and a tetanus shot.

I took her sutures out ten days later. The wound was beautiful, well healed, but she still had a mild degree of swelling.

"Elevate, exercise; you know, Barbara."

"Okay," she said.

Two weeks later she dropped by.

"Joni, would you look at my finger? Something funny happened this morning."

"What?"

"Well, I was trying to get my son off the jungle gym, and when I reached up and knocked my hand against one of the bars, I felt this ping and now my finger is stiff."

"What do you mean, stiff?" I was getting that feeling again.

"I mean, stiff." She closed her hand into a fist. All the fingers closed but one. The middle one; it curved obscenely in the air, at me. I got the old thump. I bent the finger gently toward her palm. It slowly straightened out again.

"Jesus Christ, you've got a flexor tendon." I kept staring at her hand.

"What does that mean, Joni?"

"It means I blew it."

"It just happened this morning."

"No, no, it didn't." I kept bending her finger, hoping it would stay down. "Tell me that you're not left-handed, Barbara."

"I am left-handed."

I was shaking my head. "Oh, God." I didn't know what to say.

I called the one guy in town who was really into hands and told him my tale of woe. He was at St. Catherine's, seeing a patient, and stopped by on his way home. He examined her and confirmed the obvious.

"I don't know if we can get a secondary repair to work, Barbara, but we'll try."

Barbara went to the operating room, had a general anesthetic, was in a cast, and missed six weeks of work. The repair was a success. The orthopedic surgeon wrote her up in a journal.

"Don't feel bad, Joni," she whispered to me with her hand in fourteen layers of bandage.

I had a heart-to-heart with the hand surgeon.

"I was careful, Frank, I was very careful."

"You didn't have enough exposure; the lacerated part could have been just shy of the wound edge; especially if the lacerating object went in and then down."

"Shit, what a lesson."

The following Sunday one of the surgical residents from the university brought his kid to the nurses' station with a washcloth pressed against his forehead.

"Hi, Joni," he said, "want to sew up a face?"

"Your kid?" I said.

"My kid."

"Not on your life."

# 41

I had been working the ER at the medical center for six months. By now the tension that had developed between our group of doctors and the nursing personnel was scarcely bearable. The hostility was overt, and you really had to keep your eyes open.

It was about 10:00 P.M. I had been with a patient for about half an hour. I hadn't seen or heard from any of the nurses and I assumed it was quiet. I started back toward the main patient area, glancing casually into the rooms as I went by. I was passing room one, the room we used for codes and heavy trauma. Both doors were closed. There was a child crying inside; not a baby, an older child. A female voice was talking. "Now, sweetie, don't cry. I'm just going to start this little needle in your hand." I slowed down. Who was in room one? I didn't remember anyone in room one.

"Now, I'm just going to draw some blood from your arm, so we can send it to the laboratory." It was Linette's voice. The child was crying again, and then there was another female voice. The mother, probably. I listened: no male voices. The door opened. Linette came out carrying two tubes of blood. She froze when she saw me.

"What's going on in there, Linette?"

"Oh, nothing, it's not your patient." She pulled the door closed behind her. I got a very uneasy feeling.

"What's the blood for?"

"Hemoglobin type, and cross-match."

"What's wrong with the kid?"

"He already has a doctor."

"I didn't ask you that; I asked you what was wrong."

"Oh, it's just a motorcycle accident." My feeling of uneasiness was worse now.

"Who's the surgeon?"

"Feinstein's the doctor."

"Feinstein's a pediatrician."

"I know."

"Who ordered these bloods drawn?"

"Oh, I did."

"What do you mean, you did?"

"Oh, I can do that." She shook her head defiantly. "I can draw blood for type and cross-match and start IVs if I feel it's indicated." She started walking toward the nurses' desk. I pushed the door open. There was a child shivering on the table under a pile of blankets; he was six or seven years old. His face was that superwhite that you only get when you lose a lot of blood and lose it fast. I ripped off the covers and pulled up his gown. His abdomen was hard as a rock and was pooched out. I grabbed my stethoscope out of my pocket and listened to his chest. He was getting very little air to his left lung.

"Who are you?" It was the mother.

"It's okay, I'm the doctor here in the emergency room." I grabbed around, searching for another IV. One of the other nurses came in. I walked over to her. "You get anybody," I said very quietly, smiling at the mother who was three feet away, "any surgeon in the house, any of the chest guys, and I mean anybody, and then you call surgery and x-ray." I put in the second IV. The kid was too shocky to care. The nurse looked startled. I hissed through my teeth, "Move, Pam, move; this kid is gonna cool." She shot through the door.

Luck is greatly understated in our profession. We give a lot of credit to skill, which certainly is a biggy, but we never give credit to luck. Maybe it's because we think that if we admit to luck, we will somehow be negating our ability. But all the skill and all the ability and all the judgment don't have a chance when you run out of luck and you run out of time.

In the emergency state you're dealing with the loss of life's functions, and the quantity of loss per unit of time. Time lost: till the patient is reached; till he's extricated from his car; till his neck collar goes on; till the message is radioed; till instructions are given; till the patient is loaded in the ambulance; till the unit gets to the hospital; till he's unloaded; till his clothes are off. All that time gone, and all that time, the patient is busy: he's bleeding, quietly, rapidly, faster than you can drive; faster than you can move; insidiously bleeding into his abdomen, his chest, closed spaces, unreachable from outside. How fast did he bleed? How long did it take you to get there? And, then, when you had him in front of you, how long, how long did it take you to make the diagnosis? And, once you made it, were you lucky enough; were you lucky enough to have a general surgeon and a vascular surgeon right outside the door?

Pam crashed into two surgeons on her way out. They happened to be cutting through the emergency room on their way home. Were you lucky enough to get the kid up to surgery before he ran out of blood? Or were you left sitting with your judgment and your skill, thinking what you would gladly have given for a few more lousy minutes, and wondering what you were going to tell the parents.

It was Fletcher and one of the other general surgeons. The child's condition required no introduction. Fletcher took over. I walked to the nurses' station to find Linette. My relief at seeing Fletcher was temporary; this kid could arrest any minute; who the hell knew what was going on in his left lung? He should have had an x-ray plate under him from the minute he was loaded onto the gurney. Christ, how long had he been lying in there? No doctor had known he was coming in, and no doctor had been told he was there. Linette had failed to inform me; she had, instead, called a pediatrician who could do absolutely nothing for him. Layton was right; these nurses played dirty games. I walked to the nurses' station.

"Linette, I want to see you."

"I have to discharge a patient."

"Wrong. You only have to do one thing, and that is listen to what I have to say."

She looked at me tolerantly. "Look, I really do have to do this."

"Sit down, honey, before I push your face in." She sat.

"I'm going to start with the easy and obvious question first: Why was I not informed that the patient was here?"

"We don't have to do that, we don't have to tell the ER doctor about every case that comes in."

"I see. What is it, then, that you think you have to do?"

"I think that my first responsibility—"

I interrupted her. "What was his blood pressure when he came in?"

"Eighty over forty."

"Eighty over forty. I see. So, we have a six-year-old child who was thrown from a motorcycle with a blood pressure of eighty over forty. What did you think then?"

"Well, I thought . . ."

"You thought, well, la de da, here's an opportunity to give it to Scalia right in the neck. That's what you thought, isn't it, honey?" I was getting right up there; shouting level was right around the corner. "Did you think maybe he had a spleen hanging loose in his belly? Or maybe his left lung was ripped off right at the root? Either of which could kill him so fucking fast it would make your eyes cross? Did you?" I was screaming. She was trying to compose herself.

"I don't know," she started to say.

"You don't know, you don't know, of course you don't know, goddammit, because you're not trained to know. You're trained to know what you're trained to know, and that means when you've got a baby in there with no blood pressure, and he's even been on the same side of the street as a motorcycle, it's up to you to get your ass out here and inform me—the doctor, who does know, because she is trained to know. And you don't ever play doctor in this emergency room, or any other emergency room, because your little game here may have just cost this child his life."

She looked at me dully. I grabbed the front of her uniform and pulled her off the stool. "Do you understand me!" She was shaking. I was shaking.

One of the other nurses came over. "Doctor Scalia, I hate to say this, but they can hear you over in x-ray." I let go of Linette, reluctantly. I wanted to kill her. I reported her to the nursing administration, although I knew ahead of time that it was a wasted effort.

Several days later, Hancock, the head of our group, came into the ER. "I want to talk to you," he said.

"Fine." We went into one of the rooms and closed the door. "We've lost our contract here at the medical center. They've given it to another group. There's no work after this month."

"Why? Why didn't they pick up our group? They'll never get anybody as good as the four of us."

"They don't care, they don't want us, and they *really* don't want you. You must have really burned quite a few butts around here."

"No more than you have."

"Well, I can almost guarantee you that the new group won't pick you up."

"Pick me up?" I had to think about it. "Pick me up?" Was I a commodity? An item? Hey, run down to the store and get me a sixpack of Jonis? What crap.

"What are you going to do?" I said to him.

"I'm going to try to get the contract at the county."

I looked at him. "You know, this is such garbage. I can hardly believe it."

"It's garbage, but that's the way it is."

That night Les came home and said that Neil had just told him that they wouldn't be able to go into practice together. Neil's ex-wife was driving him crazy, and he was going to go back to Chicago so he could keep a better eye on his kids. I didn't mind the loss of my ER work because I really needed the time to help Les in any way I could with the setting up of his office. He only had five months left in the Air Force.

# 42

Les's office opened in July. I gave a party for him—a combination open-your-office and birthday party. He was very excited, and with good reason. After ten years, this was it. This was finally it. His own practice.

Les had handled everything beautifully. He was so organized, he had his office site picked a year ahead of time. He knew what quantities of what he needed, right down to the paper clips in the drawers. He managed the opening of his office the way he had always done everything else. With a large degree of class.

The office would have been very comfortable on page 41 of *Sunset* magazine. The walls were white, the carpet a bright tangerine. The ceiling in the entrance was made of teak, as was the floor which rose up in an arch to form the reception desk. The lighting was recessed, and the desks and all the work areas seemed to flow from the walls in a continuous network of white laminate. The waiting room contained enormous cacti and chairs of black iron cagework. He personally tested them to make sure his pregnant ladies could get out of them with ease. He wanted his patients to love the office. They did. He loved the office. He was there constantly, and when he wasn't there, he was in the hospital.

I called the head of the emergency group at St. Catherine's. It was a small Catholic hospital, not far from our house. They had been looking for somebody to work full time. They had filled that position, but they had some people on vacation and there was practically a full schedule of shifts to work for at least several months. I took them all. It had to be better than the medical center.

The ER was tiny at St. Catherine's; it would easily have fitted into one corner of the ER at the medical center. But they pushed the same number of patients through every day. I worked from 8:00 A.M. to 8:00 P.M.

As for Les's private practice: it became obvious that the pot of gold at the end of the very long rainbow, "private practice," was not a pot of gold at all. Being in practice may be the beginning of one's medical career, but it is the end of absolutely everything else.

It is the end of your sleep; the constantly ringing phone, five, maybe six times a night, every night, interrupting your rest, breaking into your privacy because some inconsiderate woman had a fight with her husband and felt that as long as she wasn't getting any sleep, or anything else, neither should her gynecologist. They called him for their sore throats, they called him for their diarrhea, they called him because they couldn't find their birth-control pills at two o'clock in the morning. They didn't give a damn, just as long as he was a phone call away. He was available to them, but he wasn't available to me. Because if there is one thing being in practice is the end of, it is your marriage. It is the end of seeing your husband. It is the end of seeing him, and when you do see him, he is too tired to care, and so are you because you are tired of waiting for him, tired of waiting on him, tired of structuring your whole existence around The Profession and its never-ending demands, and The Patients and their never-ending needs.

I don't know when I realized how much I hated it. How much I hated the profession with all its promises. When did I realize that we had had the slickest con job of all times? We had pushed ourselves well beyond our mental and emotional limits for years. And for what? So someday we could arrive at a point where we would be pushing ourselves well beyond our mental and emotional limits? That nothing had changed since we had started, that the same bastards that were bastards before had just done a change of clothes, that the assholes now dressed a little bit more expensively, and drove a slightly larger vehicle, but they were still assholes. They had just found a place where they wouldn't be noticed, because their own kind didn't recognize their own reflections.

So I went to work, because at least I could feel that what I was doing was still important. And I did feel that way. By now I knew everyone who worked the ERs in town. I had been working ER for a year. We all knew one another; all the ambulance and fire and police personnel, we all knew each other. We had shared many a patient. The rest of the profession shunned us.

We were the freaks. We didn't have an office and we did the scut jobs that the private practitioners wouldn't come out of their offices to do, partly because they were too lazy but overwhelmingly because they just didn't know how, as I hadn't known how a year before. They didn't know what the hell to do when they had an emergency because they had been high-stepping for a little too long and glad-handing just a few too many patients. And they weren't quick to recognize things, and they weren't that fast with their hands, and they were oh so glad that "that jerk in the ER" could take care of that messy problem so they wouldn't get any feces on their new pants. Even the patients didn't want us. "Where's my doctor?" they would say indignantly. "I want *my* doctor to take care of this." It took everything to keep from saying, "Lady, your doctor doesn't want you; that's why *I'm* seeing you."

A paramedic training program was begun in town. I had an opportunity to do some teaching, and I enjoyed it, but it was incidental, really, because I recognized finally that the end of the rainbow was really the end of the line for me.

# 43

It was early morning at St. Catherine's.

We were sitting around, Susie, Jo-Ann, and I. Joey and Bill had just come in with some doughnuts. They sat down in a tired heap. "The cops lost a guy on the highway last night."

"What do you mean?" I asked.

"It was a super-bad wreck, one woman dead, and this other guy was thrown free onto the pavement. When the cops got there, they tried to keep him quiet but he got up and tried to walk away. They said he just dropped. OCP said he snapped his neck."

"Well, it's just that easy."

"I don't really understand, Joni." It was Jo-Ann, one of the nurses. "I mean, I understand they die because their spinal cord is injured, but it's surrounded by bone, isn't it? I don't see how it gets damaged that easily."

Bill said, "You know, I feel the same way. I know we put a collar on, and I know it's superimportant not to move that neck, but I don't exactly understand the mechanism."

"Look." I grabbed the box of doughnuts. "You've got seven vertebrae in your neck." I needed seven doughnuts with holes, but it looked like we only had four. I stacked the doughnuts.

"Now, you've got these vertebrae just stacked up here, and the only thing that keeps them from slipping is a series of ligaments in the front and in the back. Give me two paper towels." We supported the stack of doughnuts with the two towels held in place. "Now, in the holes in the doughnuts runs the spinal cord, soft and fragile."

"What are we going to use for the cord?" There was a piece of bacon lying on top of the microwave. Jo-Ann stood it up in the center of the doughnuts and supported it with her finger. "Okay, now we have an accident. We are propelled violently forward"—we rocked the column—"and some of the ligaments are ripped." I took away one paper towel and my hand, which was supporting it. "They're slipping."

"Yes." As we moved the column forward, one or two of the doughnuts moved forward on the others so that the holes were no longer aligned. The bacon was now almost touching the inner edge of the doughnut hole. "Okay, Joey, now pull a little more on that second doughnut."

"I'll break the bacon."

"You'd better believe it."

There was some commotion in the hall. Susie left to find out what it was. She stuck her head in the door a couple of minutes later.

"Joni?"

"Yeah, Suzanne."

"Could you please see this little lady in room one? They've been waiting for two hours for their doctor, and her son is drunk and about to take the place apart."

"Okay."

I walked down to room one. We didn't actually have rooms; they were just little alcoves, with curtains in front. You could hear every word spoken in the alcoves if you were in the hallway.

"Where the hell is he? Where the hell is that damn doctor? What the hell do I pay him for?"

I walked into the room. "Excuse me, sir, I am Dr. Scalia, the doctor on duty here in the emergency room. Would it be all right with you if I took a look at your mother?"

"I don't give a damn who looks at her. I just want somebody to give me a time on this."

"A time?"

"A time. That's right, a time. I want to know when she's

gonna die. She's ninety years old, she's blind, she needs to be helped to the bathroom, and this morning she crapped all over the rug."

I looked over at the figure on the bed. A tiny white-haired lady, in a pink flannel nightie and robe, lay totally still, staring up at the ceiling.

"I take it she's not deaf, sir," I said as quietly as possible.

"No, she's not deaf," he screamed. I turned to Susie, whose face was flushing and blanching alternately.

"Miss Rowan, would you escort Mister, uh—"

"Peterson."

"Mister Peterson out to the waiting room?" She pulled back the curtain. "This way, sir." He left without looking back. I approached the bed.

"Mrs. Peterson?" I took her hand, "I am the doctor. Are you having any pain in your belly?" Her eyes blinked and she stared up at the ceiling. "No, no, I just suddenly lost control. I've never done that before. It was all loose, and there wasn't any time."

"I'm going to examine you." Susie was back, and she helped me undress the woman. She grabbed me by the shoulders after we had finished and whispered, "I'd like to murder that man."

"I've got dibs," I said.

We walked out. Toby was at the front desk. "What do you want, Doc?"

"Just get some stuff on her. EKG, CBC, lytes, and get some x-rays of her abdomen. I didn't feel an impaction, but she's so old, she's a candidate for anything."

"I can't imagine how horrible it must be for her. Living in the house with that man. Totally helpless." Susie was talking.

"Well, that's the second thing we have to do. Get her out of there. Actually, that's the first thing we have to do."

"Why the hell doesn't he just put her in a nursing home?" Toby asked.

"Nursing homes cost money, and this beauty needs all the cash he has for booze. Listen, get Sister whatever-her-name-is down here. The one from Social Service."

Mrs. Peterson's cardiogram was like that of a twenty-year-old. Her chemistries, her x-rays, and her lab work were normal, as was most of her physical examination. She just had diarrhea.

Sister Marion came downstairs and we discussed the situation. She said she would see what she could do.

"Sister?"

"Yes."

"Don't send this woman home with him. Please. He will kill her."

"I will do my best, Doctor."

"I don't ever want to get that old, Joni. I don't ever want to have to depend on anybody to take care of me."

"Yeah, Susie, very few of us are lucky enough to have a choice."

The radio came on.

"St. Catherine's, this is Meds sixteen." The sirens were screaming.

"We have a ten-year-old." The static was terrific. I couldn't make it out. "Did you get that?" Toby shook her head. She grabbed the receiver. "Meds sixteen, you are ten-one. We cannot copy you."

They came on again. "We are code arrest, a ten-year-old male, buried alive."

"ETA, Meds sixteen?" They didn't hear us.

"Call Meds control, Toby."

We set up for the code and paged it. "Code arrest, Emergency Room, Code arrest, Emergency Room."

Toby came into the code room. "Meds control said they're outside town, that's why we can't copy them."

We heard the sirens again. It was the radio. "St. Catherine's, this is Meds sixteen."

"Meds sixteen, give us your ETA."

"Our ETA is now about ten. Please note, the father is on board. We are doing closed chest compressions."

"Ten minutes? Is that a paramedic unit?"

"No, it's just a transport."

We waited. We waited and we waited. The unit was in the driveway and was backing up to the door. The guys jumped out and raced in with the lifeless form bumping around on the stretcher. The father was behind them. He ran into the room after them. The code team and the nurses were all over the kid. One of the surgeons was there. I faced the father in the center of the room. He was large-chested and sunburned, his face full of lines. His flannel shirt was rolled up over his bulky forearms. He looked over at the flutter of activity.

"Sir, could I ask you to wait outside? Please? Let us see if we can do anything."

He didn't take his eyes away from the table. "You can't do anything. It's too late. He's dead. He was barely breathing when I got him out."

"Please, sir."

He nodded and walked out the door. I shut it rapidly behind him. He was correct. The child was undeniably dead. I checked his eyes with an ophthalmoscope, but it wasn't really necessary. Everybody was standing, waiting. The surgeon already had him intubated. "Don't put up that IV." The surgeon grabbed the stethoscope and listened over his chest; his eyes went back and forth; searching, searching for the sounds that weren't there. "He's dead." I stood my ground. He looked up. Everybody was staring at me; waiting for instructions, waiting to be told what to do, so we could all get the kid going again.

"I'm sorry, but his brain is dead, and he is dead and heaven forbid, just heaven forbid, we push some drugs and get some sort of pattern across that screen, and we have to support a heart and nothing else."

Susie came in the door and looked at me hopefully from across the room. I put up my palms, facing her, shook them, and shook my head.

"No," she said, and started to cry. I read it off her face. Her son was ten, and I'd met the boy. It was quite a likeness. I turned away from the group and went to wash my hands.

"I think you really did the right thing, Joni." It was one of the anesthesiologists. He had been in the room; I hadn't seen him.

"Yeah."

"There just really is no point in doing a resuscitation in that situation."

"Yeah," I was crying.

The EKG tech came into the workroom. "Doctor, I just wanted to say that I think that was very good that you did that. Those things are hard to stop when everybody's standing around. I've seen it happen a lot, and then the family gets charged for something that shouldn't have been done."

"Yeah, Marie. Well, I think everybody just kind of wanted to wish him off the table, me included. Will you excuse me?" I went out to the front desk.

"Toby, don't put any charges on this; it's a DOA."

"I figured."

The father was standing in the hallway with his large frame facing the wall, his head resting on his wrist, his palm flat against the tiles.

"I wish there was something we could do for him, Joni."

"So do I, but I can't think of a thing." I walked over to him. "I'm sorry, there was nothing that could be done."

He stepped back from the wall and looked down the hall, past me, over my head, and pursed his lips. "I knew he was dead; it was too long. I knew that." He turned away and walked out into the waiting room. I leaned against the desk, trying not to look at anybody, for fear I'd start crying again.

# 44

It was Sunday. We were sitting on the back porch. I was petting the dog, ruffling the short hair on his neck. My hand came over something. A lump. No, it can't be. I ran my fingers over it, carefully. A big lump, deep in to the fur of his neck. I stood up fast. Come here, boy," I said. I got him to stand for me and methodically palpated his body. There were at least four lumps and they were huge.

"Les, come feel Nero's neck." Come feel the tumor, I thought. I ran through the differential diagnosis really fast. What else could it be? What else could it be that wouldn't kill him, that wouldn't devastate his body so that his face would say, "I am already dead. I am walking around but I am already dead." A fungus? Valley fever? Could be, dogs got it all the time. But these nodes were hard like a rock. I felt again. Hard. Stony hard.

We called the vet and had him biopsied. Lymphosarcoma. Cancer of the lymph glands. One-hundred percent fatal in dogs. They could keep him alive with chemotherapy; sometimes they had a temporary remission. The words were inadequate. As inadequate as they always were whenever they were used, whenever anyone's family was informed that there was a predictable death. That their child, or their husband, or their mother was going to die. Inadequate, because they don't just "die" of cancer. They are killed, very slowly and cruelly, and everybody else dies right along with them. I was lucky; I would get Nero put to sleep. He was beautiful and vital, right up to the last minute. He never knew what hit him; his body dropped suddenly, like a weight in my arms, and he was dead. My pain was indescribable, but his was nonexistent. I thought about the little Chavez girl, rolling around on the x-ray table with nowhere to go. Nowhere to go with her living death, and nobody to end it for her. "Who's making the rules?" I thought as I left the pet hospital, "who in the name of hell is making the rules?"

I missed Nero from the minute he died. There was this unbelievable empty space. I kept thinking I'd forgotten something; or I'd misplaced something; or I'd lost something. I had. It seemed like everything that really meant anything to me had died in some form or another, and if it hadn't yet, it was well on the way.

I spent my days off looking for things to do and wandering around the house. It was so big you could get lost in it. I was lost in it. I called Susie at work.

"Hi, what's doing?"

"Not too much; we just admitted one of Hernandez's patients in one of their usual conditions."

"One foot on the code cart and the other on a tortilla?"

"That's it."

"Can you stop by this afternoon?"

"I don't know, I'll see if I can get a babysitter. I'll call you back."

She couldn't come. I wandered around the house. I turned on the soaps for a little while. They were all bad. Maybe I'd go down to the office. That was stupid; that was always an instant bummer. Maybe I ought to tell Les how I felt about things. Could I possibly tell him? I went out in the back yard. It was cold. The water in the pool was blowing. It was so quiet. The place was like a giant cemetery, it had all the dust and stone and rock to qualify. You could die here and nobody would find you for days. Nobody would look. I didn't want to die here. It was bad enough Nero had to die here, but I didn't want to have to. I was going to; I could feel it. Death was already in my house; it came for me but it took the dog instead. I went back in the house. The phone was ringing.

"Hi, sweetie."

"Hi."

"What are you doing?"

"Oh, just flopping around."

"I bet you're watching the soaps."

"No, I'm not, smartass, so there."

"Yeah, you're watching the soaps. You've just got the volume turned down so I won't hear it. You're probably watching *Edge of Darkness*."

*"Edge of Night."*

"Right, that's what I mean. Listen, I've got something exciting to tell you."

"Great, I could use it."

"I had an artist come in this morning. He's going to do a six-by-ten-foot painting for the waiting room. He does totally modern work. Isn't that exciting?"

"Yeah, it really is."

"What's the matter, honey? You sound a little down."

"No. No, I'm just a little bored today, that's all."

"Well, why don't you call up one of your friends?"

"All of my friends are in San Francisco, Les."

He was quiet. "Wow. You are down."

"Right."

"Well, straighten yourself out, and if you play your cards right, there might be something in it for you."

"Fuck you."

"That's what I had in mind."

I hung up on him. I smiled. He was so neat. So damn neat, and I loved him so much. I looked out the window and started crying. I cried for the rest of the day.

Les came home. I had put cold water on my face and hoped he wouldn't notice. He didn't. He wanted to show me the sketch for his painting. He wanted me to be as excited as he was. He was so happy. He really was.

"It looks terrific, honey."

"Listen, not only that, but I went over the books with George today, and I think the way things are going, I'm going to be able to take in a partner very soon. That way I won't have to be on call every night."

"Great!" Every little bit helps, I thought.

"Listen, why don't you get comfortable, and I'll make dinner."

"Good idea." He gave me a big kiss. "Love you," he said. Well, I thought, it looks like you are here for the duration.

Next morning I called the guy who ran the group at St. Catherine's. I told him I wanted to work full time. He told me the group was still full, but he was about to negotiate the contract, and he'd see what he could do. He only had two days for me to work the next month, and I couldn't take them because my malpractice insurance for one month alone was more than I could make for the two days. I still had a few remaining days to work.

It was Friday night. The ER was pretty quiet when the car pulled up outside in the parking lot. Somebody called for a wheelchair. "OD, Dr. Scalia."

They wheeled him by, supporting his head and shoulders, trying to keep him upright. I recognized the face when he went by. They stopped and were going to lift him onto the bed.

"Dave, it's Joni Scalia," I yelled at him. He nodded stupidly. "What did you take, Dave?" He mumbled something. It sounded like Valium. "Valium? Did you take Valium?" He raised his head up slowly from his chest and shook his head.

"Doriden," he smiled wickedly. "Doriden."

"You know, I'm going to put a tube down your nose, Dave, and you may need a catheter." He shrugged his shoulders.

"Okay, let's get started," I said.

"This guy a friend of yours?" Karen asked.

"No, not really, I've met him a couple of times." She filled out his chart. Dr. David Porter, age thirty-five, etc., etc.

His wife came rushing in. "Would you call his psychiatrist, please?"

"That the guy who gave him the pills?"

"Yes. Who are you?"

"I'm the doctor for the emergency room. Do you know how many he took and about how long ago?"

"No, I have the bottle, it was almost full. Would you call his psychiatrist, please?"

"Sure." We went to the phone. Dave Porter was an internist. Very bright, very conscientious. He had more patients than he knew what to do with. He was expanding his office. He was losing his wife; she'd just filed for divorce. We had a call in for the shrink, who was up in the mountains on a picnic. Porter's wife saw the equipment being wheeled into the room. "What are you going to do?"

"I just want to get whatever's left in his stomach. Mrs. Porter, do you want to call an internist, somebody you use, to assume his care?"

"Yes, let me think. Can I see him first?" She walked in and went over to the bed. "Dave?" He didn't move. I shook him. He opened his eyes lazily and stared up at the ceiling. She grabbed him by the chin and pulled his face over to look at her.

"Dave, this was very stupid."

He got her into focus, and then smiled triumphantly. She shook her head and walked out. We got him lavaged, and I got somebody to come in and take over his care. The nurses were all sitting around and chattering, contemplating why any doctor would consider committing suicide, with all the money they had at their fingertips, and what lazy bastards most of them were. I remember them all sitting under the crucifix—all the little "angels in white."

# 45

The last day I worked at St. Catherine's was relatively quiet until about 4:00 P.M., when we got a motorcycle accident. He was twenty-two years old. He was going sixty-five when his motorcycle hit the front end of a pick-up. He flew through the air, high over the cab of the truck, and landed in the dirt. He arrested in the ambulance and when he arrived at the hospital, his pupils were blown wide. He was still wearing his helmet, fatigues, and Air Force boots.

We opened his chest in the emergency room. His whole blood volume poured and slobbered out of the wound onto our feet. He had a hole in his aorta the size of a dime and he'd bled massively inside his closed thorax. His heart and lungs, having no place to go to escape the huge volume of blood, had been shoved over into the right side of his chest, rendering them useless. He was dead.

I walked into the workroom. Father Emmanuel was leaning over one of the utility sinks, trying not to vomit on his raiments. One of the nurses was holding a cold cloth to his head. I washed and dried my hands and reached for a paper cup.

"Dr. Scalia."

"Yes," I said.

"The Air Police are going to inform his wife. Will you talk to her when she gets here?"

"Yeah." I poured myself some coffee and walked out to the nurses' station. Two guys from the sheriff's department were filling out their report at the desk.

"Where's the chart?" The ward clerk handed it to me and I sat down on one of the high stools, preparing to write.

"Joni! Look at your feet!"

"What's wrong?" I said looking down at myself. The top of my right shoe was totally caked with dried blood and both legs were spattered. "God!" I jumped off the stool. "Give me a wet towel."

I was bending over, trying to wash my shoe.

"Hey, Doc."

"Yes." It was one of the guys from the sheriff's office.

"Mind if I ask you a question?"

"No, go ahead." I scrubbed my leg vigorously.

"What's a nice girl like you doing in a place like this?"

I laughed. It wasn't funny really, but it saved trying to think up a smart answer. Besides, what constitutes a smart answer when you're wiping a dead man's blood off your legs?

The door to the treatment room opened. Betty Carmichael, the head nurse, came out.

"What a mess. What's the matter with you, Scalia? Does it always have to be Vietnam around here when you work?" I dropped my towel in the laundry.

"You know, Betty, I can't believe that kid is dead."

"Believe it, baby."

"No, I don't mean I can't believe he's dead. I mean I can't believe he actually bled to death, dying of blood loss, for a couple of lousy minutes. No goddamn IV in the ambulance. At least, if he'd had something running around in there, even if it was Ringer's lactate . . ."

"You think it would have made any difference?"

"Yeah, I do. I think it might have. It might have just kept enough volume up, pushed a few red cells around, just enough oxygen so he wouldn't have arrested. I mean, Jesus Christ, what do you think pumping up and down on his chest in the ambulance did for him anyway, except make the hole bigger?"

Betty lit a cigarette and sat down on the edge of the desk.

"I hate to tell you this, Doctor, but, in my humble opinion, if this guy had hit that pick-up truck in the parking lot, right at the back door, and flown past the admitting desk and landed face up on a gurney in the treatment room, we wouldn't have saved him."

I looked at her. "I guess that's why you were really moving your ass in there, Betty, because you didn't think it was making any difference." She shrugged her shoulders and blew smoke in my face.

"Do me a favor, will you?" she said.

"What?"

"Let's keep it quiet around here tonight. I can't take any more after that scene."

It was quiet. We probably saw only three more patients. I picked up my stuff to go home. "Who comes on after you tonight?"

"I don't know." They all looked at the schedule.

"Hell. It's Kerner."

"Can I ask you guys a question?" They all stared at me.

"What do you say about me when I go home?"

Nobody answered me.

I didn't hear from Kerner about my job. He was sure taking his time. I knew he had to bargain for a new contract for the hospital, though, so I figured I might as well just wait it out.

One of the internists in town called and asked me if I wanted to go in with him on a part-time basis, because his patient load was so heavy. It would be office medicine, again. I didn't want that. I told him I'd think about it. I didn't have to think long, though, because he called back two days later to withdraw his offer, saying that all the local GPs who fed him patients considered it quite an insult that he'd have another GP in his office, putting him in direct financial competition with them. I told him what I thought about the other guys, and in so doing, if he was paying attention at all, he would have known I told him what I thought of him, too.

I spent my days wandering around the house, waiting for the phone to ring. It rang. It was Kerner, asking if I'd come in and work that afternoon. I had come down with some sort of viral symptoms that morning and I ached all over; I told him I couldn't. I got into bed, took two Empirin, and stared at the ceiling. I hated the bedroom. It was totally lacking in warmth. But, the whole house was like that. I felt like I'd been living in somebody else's house for three years. When was I going to go home, I wondered. Where the hell was home, anyway? San Francisco. San Francisco was home. That fog just mothered you and soothed you and took all the sharp corners off everything. And when the sun came out it was that warm sweet sun, that lolling kind of sun. Not the sun that killed you with its harsh intensity and shriveled you into a fraction of what you used to be.

The phone rang. It was Susie. She was upset; it was obvious from her voice.

"Joni?"

"Yeah, Suse, what's up?"

"How do you feel?"

"I'm okay, it's the flu."

"Listen, Joni, I've got something to tell you, but I don't know if I should tell you." She was crying.

"What is it?"

"I don't know how to say this; maybe I'm making a mistake telling you."

"Susie, just tell me what it is, please."

"Joni, they're not going to let you work here, you're not going to get any work here any more."

"What do you mean? I just talked to Kerner a couple of days ago. He said he was going to try to make a place for me, permanently."

"He's bullshitting you, Joni; he's got no intention. They had a meeting yesterday. All four guys. They don't want you. They don't want a woman working here. They said it. I heard them. I was there. The nurses on three to eleven got to them. They filled them full of lies about you, Joni; they hate you."

"That's crazy, Susie! What could they possibly have said?"

"Oh, you wouldn't believe it. They have a letter. They wanted me to sign it. It said you were unprofessional, that you wear dungarees to work, and all kinds of garbage. They tried to get me and Penny to sign it. I told them I'd quit first."

"Oh, God, Susie, don't do that."

"I mean it. I'll quit. You're the best goddamn doctor they ever had working there. You're the only one who gives a damn. I'm going to the administration tomorrow." She was sobbing.

I was exhausted. I was exhausted from just hearing it all again. It was the same old hassle. How many times had I heard it before? It still hurt. Why did it still hurt?

"It's okay, Susie, it doesn't matter."

"What do you mean, it doesn't matter? It sure as hell does matter."

"I mean, I don't care any more. I just don't care."

"Well, goddammit, I care, and a lot of other people care, and love you and know how good you are."

My whole body ached. I had a temporary image of all the little flu viruses running around trying to fight off the Empirin compound. "Susie, I'm tired; I'm tired and I'm sick, and I don't care if I ever see another patient."

"Joni!" She had stopped crying. "Is Les home?"

"No. He's got surgery this morning."

It was quiet. I could hear the humming background noise of the phone.

"You wouldn't be thinking of doing anything stupid, Joni, would you?"

Funny thing about Susie, she could always pick up on me. Anything stupid. I wonder what that includes? Thinking about it? Not really, not any more than I had over the last few weeks, the last few months. The Smith & Wesson was in my top drawer; I looked at it at least once a day, when I went for my underwear.

"Me? Sally Sue Simpson?" I said in my lousy phony Little Rock accent.

"Don't bullshit me, I'm worried about you."

"What's to worry about?" When it's all over and they carry you out in a bag, what's to worry? "Listen, Susie, I feel like hell. I just need a little sleep."

"You want to hang up?"

"Yes. I'll call you tomorrow and we'll talk."

"Call me tonight."

"Okay."

"Promise?"

"Promise."

I hung up and fell back onto my water bed, letting the waves rock me until they finally stopped. The thoughts started flooding in, and with them came the tears. Where does it all end if you don't end it by yourself? If you let somebody else write your own ending? The tears were really rolling fast, running past my ears and onto my neck. How do you know when it's over for you? Who tells you, "Now, it's now, it's today"? The white-haired bastards tell you. They know it all;

they wrote the script. My nose was running and there were no tissues. Where were the tissues? That was the thing about tissues, they were never there when you needed them. There was a soft-pak somewhere. Where did I see them? I remembered. They were in the dresser. In the drawer with the undies. I rolled off the bed and walked over to the dresser. It was right there. Next to the .38. I looked at both of them. What a choice; blow your nose or blow your brains. What a choice. Not that difficult, really, not if you gave it some thought. I reached for the Kleenex. First things first.

It seemed like I was blowing my nose for a long time before I closed the drawer. It was a stupid idea. Somebody I knew would find me, or worse, Les would find me. And then, my God, what if there were some kind of investigation? What if they would suspect homicide? That would be the end of Les's career.

I fell back onto the bed and started crying again. I lay there a while and looked up at the ceiling. I finally got up and went into the bathroom. I washed my face and caught sight of it in the mirror. It was swollen and distorted. I looked awful. I looked like somebody else.

I walked out into the expansive bedroom. The wall opposite the fireplace was lined with diplomas. They were all mine. A whole wall full of diplomas. Paper. I had sweated for every piece. I stood there and shook my head. It had not been worth it. I had lost more than I had achieved. There was very little of me left; my quality, my essence, they were gone. Did it matter that I had spent all the years that I had just to be a member? Did it matter to me? No. It didn't matter. Not any more, I knew that. And my marriage: Where was that? Was that gone, too? Another sacrifice to the profession?

I heard the back door open. Les was home. I heard him drop his keys on the kitchen table. "Joni?" I stood looking at the wall of diplomas. I heard his footsteps getting closer as he crossed through the house. "Where are you?" He walked into the bedroom. I turned around to look at him. It was the same as it always was when I saw him. Nothing could touch it.

"How about a kiss?" he said.

I walked over to him. "Les, I would like to talk to you."

"Okay, but could I get a kiss first, and take off my tie?"

"Sure," I said. "Take off your tie." I kissed him on the cheek. I watched him go over to the closet. He looked tired, and he looked older. Six months in practice and he already looked older. How would he look a year from now, I wondered? Five years from now, when the strain was already a built-in part of his face?

Suddenly it was all clear to me. It was all very clear. Everything that meant anything to me in the world was standing three feet away. Whatever might have been or would ever be expendable in my life did not include Les. There was no way anything was going to destroy this marriage. And my life. I would never give up my life, not for anything, and certainly not for The Profession.

"Now," Les said gently, turning from the closet. "Let's talk."